D1489033

Date: 10/1/18

GRA FUNA V.3
FUNA,
Didn't I say to make my
abilities average in the ne...

Didn't I Say
to Make My Abilities
Average in the
Next Life?!

VOLUME 3

PALM BEACH COUNTY
LIBRARY SYSTEM
3650 Summit Boulevard
West Palm Beach, FL 33406-4198

Reina

Pauline

Mavis

Mile

Didn't I Say to Make My Abilities *Average* in the Next Life?!

Didn't I Say to Make My Abilities *Average* in the Next Life?!

DIDN'T I SAY TO MAKE MY ABILITIES AVERAGE
IN THE NEXT LIFE?! VOLUME 3

© FUNA / Itsuki Akata 2016

Originally published in Japan in 2016 by EARTH STAR
Entertainment, Tokyo. English translation rights arranged
with EARTH STAR Entertainment, Tokyo, through TOHAN
CORPORATION, Tokyo.

No portion of this book may be reproduced or transmitted
in any form without written permission from the copyright
holders. This is is a work of fiction. Names, characters, places,
and incidents are the products of the author's imagination or
are used fictitiously. Any resemblance to actual events, locales,
or persons, living or dead, is entirely coincidental.

Seven Seas books may be purchased in bulk for promotional,
educational, or business use. Please contact your local
bookseller or the Macmillan Corporate and Premium Sales
Department at 1-800-221-7945, extension 5442, or by
e-mail at MacmillanSpecialMarkets@macmillan.com.

Seven Seas and the Seven Seas logo are trademarks of
Seven Seas Entertainment, LLC. All rights reserved.

Follow Seven Seas Entertainment online at
sevenseasentertainment.com.

TRANSLATION: Diana Taylor
ADAPTATION: Maggie Cooper
COVER DESIGN: Nicky Lim
INTERIOR LAYOUT & DESIGN: Clay Gardner
PROOFREADER: Jade Gardner, Dayna Abel
ASSISTANT EDITOR: Jenn Grunigen
LIGHT NOVEL EDITOR: Nibedita Sen
DIGITAL MANAGER: CK Russell
PRODUCTION DESIGNER: Lissa Pattillo
EDITOR-IN-CHIEF: Adam Arnold
PUBLISHER: Jason DeAngelis

ISBN:978-1-626929-61-6
Printed in Canada
First Printing: September 2018
10 9 8 7 6 5 4 3 2 1

Didn't I Say to Make My Abilities *Average* in the Next Life?!

VOLUME 3

BY

FUNA

ILLUSTRATED BY

Itsuki Akata

Seven Seas

Seven Seas Entertainment

God bless me?

CONTENTS

The Kingdom of Tils ---- *C-Rank Party "The Crimson Vow"* ----

Mile

A girl who was granted "average" abilities in this fantasy world.

Reina

A rookie hunter. Specializes in combat magic.

Pauline

A rookie hunter. A timid girl, however...

Mavis

A knight. Leader of the up-and-coming party, the Crimson Vow.

Eckland Academy --- The Kingdom of Brandel

Marcela

Adele's friend. A magic user of
noble birth.

Morena

The king's third daughter.
Intrigued by Adele.

Monika

Adele's friend. A merchant's
second daughter.

Aureana

Adele's friend. A peasant girl.

Previously

When Adele von Ascham, the eldest daughter of Viscount Ascham, was ten years old, she was struck with a terrible headache and just like that, remembered everything.

She remembered how, in her previous life, she was an eighteen-year-old Japanese girl named Kurihara Misato who died while trying to save a young girl, and that she met God...

Misato had exceptional abilities, and the expectations of the people around her were high. As a result, she could never live her life the way she wanted. So when she met God, she made an impassioned plea:

"In my next life, please make my abilities average!"

Yet somehow, it all went awry.

In her new life, she can talk to nanomachines and, although her magical powers are technically average, it is the average between a human's and an elder dragon's...6,800 times that of a sorcerer!

At the first academy she attended, she made friends and rescued a little boy as well as a princess. She registered at the Hunters' Prep School under the name of Mile, and at the graduation exam went head-to-head with an A-rank hunter.

A lot has happened, but now Mile is going to live a normal life as a rookie hunter with her allies by her side.

Because she is a perfectly normal, *average* girl!

CHAPTER 20

The Return to the Capital

I T WAS THE SECOND NIGHT of their journey home to the capital.

"Time for tonight's folktale!

"One day, a suspicious-looking old woman, who was selling apples, came to the home of a young girl who had run away from her evil stepmother and was living with some dwarves. The old woman asked, 'Do your gums bleed when you bite into apples?' The young girl used the toothpaste that she bought from the old woman and perished..."

Given that Mile had never seen snow during her time alive— either in her home world or this land—she decided to switch the name of the heroine of this tale to that of the protagonist of another in order to suit the context.

Her heroine was called...

"Cindeadella."

"And then, a perverted prince with necrophiliac tendencies showed up to kiss the young girl's corpse..."

"What?! But the seven dwarves were there, too! They'd never let him lay a hand on that girl!"

"If the search functions of that magical bell were put to military use, they would have an overwhelming effect on the tides of battle..."

"But the girl has such a strong life force. Couldn't she just use the prince's energy to revive herself?! She's a demon, isn't she?"

The members of the Flaming Wolves interjected at their leisure until Reina roared, "Shut up! You aren't supposed to question everything. This is just a nonsense tale to enjoy!"

It seemed that Reina understood the proper way to enjoy a story. In other words, she had been well trained. By Mile.

The other two were exactly the same.

The third night:

"On the way to see her grandmother, a young girl traveled deep into the forest, a red cloth draped atop her head and pinned under her chin so as to hide her cheeks. Indeed, this was because she had a toothache.

"Little Red Riding Tooth."

"What a big mouth you have! I bet you could swallow a person whole! And it's not just your mouth! What happened to your throat and stomach?"

"If you devised a plan to sneak behind enemy lines in the belly of a wolf, it would have an overwhelming effect on the tides of battle..."

"That would spread some pretty damaging rumors about wolfmen..."

"Shut uuuuuuuuuup!"

And then, the fourth day:

Finally, they arrived back at the capital. Their job of eight nights and nine days was complete.

They'd only spent a short time as guards, but the Crimson Vow had gotten quite a lot out of it; it was the first time they had worked in conjunction with other parties and the first time they had battled against not only monsters, but other people as well.

However, while the four girls still *looked* as though they had quite a bit of energy left in them, in truth, they were exhausted, both in spirit and—thanks to the lengthy wagon journey—in body.

As they stopped by the shops of each of the four merchants, the wagons and their owners departed one by one. And of course, with every stop, Mile withdrew the merchants' excess goods from her storage and collected her handling fee.

At the final merchant's shop, they handed over the goods, calculated the fee for transporting those goods held in storage, and filled in the job completion paperwork. Though the members of Dragonbreath were not with them, they forwarded the report of their completed duties as well. The job was now officially finished. Then, the merchant started in on a different topic entirely.

"Everyone, I'd like to extend my sincere thanks. Without all of your help, our caravan would have been wiped out, and it's likely that we ourselves might not have made it back alive. We'll never forget all that you've done for us. Should the chance ever arise, we would be grateful to have you take on our requests again in the future."

The merchant bowed his head to all of them and quickly continued.

"And um, Miss Mile, if it should suit you, we would be happy to adopt—"

"No thank you!"

"No thank you!"

"No thank you!"

Before Mile could even speak, Reina, Pauline, and Mavis had replied in her stead.

The merchant slumped in disappointment.

"Who does he think he is?!"

"Honestly! What kind of nonsense was that?!"

Reina and Pauline ranted about the merchant's impertinent invitation all the way to the guildhall.

Upon seeing the girls, their usual, favorite clerk shouted, "I heard all about it! You all were really amazing!"

Hearing this, everyone in the hall turned to look at them.

Forgive me... thought Mile, a mortified look on her face, but the other three were beaming. Naturally, the Flaming Wolves were as well.

"Honestly," said Mile, "it was all thanks to the five members of Dragonbreath, as well as the Flaming Wolves here."

Suddenly remembering their position, Reina and the others nodded as well.

However, the guild staff and other hunters had known the Flaming Wolves for some time, and were well aware of their abilities. Furthermore, while it was well established that Dragonbreath were powerful hunters, close to B-rank, they certainly were not the sort of party who could face over forty soldiers and make it out unscathed. So naturally, the Crimson Vow, the wild card in this situation, fell under suspicion. Nonetheless, questioning one's fellow hunters was considered a taboo, so while a private inquiry was a different matter, no one dared to cross-examine them in front of such a crowd.

Just then, a shout came their way.

"Brett! Congratulations on your big win! We're so proud to be part of your party! I bet you got a huge reward, didn't you? We should celebrate tonight and discuss our party's plans for the future!"

The Crimson Vow looked around in surprise and saw a pair of girls nearby. One got the impression that they had been waiting for the Flaming Wolves this whole time.

"A celebration for our party members, huh...? That might be good. We did earn a lot this time, and it's helped our reputation. We should party with some cute girls to celebrate our bright future!"

"Oh, that's a good idea!"

"Totally!"

Chuck and Daryl agreed with Brett's proposal.

The two girls smiled in satisfaction. "We've been staking out some places. What do you think about the Wingtip?"

"Huh?"

Brett looked perplexed at the girl's suggestion. "Why exactly are *you* proposing the place?" Chuck and Daryl looked equally confused.

"Huh? Well, it's a party celebration... So, the five of us should..." the girls started.

Brett replied wearily, "A five-person party? No, the Flaming Wolves are a three-man band and have been for several months. You girls' fellow party members are those four handsome fellows, aren't they? You all cast us aside, saying we were nothing but pathetic country bumpkins. We're nothing more than some guys who *used* to be your allies. You have no business with us now.

"If anyone should be celebrating with us tonight, it should be the people who fought alongside us. Those girls over there best fit *that* bill. Besides, isn't alcohol bad for an unborn child?"

As Brett spoke, he, Chuck, and Daryl all stared at the girls coldly.

Ouch...

Mile and the girls, along with everyone else present, could all see the misery in the two girls' eyes.

The pair was frozen for several moments, but as soon as they noticed the countless pitying and contemptuous stares directed their way, they hastily retreated.

"They won't be coming back again, will they?"

"Who knows... Well, even if they do, I don't intend to deal with them again, so it's none of our concern."

"Ah, guess you're right."

In truth, this could not be thought of as a betrayal. All the people involved had simply chosen what was best for them. It was as simple as that. The two girls had thought that those four handsome men were the best choice for them.

And naturally, the Flaming Wolves thought that caring for a pair of girls who had made that choice—and were now carrying other men's children—was not.

Members of a party had to entrust one another with their lives, so it was out of the question to have people in your party whom you could not have total faith in. Furthermore, it was likely that those girls would not be able to work as hunters very soon. They were already showing.

The Crimson Vow handed over their job completion certificate, marked with an A-grade, along with the merchants' report about Dragonbreath, asking the clerk to keep her voice down so as not to attract any more attention as they collected their pay. For the four of them, there was 96 half-gold in total.

So that it would be easy for the party to divide, the clerk handed them 8 gold and 16 half-gold pieces. She was very diligent when it came to matters like these.

Though it would be nice if she paid more attention to *other* things, Mile grumbled internally.

They had already received their payment for the bandits and soldiers back in Amroth, so this part was merely the promised pay from the merchants. With this, their assignment was now well and truly complete.

"Oh! There were some letters for you as well," said the clerk.

Mavis grimaced, and Pauline's shoulders slumped. The clerk handed them two letters apiece, which they immediately shoved into their pockets, unread.

And then, as they started to head back toward the inn...

"S-say, why don't we celebrate the end of our job?" asked the Flaming Wolves.

"We'd better hold off," the girls replied. "Little Lenny gets mad at us if we don't eat our meals at the inn when we're in town..."

"I can't drink anyway..."

"And we really need to go count our money..."

"So then!" they all finished in unison, and promptly departed, leaving the three Flaming Wolves with blank stares.

"We're back!"

"Welcome home!"

As always, Lenny greeted the girls from behind the counter.

Actually, now that they thought about it... they had never seen anyone *besides* Lenny behind that counter. Was she not just a helper, but actually a full-time employee?

While Mile puzzled over this, she retrieved the dried fish from the loot box.

"Here, a souvenir."

"Whoa, these are fish, aren't they?! Did you all go to the ocean? If I'd known, I would've asked you to buy some smoked fish, too..."

As Lenny started to pout, Mile pulled out some of the smoked fish from her loot box as well.

"O-ohhh..."

From the looks of it, Lenny was not interested in serving the fish as a meal at the inn, but rather, in eating it herself. In her usual loud voice, she called over the innkeeper and his wife, who graciously thanked the girls and accepted the goods.

That evening after dinner, when those patrons who had come only for the meal had returned home, and those guests staying overnight had retreated to their rooms, a scene of carnage unfolded on the inn's main floor.

"No way!" Lenny screamed. "Have you forgotten all the favors we've done for you up until now?!"

"No," Pauline replied coolly, "This is a perfectly fair transaction. As I recall, the agreement that we made was *mutually* beneficial."

Indeed, under their agreement, they had helped attract customers in exchange for a discount. Now that they had stayed at the inn for a whole month, the time that they had paid for in advance was up. Lenny had hoped that they would renew their contract under the same terms, but the Crimson Vow's initial timidity, which they had felt when their future was uncertain and they needed to pinch their pennies, was gone. Now, their pockets were full.

"Anyway," said Pauline, "we're tired of waiting on the other guests. We have more than enough funds now, so we'll be relocating to an inn that has its own bath—"

"B-but..."

Lenny, the innkeeper, and the matron were speechless.

Sure enough, ever since the Crimson Vow had begun their stay, the inn's profits had been steadily rising. There was an increase in the number of patrons as well—both those who stayed overnight and those who stopped by only for meals. In the nine days that the girls had been gone, the owners had received question after question about where they were, and sales had already fallen.

And now, just when they had finally returned, bringing with them a sense of hope, they suddenly declared they were leaving. It was as good as saying, "This place isn't good enough, so we're going elsewhere." Naturally, the owners were dumbfounded.

"Just what exactly are you so dissatisfied with here?!"

"Well, I mean, we've already told you this plenty of times: we're tired of being the entertainment, and there are no baths."

"Well... what if we get rid of your duties and just offer you the room at the standard rate...?"

"Is that really supposed to be an incentive to stay at this place without a bath?"

"If we're paying the standard rate, wouldn't it just be better for us to pay a bit more and relocate to somewhere with a bath?"

At Reina and Pauline's rebuttals, Lenny fell silent.

"Well then... what if we kept the rate what it is, but just decreased your job requirements a bit...?"

"I'm telling you, money is no longer an issue for us. We're not doing it anymore!"

"Plus, the way we've done things until now is expensive, comparatively. We didn't even stay at the inn for a third of this past month. Unlike other hunters, we don't need to leave our things in our room while we're traveling, so we've come to realize that actually making a room reservation is a frivolous expense..."

"Guh... Er..."

They'd figured it out. Lenny chewed her lip as she thought.

Previously, just after the Crimson Vow had left on their rock lizard hunting trip, Lenny had entered their room to clean it. Seeing that not a single item of the girls' luggage remained in the room, she had come to the same realization Pauline and Reina had, thinking: *Oh! There's really no reason for them to have reserved their room in advance, is there...?*

With that in mind, their discounted rate, which at a glance was an excellent deal, was not so great once you took into account the number of nights that they actually stayed in the room, plus the work they did waiting on other guests.

Furthermore, the souvenirs that Mile brought back now and then were nothing to sneeze at. The rock lizard tails she brought them before, for example—wholesale prices for them were one matter, but buying them at retail price was fairly expensive. Plus, it had been an entire tail. It was more than enough to make meals for the guests. It could also be preserved in various ways, such as smoking and drying, and what was left over could be resold to other inns. It was incredibly profitable. It was the same with the orc meat before that, and the fish this time.

She had no choice but to give up hope that the inn could profit from their lodging fees, but there had to be something else that she could squeeze out of them...

With that in mind, Lenny the negotiator came out in full force. (Incidentally, Lenny's parents were complete non-entities in this conversation.)

"Okay. I'll give you a four-person room—meals not included—for six silver a night! You only have to pay for the nights you stay, and you only have to interact with the other guests as much as you would with anyone else lodging in the same place you were, so..."

Lenny was grinding her teeth, looking as though she were about to vomit blood.

However, what she was offering was nothing more than a simple discount. All the other amenities were exactly the same as those they could get in any inn. Even if the discount was rather steep...

Yet seeing Reina and Pauline's dispassionate reaction to her proposal, Lenny made a determined face.

If what they really cared about was the amenities, she could try offering them free lodging. But she could not possibly bring herself to make that decision.

This was still an inn, after all. They earned their profit from the guests who stayed there. Therefore, if guests stayed there without contributing any income, they would no longer be an inn. They could offer discounts now and then, and depending on the generosity of their guests, they might even earn some favors from time to time. Still, they could not violate the founding principles of an inn!

True, even if they were to let the Crimson Vow lodge for free, there would still be some profit to them in the situation. But even knowing this, she could not choose that route. She could not betray her pride as an innkeeper's daughter. No matter how much her father, beside her, tried to convey an aura of, *It doesn't really matter, so just let them stay for free.*

"Um..." The voice came as Lenny crumbled into despair.

It was Mile, who, up until now had merely been standing quietly beside Mavis.

"If we can make that agreement, then I think as long as two other requirements can be met, we should be able to keep lodging here..."

Though Reina and Pauline glared at her, with an air of, *Just what are you trying to say?* Mile continued to speak.

"The first requirement is: We need to abolish the expectation that we eat our meals here when we're in the capital."

Tacking on a reassurance to the innkeeper, who looked like he had taken a grave blow at the implication that his cooking was somehow lacking, Mile continued.

"I mean, it's not that the food here isn't great! It's just that there are so many shops around—I'd love to try eating more things. Plus, sometimes we might get invitations from our friends and that sort of thing..."

"The second is: I'd like you to lend us part of the courtyard."

"Huh???"

This time, it was not only the innkeeper, his wife, and Lenny who were flabbergasted, but also the three other members of the Crimson Vow.

"Just what are you planning...?" asked Reina, eyeing Mile with suspicion.

However, Mile being Mile, there was nothing she could do but shrug.

Most inns typically had wide-open backyards or courtyards. After all, they often housed hunters and soldiers, as well as many other travelers and merchants with an interest in physical pursuits, who liked to do their daily training early in the morning. Throughout the day, the same space was also used as a space for drying large amounts of laundry. This inn, like others, had a decently spacious courtyard, so it would be no issue for them to relinquish a small corner of it.

The Crimson Vow had just finished a big job, and so they decided to take several days' break, with each of them free to do their own thing.

Mile spent this time flitting to and fro. To the blacksmith, to the lumber mill, and even to the dump...

And then, one day, the guests of the inn suddenly realized that something odd had appeared in a corner of the courtyard, as if out of nowhere.

"Oh my! Is it finished?" asked Reina, who had come to see.

"Yep!" Mile happily replied. "And tonight's the grand opening!"

That evening, after dinner...

Lenny, her mother, the members of the Crimson Vow, and a number of female guests who had come to look on with interest gathered before a nine-meter-square structure that had been erected in the courtyard.

What stood before them was a modest-sized wooden shack, with a water tower beside it.

The water tower had four tanks placed upon a platform about two meters high. The tanks were made up of a random selection of items, gathered from whatever happened to be suitable. Two of them were large wooden tubs, and the other two were giant pots of the kind that might be used in the kitchen of a military base. Spouts ran from openings in the bottoms of each of these containers into the small room.

Mile climbed the stairs that were built into the tower, explaining her creation to everyone from above.

"This is a water-supplying apparatus. Cold water goes in the wooden buckets, and hot water in the iron pot. If either side becomes empty, it can be replenished while you're using the other one. The hot water supply assumes you'll be using magic—it can't function to boil the water itself."

As she spoke, she filled the respective tanks with hot and cold water.

"You can put the hot water in directly with magic, like this, or fill the pots with cold water and then use a fireball or whatever to heat the pot and prepare the water. Ah—but please be careful not to overdo it and destroy the tanks."

She then climbed down from the tank and opened the door to the shack.

"When you first enter here, there's the changing room. This is where you undress..."

She slid the second door to the side.

"And this is the bath. It has a soaking tub, a washing area, and a shower. You can use this part to regulate the temperature of the water by mixing hot and cold. Please take care not to scald yourself!"

"Woohoo!" The whole crowd cheered.

Indeed, the bathhouse was now complete. However, it was for ladies only.

What about the men? They could just draw water up from the well and douse themselves, couldn't they?

At any rate, with this, the Crimson Vow no longer had any reason to move to another inn.

"Th-thank you so much, Miss Mile!" Little Lenny's eyes were overflowing with tears of joy. "Now, we'll get even more guests, and we can charge admission just for the baths!"

"And you'll be paying us a usage, provision, and water-heating fee, won't you?" Pauline asked with a smile.

"Er..."

Lenny's face darkened a bit.

"Of course, when we aren't here, you'll need to recruit someone from among your guests, if there is anyone who can use magic—or figure out if there is someone nearby who you can pay to do it. Or, you could put in a request for magic-users at the hunters' guild. I think you should be able to attract a few takers just by promising them snacks and ale."

As she spoke, Mile provided an example for what to do when there was no one available to produce hot water directly, filling the bath with water and then producing a fireball, which she did not release, but rather, submerged gently into the water. There was a burbling sound, and the temperature of the water in the bath rose slightly. She did this a number of times until steam began to rise from the surface of the pot.

The hut had no windows except those situated up high to let in light, so it was designed to let steam out through gaps in the ceiling. Also, though it appeared to be wooden from the outside, there were stainless steel plates sandwiched between the boards.

Additionally, inside the washroom, there was an emergency lever which, if pulled, would bring down another stainless steel plate across the doorway, sealing off entry from the outside, while a chute would open in the wall of the washroom, and the bather's clothing, weapons, and armor would come out for rapid dressing.

It was possible that people might plan to attack someone while they were in a place where they were unarmed, so Mile had installed these features as a precaution. Furthermore, there were escape hatches installed in the floor and ceiling, just in case. Naturally, there were traps for snaring any potential pursuers, as well.

Just what sort of battles was Mile intending to wage here...?

Had she been so inclined, Mile could have foregone the trouble of buying and gathering all her construction materials, and simply alchemized the whole thing using earth magic. However, that would have made her stand out far too much and attracted suspicion. Therefore, she had taken pains to make the bath appear, as much as possible, like something that had been haphazardly cobbled together from odds and ends. The kind of thing any normal, average C-rank hunter might produce.

Yet, once again, there was something Mile had neglected.

It was the fact that there wasn't a single normal, average, C-rank hunter in the world who could build an entire bathhouse in just two or three days...

"Now then, Lenny! Why don't you do us the honor of being our first-ever bather? Show us all how it's done!" said Mile, already beginning to strip Lenny of her clothes. If she didn't, she suspected that that "honor" would fall on her, so she thought it best to take the initiative.

"W-wait Miss Mile, what are you—?! No, d-don't—!!"

In a quick move, Mile stripped the embarrassed Lenny of her smock and went to remove her... undershirt...

Mile suddenly found herself frozen, unable to move. Reina looked on in horror.

Apparently, Lenny was incredibly well developed for a girl of ten.

Yes, even more so than Mile. And Reina too...

After that, the other female guests joined the girls, and they
all stepped into the bath together. Everyone fussed over Lenny,
while Pauline relayed to them all the "Way of the Bath" and the
"Bath as a Lady's Etiquette" talks that Mile had shared with them
previously. Mile and Reina, meanwhile, took to the corners of
the tub, where they sank into the water up to their ears, staring.
Consequently, the rest of the bathers left them very much alone...

"Time for another folktale..."
Mile did not seem pleased about it.
Apparently, she had yet to recover from her grave shock.
"'The Wyvern Returns'..."
And so the story proceeded.
"And then the wyvern plucked out one of its feathers for each
of them..."
"A wyvern's wings don't have any feathers!"
"Oh..."

"'The Ugly Goblin Child'..."
"But *every* baby goblin is hideous!"
".........."

She was in a funk. Normally, Mile would have told the story
"The Dragon Returns," about a dragon peeling off its own scales
to make armor.
"I'm going to sleep."
"Me too."

"Well, I guess I'll sleep too, then..."

Mile snuggled into bed, followed by Reina and Mavis.

Only Pauline remained awake, engrossed in her nightly ritual of counting coins.

"Oh, g-good morning..."

The next morning, when they went down for breakfast, Lenny greeted the girls with a somewhat sheepish expression.

In fact, she was wearing the same baggy smock that she always did, but for the first time ever it occurred to Mile and Reina that this might have been out of consideration for them.

However, Lenny's pity only stung more.

"G-good morning, Miss Lenny," they both replied.

"Wh-why are you suddenly calling me 'Miss'?"

It seemed they had both unintentionally acknowledged Lenny as the victor...

Several days later...

As the girls were calculating their pay after a successful day trip of hunting and harvesting (gathering orc meat and the like), the clerk whispered to them, "The guild master wants to see you in his office."

The girls silently nodded, then slipped surreptitiously up to the guildhall's upper floor.

"Oh, you're here."

Once they entered, the guild master began to explain.

"To tell you the truth, girls, there are some folks who have been asking questions about you lately. It seems like they're strangers to this town. But no one knows what they're after. I have some guesses, but I really couldn't say more than that."

It was a blunt way to break the news to them, but unfortunately, he told the truth.

Maybe it was someone who had seen them at the graduation exam, or some noble who had heard the rumors about it. Or perhaps it was someone who was keen on Mile's storage magic, or an agent of one of those merchants, or a group of imperial soldiers...

Or perhaps it was even someone interested in their marriage prospects...

Certainly it's not that last one, the girls assured themselves. Still, as the guild master had said, there were so many possibilities they couldn't possibly guess which was most likely. They could only laugh awkwardly.

"I'll be keeping an eye out for you, but do be careful. That is all."

"Honestly though—who, exactly, would be investigating us?" asked Mile on the way back to the inn.

Yet just as they turned the final corner, they came upon a young man standing before the entrance. He was around twenty years old, determined-looking, and fairly handsome.

The moment he saw them, he ran toward them at full speed. Instinctively, the girls took on a defensive stance. However...

"Huh?"

He was tall, with golden hair, a taut and resolute face, and shining eyes...

He was most certainly no one that Reina, Pauline, and Mile had ever met before, and yet somehow he gave them the impression of being an old friend.

And then, Mavis screamed.

"Third Brother!"

Of course.

They had heard much of this fabled Third Brother. Perhaps more than anyone in the world, outside of Mavis's own family. The number of times they'd heard the tales in their six months at school was so high they'd lost count...

This Third Brother came to a halt just in front of Mavis.

"Wha—? Mavis...? Y-your hair..."

"Huh? Oh, yeah. It was getting in the way, so I cut it."

"Gaaaaaaaaaaaaaaaah!!!"

The girls tried their best to bring Third Brother out of his tizzy as they moved into the inn. Naturally, it would look suspicious for four young ladies to bring a man up to their room, so they picked a corner of the dining room to chat in. After some time, when it seemed that he had finally calmed down somewhat, Mavis began to speak.

"What are you doing here, Third Brother?"

"Isn't it obvious?! I came here to get you. Father has sent you countless letters, but you never returned home—you never even replied! Now, we're going back home. Pack your things!"

"Sorry, but I am no longer Mavis von Austien, eldest daughter of the Austien family. The girl you are looking at is plain old Mavis, rookie C-rank hunter and forward guard leader of the Crimson Vow, who aims to become a knight someday."

"What are you saying?! You're our family's only..."

Pauline interrupted him. "Please wait, Third Brother."

"It's Ewan. *You* shouldn't be calling me that."

"Ah, right..." she replied earnestly.

She had only called him that because, whenever Mavis spoke of her brothers, she referred to them as First Brother, Second Brother, and Third Brother. So naturally, those were the names that Pauline had come to associate with them. And, of course, she hadn't known Ewan's actual name. It wasn't as though she *wanted* to call him "Third Brother."

"Well then, Mister Ewan," she said. "Are you aware that Mavis ran away from home because *your* family ignored and even opposed her own dreams of becoming a knight? If she were to return home now, just what would happen to that?"

"Well, of course, we wouldn't permit that! Our dear, precious Mavis's place is with us! Mavis isn't a knight to do the defending—she's our fair princess, who *we* should defend! Why else do you think my brothers and I all became knights in the first place?"

"Err..."

The three third wheels shrank back, and Mavis sighed wearily. Lenny was all ears, listening wide-eyed, while the other guests looked flabbergasted.

It's just like the Kellogg's slogan! thought Mile.

She was only partly right—there weren't any roosters around, but this sure had been a wake-up call.

"What are you so shocked for?! Here, take a look at this!"

"D-don't! Third Brother, please don't!"

As Mavis tried desperately to stop him, Ewan jerked away and pulled from his breast pocket some kind of small parcel, which he then began to unwrap.

"Now then—feast your eyes!" said Ewan, handing something over.

It was a palm-sized portrait of a cute young girl, around ten years old. She had golden hair all down her back, big round eyes, and a precious smile. She looked just like a princess from a fairy tale.

"Who is this?" the girls asked.

"It's me..." Mavis replied ruefully, scratching the bridge of her nose.

"Whaaaaaaaaaaaat?!?!" they all screamed.

Just as they noticed that there was one voice too many among them, they realized that Lenny, who was supposed to be at the inn's counter, was gazing at the portrait as well.

"W-well... I guess if Miss Mavis grew her hair, and put on a dress, and opened her eyes wide, and smiled... She would look something like this..." Lenny mused.

"Right?! You get it!" Ewan nodded emphatically.

"Ah, yes, it is just as you say, Mister Ewan..."

"*You* can call me Third Brother—I don't mind."

"Uh..."

Lenny gaped at him.

"And, I don't mind if *you* do, either," he added, pointing to Mile.

"What?"

Mile gaped at him as well.

Snap!

A sound rang in everyone's ears.

As everyone looked curiously around the room, as if to ask, "Did anyone else hear that?" they saw Reina and Pauline, their veins bursting in their foreheads.

Oh nooooooo!

Clang!

Clatter!

Everyone in the room moved their tables and chairs as far away from the Crimson Vow as possible.

He had made an enemy of Pauline and Reina. There was not a single soul among the staff and guests who was not well aware of what that meant...

Didn't I Say
to Make My Abilities
Average in the
—— Next Life?!

CHAPTER 21

The Assault

"**...S**O, YES, that's how it happened," Ewan said, wrapping up his explanation. He slicked back his prized golden—and now slightly singed—hair, pressing a hand over his heart, which was ringing like an alarm.

Apparently, there had been several nobles watching the graduation exam who had recognized Mavis and brought reports back to her father at home.

After finally tracking Mavis down, the Austien family had sent her countless letters by way of the guild; however, never receiving a reply, they began to grow worried, and finally decided to dispatch someone to look for her in person. The one who was selected was this third brother, Ewan, who had been taking it easy, having just returned from a distant operation with his company.

"I absolutely must bring you back home with me. If I don't..."

"If you don't?"

"Our father and brothers will murder me!"

"Ah..."

The other three understood.

"I told you! I refuse to come back home!" Mavis shouted.

"You may not refuse! I'll bring you back whatever it takes! I mean honestly—hunters are such... No, never mind..."

Ewan trailed off under the threat of Reina's glare. He was rather wimpy, as far as knights went. For her part, Mavis had lost the usual masculine edge to her voice and was now speaking in a more "ladylike" manner. Perhaps it was because it was her brother she was speaking to? It gave Mile and the others a sense of... well, it gave them a very strange feeling.

"What will you do if you get injured and it leaves a scar?!"

"Pauline can heal me, so that shouldn't be a problem."

"What if you're attacked by bandits?"

"Just recently we defeated over forty of them. And in reality, those weren't even bandits, but soldiers from another country..."

"Wh...?"

Ewan was horrified.

She had neglected to include the fact that there were other parties fighting alongside them during that incident, but still—it was the truth.

"D-don't tell me you're talking about that rumor that's been going around...about a small group of hunters capturing a platoon of imperial soldiers..."

"Oh, so you've heard about it?"

That was when Ewan remembered.

His own unit had just returned from a practice tour when he heard about the so-called Amroth Regional Guerilla War. The thing that stood out the most about the story was that four young girls had been involved in it. There was "Firebomb," who let off endless explosive flame spells that could pierce through even defensive barriers; the "Saintly Maiden," who could use healing magic; the "Little Demon," who let off the loudest, most ostentatious spells; and then... But no, surely...

As he thought, he looked over at all of them.

There was the redhead girl who seemed fond of burning people—i.e. *him*, just a few minutes earlier.

There was the silver-haired angel who looked as though she must have fallen from heaven, who made one feel at ease with a glance.

And then, there was the black-hearted, busty girl.

The Austiens had a bit of family wisdom: Never trust a busty girl.

But all this meant that the "Godspeed Blade" he had heard about...would have to be...Mavis? Were they talking about Mavis?!?!

It was true. Reports of the Crimson Vow's activities had made it from the mouths of the captured soldiers that the girls had been unable to silence all the way to the palace military commanders.

This was bad.

Ewan was panicking.

If even a quarter of what the rumors had said about the

Crimson Vow were true, he would never be able to win against all four of them at once. Unlike his brothers, Ewan could only fight against four or five enemy soldiers simultaneously—at best. These girls could take on scores of enemy soldiers and make it out unscathed, and there were *four* of them. There was no way he could possibly best them. He wouldn't underestimate his opponents based on gender or age. As such, this was the only objective conclusion Ewan could reach.

In any case, he had no intention of harming Mavis or her friends, though that did not mean that he had not been prepared to use at least minimal force. Now, even that was no longer an option.

"At least show your face, Mavis! Just once, come see Mother and Father and let them know that you're all right!"

"And when she does, you'll trap her in the house, won't you?" Pauline interjected.

Ewan glared.

You snake! I guess it's true what they say about busty women...

He clicked his tongue against his teeth.

They continued to talk for some time after that, but they could not seem to reach common ground. Finally, some of the guests came to request that the girls run the baths for them, so they took the opportunity to draw their discussion to a close.

Ewan proposed reserving a two-person room at the inn so that Mavis could share it with him, but naturally, she refused.

After that, they were faced with Ewan's unfortunate attempt to accompany Mavis to the bath, but everyone barred him from following through with that.

Because the bath had no windows except the small ones that allowed light to filter in from the ceiling, and because the small structure had been built in the corner of the courtyard, anyone who approached would be clearly visible. Peeping was impossible. There weren't any thieves or assassins around, but if there were, it would be unthinkable for them to try to make a grand entrance through the front door.

Thus, everyone barred Ewan from entering with Mavis quite easily.

But, Ewan explained, back home, they had bathed together until age thirteen—something Mavis hurriedly tried to deny.

"Until you were *thirteen*?"

"Huh? Is that weird?"

"………"

The next morning, when the girls went to eat breakfast, Ewan was nowhere in sight.

Perhaps he had already finished, or perhaps he would eat after. Either way, they were not terribly concerned.

Of course, when they started to head out to the guild, and Ewan still had not shown his face, they began to grow suspicious, which is when Lenny explained:

"Oh, if you're looking for Big Brother, he went out super early this morning."

"Huh...?"

The girls were all perplexed.

What with the way he had been acting, they had felt certain that

Ewan would try to accompany them on their job, but it seemed their troubles had come to a rather anti-climactic resolution.

They set out at once, before he could return.

"All of these suck..."

There wasn't a single appealing request on the guild's job board.

There were a decent number of postings, but nothing that suited them. Either the rank was too low, or the rank was too high, or the pay wasn't worth it, or they were somewhere far away...

They would feel awkward taking on a job that required overnight travel while Ewan was around. But still, taking on a D-rank task was unforgivable.

"Guess we've got no choice. Time to take on some dailies and prepare for some gathering..."

After a while, they arrived at the hunting grounds designated for C-rank hunters.

Occasionally, orcs and ogres appeared in this area, so it was never frequented by E-rank or lesser hunters. Now and then, some D-rank hunters might show up, but it was mostly C or B-ranks who visited these woods.

Mile activated her detection magic the moment she stepped onto the grounds. Normally, she did not use it while in town. There would be too many things for her to detect, for one, and that would be irritating. Plus, even if she were to exclude humans, she wasn't sure what she would do if she discovered something that *wasn't* human in the vicinity. So, it was easier just to forego it.

Even while hunting, Mile did not point out each and every creature she detected to her fellow party members. If they came to rely on her for every little thing, then if their party ever disbanded—or if Mile ever took part in a separate operation—the rest of them would be completely lost. That simply would not do, so Mile made the independent decision to limit her aid, helping the party with the things that she alone could do—like supply-carrying and defense—only in truly dire situations.

"Oh?"

Mile paused, looking suspicious.

"Is something wrong?" asked Reina.

"Ah, no, it's nothing."

I sense some people nearby...but they aren't speaking or making any other sounds.

Mile thought this rather curious, but they *were* at a hunting ground. It wouldn't be peculiar at all for other hunters to be here as well. If they were quiet, it could be because they were resting, or because they were attempting to sneak up on some prey....

In fact, it would be much stranger for them to be making a racket in the middle of hunting.

Even as she had this thought, Mile continued to scan for prey visually along with her cohorts. Of course, her detection magic was still activated, but that was for safety's sake more than anything else—not for the sake of making hunting easier. Except, of course, when they weren't catching much the normal way.

They're following us...

Mile had noticed from the start that the humans she had sensed earlier seemed to be keeping a fixed distance from them.

One was ahead, with four others behind. This was most definitely the pattern of pursuers trying not to be noticed by their prey. This was bad. Mile gestured for the other three to come closer.

"What is it?" asked Reina, sidling toward her as they walked.

"We're being followed," Mile replied. "There are five people heading our way. They're closely grouped."

"Hmm? Well then, we'd better find a good place to meet them."

Mavis and Pauline nodded silently.

About ten minutes later...

Mile and the others stood in front of a tree with a trunk the circumference of several adults' arm spans. Suddenly, five men appeared. Reina and Pauline were closer to the tree, with Mavis and Mile in front.

To the men, this looked like a prime opportunity, as the girls stopped for a rest with the tree blocking their rear exit, so they could not escape. However, naturally, the Crimson Vow had chosen this location so that they would not be attacked from behind.

"Huh? Who are you all? Do you have some business with us?" asked Pauline, timid and bewildered as the men approached with grins on their faces. She was a splendid actress.

"Heh heh heh, well, we was just thinkin' you girls might like to tango with us a bit..." said the fellow who looked like their leader, a nauseating sneer on his face. "Don't hate us, all right? We're just tryin' to fulfill a request here. This ain't nothin' but a job... Heh heh, and we're very passionate about our work."

The man's face morphed from a smirk to a grin as Reina looked on suspiciously.

"Request?"

"That's right. A request from a certain family: 'Mess up those girls that travel with her so they can't hunt anymore.' Seems like they were hoping that it would persuade you to give up your hunting career and come back to live under your family's thumb. Your folks are a real piece of work, huh? Hahaha!"

"Huh...?"

The girls were all stunned.

"All right lads, just keep yer hands off the big one. Don't hurt her. The rest of those girls— you can do whatever you like!"

"Wh...?"

Mavis froze.

"Th-this can't... They wouldn't possibly..."

Mavis was pale as a sheet.

Her family. A family of proud nobles.

Her father and her brothers, who valued their knightly pride above all else.

She couldn't believe it. No, she didn't *want* to believe it...

Mile hurriedly moved to support Mavis, who looked as though she were about to faint.

The others couldn't believe it either. They had heard so many tales of Mavis's family. The family that appeared in those stories loved Mavis with a fierce intensity, but furthermore, they were extraordinarily proud and dutiful, as nobles went—the embodiment of *noblesse oblige*. Was all of that just...

Could her family's fierce and intense love for Mavis explain what was going on now?

Her family was attacking her friends, in the name of loving her. For *her* sake...

Mavis crumbled, dropping to her knees.

"Mavis..."

Reina called out to her, worried, but Mavis's eyes were dull with despair. Neither Mile nor Pauline knew what to say.

The man, however, had already continued speaking.

"Alright lads, take your pick! Anyone but the brunette, the big one!"

Hearing this, all four of the Crimson Vow screamed in unison: "*When you said 'big,' were you talking about her booooooobs?!?!*"

"Y-you bastards!"

Mavis was angry.

She was utterly livid.

It was the first time that the others had ever seen an expression of true rage on Mavis's face.

Actually, she looked... pretty cool.

"You really gave me a shock! And you dared to make *me* question my own family... I won't forgive you. I'll cut down each and every one of you!"

"Mavis, wait!" As Mavis reached for her sword, Reina held her back. "You only get to take two of them! At least leave one each for the rest of us!"

"Got it."

Mavis would channel the rage she felt toward herself into striking down the men. How could she have doubted her family, even for a moment?

Reina, Mile, and Pauline—their true targets—all felt a similar urge to kill.

"Oh, so the little ladies from the Hunters' Prep School are tryin' to look tough? We've been C-rank hunters for twenty—"

Cling!

The bandit leader gaped as the sword in his hands was struck down by Mavis's interrupting attack.

"Pick it up."

"Huh?"

"Pick up your sword. I'll wait."

"Ugh!"

His face twisted in humiliation, the leader swiftly retrieved his sword, taking several steps back.

"You think you can make fun of me?! You'll regret not taking that chance while you had it! Oy! You lads, get in here!"

Rallying his companions, the leader squared off against Mavis again. Another of them joined him, sword in hand. Each of the other three faced Mile, Reina, and Pauline, respectively.

Mile was wielding a sword, so they assumed she was a sword-user, but she was still a child of no more than eleven or twelve. The other two were clearly mages. It would be dangerous to allow them to use magic, but at least from this distance, if they leapt in the moment the girls started a spell, they could easily take them down before the spell could be finished. Mavis was a fierce opponent, but she was clearly still a rookie with minimal experience, so against two veterans, it would be no contest.

Or so the men thought.

Fwoosh!

Two attacks flew toward Mavis at once, but thanks to her training against simultaneous attacks from Mile and Veil, she could take on several enemies at the same time. Even in that split second, she saw each attacker clearly. The leader was slightly quicker, and she clashed with his sword first. With their blades still interlocked, she repelled the second attack as well. Both of the men's stances were ruined, so she could have easily pursued them both. However, Mavis did not move.

"Wh...?"

The two men were stunned to see their dual-attack—a certain victory—repelled so easily, though in reality this was not all that mysterious.

What the leader had been about to say was, "We've been C-rank hunters for twenty years." In other words, even after over twenty years with the guild, they were still just shy of B-rank. Apparently, they couldn't make a living without taking on illegal jobs that the guild would not have endorsed, and judging by their bedraggled appearances and gear, they were low-ranking even amongst C-rank hunters. Here they were, broadcasting all that to the world, when they clearly had nothing to be proud of.

By contrast, the graduates of the Hunters' Prep School had been recognized for their exceptional ability and undergone half a year of intense training. They were completely different from those who had scraped to be promoted from a D to C-rank. Each of the members of the Crimson Vow were somewhat—no, very much—part of a special group.

Mavis called to the men coolly.

"Bring it on."

The remaining three bandits were in a panic.

Once the mages began casting their spells, the bandits had planned to rush the child sword-wielder in front of them and knock her down. The rest of the girls would be too frightened to act after that, and the bandit leaders could deal with them easily once they had finished taking down the knight. The task was simple.

Or so they had assumed. Shockingly, the leaders were losing even their two-on-one fight. Just as they started thinking that they wouldn't be able to go to the aid of their leaders until the girls before them were vanquished—so as not to be attacked from behind—the members of the Crimson Vow who were supposed to be their quarry began to speak.

"Well then, I suppose we ought to get started as well," said Pauline.

"It looks like they're disgraced hunters from another town's guild. Seems like they don't know anything about us," added Reina.

"Taking them all on one-on-one isn't really that fun. Why doesn't each of us take one-third of each of them?"

"There's an idea!"

All three chimed in at once: "That's what we'll do!"

Whsh-whoosh!

Mile swung her sword playfully, and with a clatter, all three men's armor fell to the ground.

"Wh..."

Unable to comprehend what had just happened, the men stared, dumbfounded.

Mile had removed the men's armor as a consideration to Reina and Pauline, who could not easily strike someone without a weapon—as well as to make Reina's fire magic more effective. However, in reality, the party's mages were in need of no such advantages.

While the bandits were still in disarray, they began their incantations.

"Ignite!"

Reina had used an Igniting spell—the most basic of basic, everyday kind of fire spell. Three of them, actually, of decent strength.

"Gaaaaaaaaaaaaaah!"

The three men's heads went up in flames like torches.

After stoically watching this display for several seconds, Pauline was up next.

"Waterball—Ultra Hot!"

As Pauline's words rang out, three spheres of water appeared above her head. They were made of red water.

"Fire!"

The spheres flew forcefully toward the men's heads, struck them, and extinguished the burning flames.

How thoughtful of her, Mile thought... until the men began to scream, just as loudly as they had when they had caught fire in the first place.

"Eurgaaaaaaaaaahhhh!!!"

That was when Mile remembered.

Come to think of it, I guess the idea of a crimson "Ultra Hot" attack came up when I was talking with Pauline about water magic attacks.

However, "hot" didn't just mean "heated."

Indeed, this "hot" was more of a "spicy." Furthermore, this was "Ultra Hot."

It seeped into their eyes, their noses, their mouths, and the burns on their scalps. They were trapped in a living hell, where they could neither scream nor even see. They completely lost the will to fight.

Seeing this, Mile realized that there had been no point in cutting their armor off after all.

The leader and his cohort continued to fight desperately in order to fend off Mavis's attacks. Judging by the screams of their companions, which rung out as though from the depths of hell, they had a fairly good idea of how well things were going for them. Unfortunately, there was nothing they could do about it.

Ka-cling ka-cling!

The two men's swords were struck out of their hands for the umpteenth time.

"Pick 'em up," Mavis commanded, expressionless.

The two were already at their wits' end.

She could have killed them at any point, but again and again she struck their swords down, and then forced them to pick them up once more. They were close to despair, but they had managed to hold out hope all the while—until now. They had hoped that their companions might render the mages defenseless and come to their aid, or that they might capture the mages and use them as hostages. Then they would have been able to turn the fight around. The bandits had been biding their time, holding on to that hope.

However, that chance had been extinguished.

Of course, if they thought about it, they could see it made sense. If there had truly been a danger of the mages being taken captive, this knight would not have taken her time fooling with them. Her allies were completely safe. Only with that firm conviction would she be able to sit around tormenting the men. She was as good as a cat, toying with a pair of mice.

And sooner or later, she would get weary of them and strike the final blow...

Even if they were fortunate enough to get in a hit and turn the fight around, those mages, who were strong enough to take down their three companions in an instant, were close enough that they might turn their aim toward the bandits' leaders. Yet given the obvious difference in their strength, it was unlikely that the bandits would even get that decisive blow in the first place.

If one were to look up the word "despair" in the dictionary, there would be an image of this scene right next to it.

"Please, spare us..."

The two had finally lost the will to rearm themselves and collapsed to the ground where they had stood.

"We had no idea you were so strong! We were told that you were a new C-rank party, all girls in your teens, so it would be an easy victory... We were deceived!"

The leader spoke through tears, but in truth, the report had not been incorrect. It had just left out several critical details.

"My, don't you think that it's a bit selfish to ask that only you two make it out of this unscathed?"

The leader whipped around as a voice came from behind him.

"It would be unjust if you didn't suffer the same fate as your companions, wouldn't it?"

The bandits followed Reina's gaze to see their three companions, wheezing, but unable to scream, burns covering their now-hairless scalps.

"Ee..."

Both of the men cringed.

"W-we'll talk! We'll tell you anything you want!"

"That's fine for you to say, but didn't you *already* tell us everything, just now? You took on a request from someone connected to my family, that is to say, the owners of the Beckett Company, and attacked us in order to send me back home. What more could you possibly have to say that would qualify as useful information to us?" asked Pauline.

"Er..."

The leader was lost for words. What a fool he had been! They had intended to kill the girls after having their way with them, save for Pauline. Even if they released them after incapacitating them enough that they could no longer work as hunters, it wasn't as though they lived in the capital—the girls would not have known their names. Either way, as long as they took Pauline away from the capital, there would have been no danger of their true identities being found out...

For them to give away both their employers' and their own motives so freely, they were truly scraping the bottom of the barrel. Even a party still amongst the lowest of C-rank hunters after over twenty years should know better than that.

"Pauline, head back to the guild and let them know what happened. Tell them that we require an escort wagon, if you would. Since we were attacked by C-rank hunters, the guild should cover the cost. It'll be easiest to explain if the one who they were after goes."

"All right. Got it."

After Pauline had left the area, and they had tied the crooks up, Reina turned to Mavis and Mile.

"Now then, let's discuss how we launch an attack on Pauline's household."

"Ah, yeah. I figured it'd be something like that, since we sent Pauline off. Right, Mile?"

"Huh...?"

"Huh?"

"Huh?"

Apparently, this thought had not occurred to Mile at all.

CHAPTER 22

The Counterattack

"**P**AULINE WILL PROBABLY TRY to say something like, 'This is a matter for me to settle on my own,' but now, it's become a problem for all of us. Even if we *hadn't* been attacked..."

"We're allies, bound to the soul!"

At Reina's prompting, Mavis and Mile chimed in to complete their motto.

"That's right, the 'Crimson Vow'!"

The conference of three determined, as a party, that they were set on invading Pauline's home. Even if Pauline were to object, these group decisions were a matter of majority rule, so there could be no arguing it.

It was after this that they began to interrogate the bandits.

Mile used her magic to heal all of them—including the three who had become human torches—just enough that they could talk. The greater the number of bandits they could interrogate, the greater the likelihood that one of them would betray the others.

"First off, are you truly all active hunters? Or might you be disgraced, *former* hunters?"

As Reina questioned them, Mile stood beside her, toying with a fireball and red waterball, which floated above each of her palms. Since she and Pauline had thought up the "Ultra Hot" spell together, she naturally knew how to use it as well.

This sight sent a shiver down the men's spines, and they thought hard.

They had lost their weapons and armor, they were tied up tight, and in a few hours, a wagon with other hunters would be coming to the girls' aid. It was unlikely that they would be able to escape their bonds at any point before then. Furthermore, even if they did manage to work themselves free, three of their companions were no longer able to fight. Given that they could not fight with their full forces, there was no way that they could win.

Seeing that there was no longer any means of counterattack available to them, the men had no choice but to think of some way to lessen their eventual punishments. At this rate, even if they were to escape hanging, the next-best scenario would be indentured servitude, as they worked out the rest of their lives in the mines. Of course, "the rest of their lives" might not be long, given the harsh conditions and strenuous work they would face day in and day out.

However, if they stayed on their best behavior, it was possible that they could receive a shorter sentence, in a less harrowing position, where they would be released after several years. And, if fortune was on their side, getting out of this with only the punishment of being stricken from the guild roster was not an impossibility.

If they could somehow pin all the blame on their employers, claiming that they only took the job not knowing much about the circumstances and that they had been deceived...

Realistically, there was only the smallest chance that anyone would ever buy such a story, but the men lacked the luxury of choice: they had no options now but to gamble. They would wager on that distant hope and pray that they could appeal to their captors' good will, if even a little...

The criminals who had attacked the girls needed to engender good will among those same girls.

It was a hopelessly reckless experiment.

And so, their depositions began.

"W-we still have our hunters' certifications! We're all C-ranks..."

The questioning continued until the escort wagon arrived, the findings being that all the men were active C-rank hunters, and while they were already in their forties, they had not put much savings away. Now that their bodies were weakening, they were doing anything they could in the time that they still had to save some funds—including taking on illicit jobs, outside of the guild.

Of course, taking a job from outside the guild was not necessarily illicit in and of itself. It just meant that, should anything go wrong, they would not be able to receive the guild's aid.

What made it illicit was what they were actually doing.

It was a job that asked them, among other things, to be murderers, abductors, and attack young girls in a way that would make them unsuitable for marriage. The main objective of this job—a family's request to bring their daughter back—was not inherently illegal. It was the *how* of this request that presented the problem.

They were going to attack and harm young girls, injuring them so badly that they could no longer work. And then they were going to capture another girl and drag her home by force, against her wishes. Furthermore, these girls were citizens of the capital, so this was an attack on citizens under the direct rule of the Crown.

According to the men, their intention had been to ignore the details of their employers' instructions so long as they achieved their objective—they had planned only to threaten the other girls a bit, maybe inflict a bit of pain by kicking them around, but not to put them through anything particularly horrible. Of course, whether or not this was true was incredibly dubious...

"It's true!" the men desperately pleaded. "That's why we spilled the whole truth and didn't hide anything from you! We thought if you knew that our employer was the father of your friend, you could bring it to the attention of the guild or the town guards, and disavow yourself of the girl who brought this plague down on you... Really, we took this job out of good intentions! If we hadn't taken it, some dastardly criminal might have, and things would have turned out very poorly..."

Yet there had been that detestable, vulgar laugh that the man had let out earlier. If *that* was acting, then he'd have had better luck making his living on the stage.

The men were able to confirm, once more, that the one who had requested this job was in fact, Pauline's father, the head of the mid-scale mercantile operation known as the Beckett Company, which was based in the lands controlled by Viscount Boardman, some four days' distance from the capital. This man was known for placing various unlawful job requests through back-alley means, and he didn't care if people made a mess doing them. As long as they didn't get caught, they got paid.

"I'm begging you, tell one of the higher-ups in the guild or the city guards! We were going to let you get away with just a few blows! I mean, honestly, we truly didn't lay a finger on you girls. We were just on a job, a job from a father who only wanted to see his daughter back home—and that's not such a strange request, is it? We're all hunters here, ain't we? You gotta help us out! Like, someday, when you girls get older, you might find yourself anxious and without savings, and then *you* might have to take some jobs outside of the guild! C'mon, please, give us a hand here...!"

All three of the girls' responses were cold.

"If I'm not mistaken, it wasn't that you *didn't* lay a finger on us—it was that you *couldn't*," said Reina.

"And also, there was that opening move, where both of you attacked me at once. That was clearly intended as a killing blow, yes?" asked Mavis.

"We don't know what the truth is here, so we have no choice

but to defend ourselves. Therefore, we'll only be telling them the facts as we saw them. Feel free to present your own defense to the guild and the guards. We won't be the ones to decide your charges or your sentence," Mile concluded, as plainly as the other two.

"Th-that's..."

The men's faces were steeped in despair.

"If all that you've told us is true—and if, furthermore, you're able to *prove* it, then you'll probably get a lighter sentence. How nice for you, to get off so easily..." said Mile.

She was grinning.

Naturally, she was being sarcastic. It was rare for her to show true anger like this.

"Mm-hm. I'll be sure to honestly attest to the skill, speed, and strength with which you both simultaneously swung your swords at me. Don't you worry about that." Mavis was angry. Very angry...

"Well then, until Pauline gets back with the wagon, how about we drink some tea?" said Reina.

Mile and Mavis nodded.

By the time Pauline returned, with a wagon and several knights on horseback in tow, it was nearly midday.

Considering the time it would have taken to get to the guild-hall, explain what was going on, and then acquire the wagon and all the necessary people, this was actually quite speedy.

"Mavis, are you all right?!"

The first to leap from the cart was Ewan.

"Third Brother..."

Mavis gave a pained, troubled smile and Ewan rushed to embrace her.

Guess she can't deny him... the others thought, looking on.

"So you're the fiends who attempted to harm my dear Mavis?!"

As this noble-looking young man began to question them, the men sputtered an apology.

"N-no! We were just trying to scare her a bit..."

"What?! You were threatening my Mavis? I'll see you hanged for this!"

"Whaaaaaaaaaaaaaaaaaaaat?!"

Ah, of course...

Just as they thought.

The girls all nodded in agreement at Ewan's completely natural response.

Mile and the others greeted the hunters and guild employees who climbed down from the wagon along with Pauline, then watched as the criminals were loaded on.

"By the way... why weren't you at the inn this morning, Third Brother?" asked Mavis.

"I went out first thing to request a courier to send the letter that I penned to Father last night. When I returned to the inn, you were gone, so I rushed to the guild in a panic, but...as there was nothing I could do, I decided to remain at the guild and await your return. Then, suddenly, I overheard that demon...strably useful lackey of yours telling the guild staff that you had been attacked..."

Though he had stopped mid-sentence and quickly tried to disguise his insult, his correction was just as rude. Plus, he was speaking only to and about Mavis. He apparently didn't care a jot for her companions.

"I-Is that so...?"

For some reason, Mavis was still hanging her head, shifting her weight back and forth. In truth, she was mortified that she had doubted her brother, even if it had only been for a moment, and she was standing there wallowing in shame. Ewan, of course, knew nothing of the circumstances, and assumed, *Ah! She's so happy to see me, she's gone bashful! How precious!*

"Mav—guh!"

Ewan tried to embrace Mavis again, but the other three girls, now very irritated, grabbed him by the collar, throttling him, and instead he could only let out a cry of pain.

As they walked alongside the wagon, which progressed at a leisurely pace, the Crimson Vow discussed what to do going forward.

"We have to go to Pauline's home," Reina announced, to Pauline's bewilderment.

"Huh...?"

"What are you so surprised for? Isn't that obvious?"

"B-but, this is a matter for me to settle on my own..."

"There it is!" Mavis and Mile both spoke immediately. The response was just as predicted.

"Huh?"

Pauline still seemed perplexed.

"In any case, your father was the one who hired those guys..."

"Huh? But, the president isn't my father."

"What?" all three asked.

"I told you when I first introduced myself. My mother is the lover of the head of the Beckett Company, a mid-sized mercantile operation. Just his lover. I never said a word about the president being my father."

"Wh-what are you saying?!?!"

A shocking truth had come to light.

And so Pauline began her tale.

Pauline's parents had managed a shop.

Her family consisted of four people: a pair of loving parents; Pauline; and her younger brother, four years her junior. The shop was moderately sized. Beneath the head clerk, there were several regular, full-time employees, as well as a healthy number of interns, drivers, and door-to-door salesmen on the roster. Her father was sweet-tempered with his wife and children, but when it came to his business he was stern and steadfast. He never showed any greed in his transactions. Perhaps because these were such valued qualities in a merchant, the business thrived. Until one fateful evening...

On the night in question, the shop was ransacked by thieves.

The thieves bound Pauline's family and their overnight employees, stole the contents of the safe, and murdered Pauline's father.

Then, as Pauline's mother sat, stunned with grief, the thieves shoved a single piece of paper her way: a "Transfer of Shop Ownership."

This deed, in her husband's name, would turn over all the assets of the shop to the head clerk.

Everyone thought there was no way this could work. However, the officials deemed the document valid, and the clerk took everything.

All the long-term employees who protested were let go, and various people to whom the clerk had taking a liking were hired on to fill in the gaps.

And then, the clerk said to Pauline's mother: "Become my mistress, if you don't want to see your children lost somewhere off the side of the road."

And so, her mother agreed.

When Pauline berated her mother for accepting the clerk's proposal, her mother had said only, "My duty as your father's wife has ended. Now, as a mother, my duty is to raise his children. Once the two of you are all grown up, then..."

A harsh smile spread across her mother's face.

"I'll fulfill my final duty as your father's wife..."

Pauline's brother was only eight years old at the time. For a single mother without a cent to her name, scraping out a living for two young children, let alone raising them both right, would be quite an ordeal. Furthermore, if she refused the clerk's proposition, there was a chance that some harm might befall her daughter and son.

And so, she chose the path of vengeance.

It was in the time after this that Pauline began to pour herself into practicing and studying.

She had no doubt that, when she became an adult, the clerk—no, the man who had now become the president of the Beckett Company—would likely sell her off as a bribe to some noble or wealthy merchant somewhere.

She would have to escape before then, and amass her own money and power to launch a counterattack. At the very least, if she could get herself married off to someone with as much influence as possible, she could sway her new husband into launching a takeover of the Beckett Company on her behalf.

In order to do that, she had to become the most valuable commodity possible.

Thankfully, she had some talent as a magic-user. She would cultivate that talent. She needed to know about commerce as well. And she needed a heart as cold as ice.

In this way, the meek and personable little girl who had lived a carefree, happy life, surrounded by her family's love, vanished. On the outside, she appeared the same, but inside her, a beast was born. A "wolf in sheep's clothing," some might say...

Pauline was twelve years old at the time.

"........"

The other three were speechless.

In that silence, Ewan, who had also been listening, spoke. "The evil of men gives birth to demons of vengeance..."

Was he talking about Pauline's mother? Or about Pauline herself...?

"It's time to launch our counterattack," said Reina.

Mile and Mavis nodded silently.

When the wagon and its escort arrived in the capital, they proceeded to the hunters' guild. Upon arriving, they were received by the guild master, the rest of the guild staff, most of the other hunters, and the capital's city guards. It seemed they had all heard the news and come running the moment the procession made it through the gates.

"You girls have done well. Is anyone hurt?"

After tending to the Crimson Vow, the guild master addressed their would-be attackers, who were brought down from the wagon. "I hear that you are active C-rank hunters. Is that true?"

After briefly confirming the circumstances of the incident, one of the riders had gone ahead as a messenger and informed the guild master of at least that much.

Once the men had confirmed this information, the guild master said to them coldly, "Though you may be hunters, your criminal acts were conducted outside the auspices of the guild. Therefore, you will not receive any support or backing from the guild in this instance. Furthermore, you launched an attack on hunters affiliated with the guild, and by extension, on the guild itself. Therefore, you will be permanently banned and turned over to the city guard on the charge of attempted murder. Any questions?"

"W-wait! It's true that we took on an illicit request—there's no doubting that! And of course, it's only fair that you would expel us. But we weren't going to kill them! We were just threatening them. C'mon, you all tell them it's true!"

They were pleading desperately with the Crimson Vow, but the girls only shrugged.

"You can tell that to the guards. Once we hand you over, the guild has no hand in this matter. The long and short of it is that you laid hands upon young girls who are citizens of the royal capital, a region that is directly under the rule of His Majesty, the king. I'm sure there's a strict interrogation and punishment awaiting you. Now then, we're handing over these criminals. Please, take them away!"

The guardsmen nodded in acknowledgement and pulled the prostrate men to their feet.

They would, of course, be expecting a testimony from Mile and the others, but that would come after their preliminary investigation, as a means of verifying whether or not the men's claims were true—likely the next day, or the day after.

"Now, would all of you please come to my office?"

And so, once again, the Crimson Vow received an invitation to the guild master's chambers.

Upon entering the room, they were directed to sit down and served hot tea straight away.

"I've already heard the gist of the situation from this young lady. Now, you all aren't thinking of doing anything strange, are you?"

"Strange? Why, no! We would never think anything like that!"

While the other three averted their gazes, Mile looked the guild master straight in the eye and added, "Just a little counterattacking, revenge, overthrowing, and annihilation! That's it! Nothing strange at all!"

"……"

The guild master slumped back at this setback.

"The guild is ready to assist in the current matter. An area merchant has picked a fight with the capital branch of the hunters' guild—we can't possibly keep silent about that. We need to teach them what it means to mess with our people."

Indeed, if anyone picked a fight with someone associated with the guild, it was as good as picking a fight with the guild itself. If the guild let itself be trifled with even once, there was no turning back. This incident was not something they could overlook.

Even the fact that the captured men had been handed over in front of the guild, rather than being taken straight to the guard's holding cells, had been for the sake of putting on a show for the other hunters. The implication was, "If you take on illegal requests, this is what will happen." There was no better way to reiterate the fact that it was much safer to only take on jobs through the guild.

If they went outside the guild, the guild wouldn't be there to help them when they got in trouble.

"There's no point in trying to stop you, is there?"

The girls shook their heads.

The guild master sighed, resigned.

"I guess it can't be helped... Just promise me this: when you go, please take just one person from our ranks with you. They can serve as a witness afterward, and they can negotiate for the cooperation of the guild there. Plus, if the number of people in your party is different, it will be easier to deceive your opponents, which should give you an added advantage."

While Mile worried over a reply, Reina spoke up in her stead.

"I suppose we have no choice..."

Thus, it was decided that the Crimson Vow would take a "plus-one" along with them on their trip to Talwess, the capital of the lands under the control of Viscount Boardman, and the home of Pauline's family.

"We can take a scheduled carriage toward Talwess three days from now. Until then, we should prepare ourselves and lay out a battle plan," Reina proposed on the way home from the guild.

Of course, it wasn't smart to say much more than that while they were still on the road. The rest, they would discuss back at the inn.

On their return, Mile headed to the reception desk to inform little Lenny of their upcoming absence.

"Oh, Lenny, in three days' time we're going away for a little while. Have you managed to find a mage who you could ask to run the baths?"

"Whaaaaat?! Not yet! I've gotta hurry up and look then! Mommmm!!!"

The news was received with panic.

And so, three days later...

The Crimson Vow stood waiting at the passenger carriage station, along with a girl who appeared to be around fifteen years old.

She wore a fluttering skirt and a loose jacket, with the but-
tons undone. Otherwise, the girl who greeted them looked just
like any normal townsperson.

"My name is Theresa. I'm from the guild. I'll be working with
you on this operation. Pleased to make your acquaintance."

"Oh! Pleased to meet you, too. Since we'll be party allies for
the time being, would you mind telling us what your special-
ties are?" As the party leader, Mavis had to ask this necessary
question.

"Ah, of course. I'm a C-rank, backline fighter—a knife wielder."

"Huh?"

Three of the Crimson Vow tilted their heads in unison.

It was fine that she was a C-rank hunter. If she had started as
an F-rank at ten years old, and she had the aptitude and worked
hard, then reaching a C-rank by the age of fifteen wasn't all that
strange. The Crimson Vow were C-rank hunters of about the
same age, after all. Perhaps Theresa had even graduated from the
prep school, too.

What they found troubling was that she was both a backline
fighter *and* a knife wielder.

How could she fight on the backline while using a weapon with such short reach?

Normally, a knife was a supplementary or backup weapon, something used for cutting up hunted prey and the like. Its reach was short, and if you threw it, you wouldn't have a weapon anymore. Therefore, a hunter whose main weapon was a knife was more or less unheard of.

"A knife? Are you s—ow!"

Just as Mile started to ask an innocent question, a kick in the leg cut her off.

"Wh-what was that for, Reina?! That hur—eek!"

She turned to complain to Reina, who had struck Mile with the toe of her boot, but when she saw the terrifying look on the other girl's face, she let out a small shriek.

"N-never mind..."

Mile, who had raised her voice more from surprise than hurt, quickly withdrew her question.

"My primary function will be to act as an observer from our guild, as well as a liaison with the higher-ups at the guild branch in Talwess. Though I'll be pretending to be a member of your party, I won't be participating in any battles, nor accepting responsibility for any actions that you take. In exchange, I will not make any move to stop you all from doing anything that you choose to. You are free to act however you like," Theresa explained. At this, the other four nodded.

They were most grateful to hear that she was acting primarily as a witness and would not interfere with any of their plans.

After that, Theresa excused herself to find a restroom before their departure. When she was out of sight, Mile asked Reina, unhappily, "What was that about earlier?!"

In a hushed voice, Reina replied, "Quit asking about her profession. It's pretty clear what her job is if her main weapon is a knife, isn't it?"

"Huh?"

"Just think about it. What kinds of circumstances would allow a girl to earn her keep as a knife wielder?"

Mile thought hard.

"Umm, you could sneak into places while pretending to be a normal girl, or secretly work as a guard, or assassinate someone... Or assassinate someone... Assassinate... Oh..."

Earlier, when Theresa had announced her specialty, Reina had been the only one not to tilt her head in confusion. This was because, of course, she had already pieced it together.

"Got it? So don't go nosing around. Both because that's the unspoken rule of being a hunter, and also because it might help prolong your life a bit."

Mile, Mavis, and Pauline nodded, all looking slightly queasy.

After a short while, Theresa returned, and they all boarded the carriage together. Just behind them, a man boarded as well.

"Third Brother..."

No one at all was surprised.

Of course he would follow them. Everyone had expected this.

So that they did not stand out as a party of all girls, followed by a single man, they reluctantly elected to pass themselves off as "a party of six, with five women and one man." It was a one-time party for a temporary gig. Unlike Theresa, Ewan would probably be participating in battle along with them, so they needed to let him in on their plans.

When Ewan wasn't busy pouting, he was, in fact, a full-fledged knight. It was likely he was genuinely talented, and observing a real knight's strategy and fighting style from a close proximity would be a useful tool in their own growth. When they thought of it that way, perhaps Ewan's presence wasn't such a raw deal after all.

As the carriage traveled on, the Crimson Vow chatted inside with Theresa. Naturally, Ewan elected only to listen, wary of cutting into a conversation between the girls. Of course, because other passengers were present, they could not have a particularly in-depth discussion—they were limited to "girl talk" and other general topics.

"So Miss Theresa, did you attend the Hunters' Prep School as well?"

"No, when I graduated to a C-rank, the prep school still had yet to be established."

"Wha...?" asked a perplexed voice.

"I was promoted in the normal progression, starting from F-rank."

"Huh?" joined another.

How odd.

Even if one were to join the guild proper as an F-rank hunter right at ten years old, it would still take at least four years to make it to a C-rank, no matter how much of a prodigy you were. Yet somehow, when she achieved that rank, the prep school hadn't existed? The same prep school that had been established a full six years ago?

It didn't add up.

"When my children were born, I retired as a hunter and started working as a member of the guild staff."

"Whaaaat?" three voices chimed in.

"And then my husband became the principal of the school, which had just been established."

"Whaaaaaaaaaaaaaaaaaaaat?!" came the full chorus.

It couldn't be. She was Elbert's wife?!

"W-w-w-wait a minute! If that's true, Miss Theresa, just how old—"

"Asking about a hunter's private life is against the rules!"

"Bu-b-b-b-but..."

As Mile wailed in confusion, behind her, Ewan, his face pale, crossed himself for safety.

It was the first night of their carriage journey.

Mile and the others had already more or less established their plans, but now that Theresa and Ewan were in the mix, they would need to go over everything once more.

As always, this took place inside the tent that Mile carried with her. Just in case, Mile put a sound-dampening magic around them as well.

"...In any case, we first need to establish what the charges are. We need to confirm whether or not what those men said was the truth. Even if they weren't lying, they might still have taken the job from someone pretending to be associated with the company, so we'll need to collect evidence regarding that as well..."

As Mile went through her re-explanation, Reina grumbled that it shouldn't matter, since they already knew they were bad guys. But in her heart, she understood this as well. She had raised the same complaint during their initial discussion, but eventually consented to Mile's way of approaching things.

Furthermore, it shouldn't take a particularly substantial effort to confirm the details of the job request. The incident of long ago involving those thieves was one matter, but with a little questioning it should be fairly easy to confirm whether or not someone had hired those C-rank hunters. Instigating the abduction and murder of citizens from the capital was enough of a criminal act in and of itself, so if they could establish at least that much, there should be no difficulty convicting the parties involved.

Naturally, they would ask the authorities to give them the third degree, in the hopes of getting them to confess to crimes from the distant past while they were at it.

Theresa had no intention of interfering with the girls' plans, and so she positioned herself to listen only as a precaution. For his part, Ewan agreed that it was necessary to undertake a thorough preliminary investigation, so there were no objections from either of the pair.

And so, on the fourth evening of their journey, the carriage finally arrived in Talwess, the capital of the lands of Viscount Boardman and the town of Pauline's birth.

Though Talwess was the capital, this was merely owing to the fact that it happened to be the largest in the territory, and one that the main highway passed through. In truth, it was only of moderate size, and one would be hard-pressed to really call it a city.

"Well then, we had better find ourselves somewhere to stay," said Reina, taking the initiative as always.

After a brief rest, they headed toward an inn.

Pauline had recommended the place on the basis of it being "the sort of inn where the clientele isn't so great, so even if you're sort of suspicious-looking, you won't stand out." There, they would rent one four-person room and two singles.

"Do you have a four-person room and two singles available?" Reina asked the man at the reception counter.

The man's eyes opened wide in shock. This inn was not the sort of place that young girls stopped by very often. However, the rooms were cheap, and it was a place where slightly suspicious-looking people would be able to stay without hassle, so now and again they did receive female guests. Yet what the man was most shocked by was not the fact that these new guests were a party of young girls, but rather, by the appearance of the young girl behind Reina.

Short black hair spilled from the edges of her hooded visage, with only a pair of eyes peeking out from the gaps between the bandages that covered her face. Even for a receptionist accustomed to suspicious customers, this one was *exceptionally* suspicious. Perhaps even the most suspicious he had encountered this entire month. By a landslide.

However, this man was a seasoned veteran of his profession. While he was a tad surprised, he quickly collected himself, and replied, "We have the rooms. How many nights are you planning to stay?"

"We aren't sure. We'll let you know the day before we plan to leave," Reina informed him, after which they discussed the lodging rate and amenities, and he handed over the key.

The black-haired girl, of course, was Pauline.

Her hair had been colored since before they boarded the carriage, but she had waited until after they disembarked to slip into the shadows and wrap the pre-prepared bandages over her face. If she had worn them from the start, she would have attracted far too much attention from the other passengers while they rode—something that would have been both inconvenient and unbearable, in light of Pauline's shyness.

She could have used magic to color her hair, but this came with concerns about the spell's longevity, so instead she decided to use dye, which was convenient and had a proven track record of being secure and combat-proof. Using dye had the potential to damage one's hair, but Pauline, at least, would be able to repair—that is, heal—it easily. Any change in color could be mitigated by using cleaning magic to break down the components of the dye as well.

The Crimson Vow headed straight to their room to rest until dinnertime. They had done nothing but ride in the carriage, but between the harsh jostling of the road and the stress on their aching backs and bottoms, they were exhausted. Ewan seemed to be heading off to his room to rest also.

Theresa delivered her luggage to her room, and then set out again to make an appearance at the guild.

The next morning, after breakfast, they all set out together.

It would be conspicuous for a group of six to move as one, so they split into three pairs. Today's mission was mainly one of reconnaissance, so by splitting up, they not only stood out less, but would also be able to gather more information.

The first team consisted of Mavis and Ewan, who likely would not have consented to teaming up with anyone else. Pairs two and three were Reina and Theresa, and Mile and Pauline.

As they still had yet to make a move, the chance of danger befalling anyone but Pauline was low. Therefore it was decided that she should be accompanied by Mile, who, among the other three, was the most self-sufficient. Furthermore, it would be unwise to place Theresa—who had come with the intent of having the smallest possible role as an active party member—with Pauline, as she was perhaps the most belligerent. Even the notion of having any other team arrangement was unthinkable.

As someone who was their senior had been dispatched with

them, it would be questionable if that person were not treated as their leader for the duration. Therefore Theresa, though she was similar in appearance to the Crimson Vow, was selected for this role—in such a way that she would neither stand out nor truly take the initiative, remaining on the sidelines. Still, there was no sense in pairing her up with the leading actress in this production.

Theresa seemed as though she wanted to team up with Mile, but it was not her place to make that decision, so she kept her mouth shut.

And so, the three teams set out to their designated destinations to investigate.

Team Reina headed for the guildhall. Team Mavis turned toward the area where the merchants congregated. And Mile, along with Pauline—her eyes to the ground and her face hidden deep within her hood, completely obscured by tightly wrapped bandages—headed toward the residential district.

That evening, after each team had concluded their investigations, returned to the inn, and finished up their dinner, the whole group gathered in the largest bedroom.

"All right, let's go over what everyone found out."

As always, it was Reina who kicked off the discussion.

"First, let me give a rundown of what we learned at the guild: Apparently, the five-man band of C-rank hunters, employed now and then by the Beckett Company, hasn't been seen around town in about ten days. The Company often employs them for tasks outside the guild, when they need someone to do work that seems shady. Judging from their names and appearances, there is no doubt that those are our guys. On an unrelated note, it turns out that the Company often hires people without hunters' certifications to serve as their bodyguards. These are folks who specialize in guard work and nothing else."

"What we found out in the commercial district follows what Pauline told us to a "T." The Beckett Company is known for its forceful business practices and near-criminal tactics—which is to say that even when they do things that are blatantly illegal, they always manage to play the victim when the authorities get involved. There are quite a few other merchants who the Beckett Company has made trouble for, or who otherwise hold grudges against them. My brother here was able to get a lot of information out of the female shop employees."

At Mavis's explanation, Ewan looked rather proud of himself. The four other ladies listening noted the fact that Ewan had *only* interviewed women.

As Mile and Pauline had concentrated their energies on paying a surreptitious visit to Pauline's mother and brother, they had nothing in particular to contribute to the report.

"So far it seems that the testimonies of the men being held back in the capital haven't changed. If there were any new contradictions in their stories, the guild master would contact me without delay. It's been approximately seven days since they were handed over to the city guard. On a particularly fast horse, a messenger could reach here from the capital in about a day and a half. In other words, we know that nothing has changed in five and a half days, at the very least. They don't seem like the type who could stand up to interrogation from the guardsmen for very long, let alone withstand the techniques of the palace's own information extractors."

Theresa's report clinched it: there was no possibility that the captured men had falsely accused the company president.

At first, the girls considered getting themselves into the employ of the president, who would no doubt be irritated that the men he hired had yet to return. However, as they discussed the specifics of passing themselves off as down-on-their-luck hunters willing to take on illegal work, one look at each other's faces assured them that this would never work. So, they rethought their plan. Clearly, they wouldn't be fooling anyone.

Well, Mile thought, the justice system here was different enough from that of modern-day Earth that even circumstantial evidence should be enough to convict them.

She had proposed frightening the man and beating him within an inch of his life. However, everyone else had declined this offer. In order to preserve the business and let Pauline and her family take back possession of the shop, they couldn't simply fell the bad men with some pseudo-assassination.

It was a sound argument. If they went about this poorly, then they would be deemed criminals as well.

Their goal was not merely to take down the president and his crew, but to see Pauline's family's honor restored.

The members of the Crimson Vow racked their collective brains.

The next morning at 9:00 AM, just after the Beckett Company had opened shop for the day at the ringing of the second morning bell, four figures appeared outside their door.

They were four girls. From among them, the smallest, a girl of around eleven or twelve, produced a simple-looking item.

Bwooong!

Suddenly, a loud and unusual sound rang out, and the people around stopped in their tracks, turning to look at the girls.

Bwong-bw-bwooong!

After the sound had rung out, the girl cried out, "Vengeance is nigh! Vengeance is nigh! A young girl's father was murdered, her mother and brother and the shop her father built were all stolen away! Now, her vengeance is nigh! All ye gathered, please take care not to stand in the way, nor take injury from the fearsome spells that will soon fly!"

The forty-seven ronin (minus forty-three) were making their stand at the lord's mansion. There was no snow on the ground, but it *was* at least the early morning.

The spectators' eyes were sparkling.

This was a world of few amusements. The citizens of this town scarcely ever came across interesting events, let alone ones that they would be able to tell others about for decades to come. Furthermore, the stars of the show were a group of lovely young women, and their foe was an unscrupulous merchant, steeped in infamy. It took very little effort to guess which party was in the right, and which was in the wrong.

People began to gather around, and by the time the merchants stepped out to see what was going on, a sizable crowd had surrounded the Beckett Company headquarters.

Reina, meanwhile, muttered to herself, "What does 'nigh' even mean, anyway?"

"What is going on out here?!"

Perhaps having been informed by his employees about the commotion outside, the president of the Beckett Company—in other words, the very man who was Pauline's sworn enemy—stepped out of the door with some fellows who looked like bodyguards by his side. What he saw was a crowd surrounding his shop and four young girls standing before them.

"P-Pauline!"

Indeed, there stood Pauline, the dye cleansed and the brown of her hair restored with magic. Her bandages had been removed, and her face was plain to see.

"You've come back on your own! What is the meaning of all this?!" the president demanded, looking out over the crowd.

"This is your audience. They've all come to bear witness as you are captured and brought to justice..."

"Wh-what are you saying?!"

The president was stunned at these unexpected words from the usually meek and mild Pauline.

"Two and a half years ago, you hired bandits to kill my father and took over our shop using forged documents. I won't let you dare say that you've forgotten that! Furthermore, you have committed another crime, and this time, there's no hiding it: you attempted to harm citizens of the royal capital, which is under the direct control of His Majesty, the king himself. This is an attack on the king's own ground—an act of treason!"

At these wild accusations, shouts of anger began to rise from the growing mob.

"I-I've no idea what you're talking about! What proof do you have…?!"

The president panicked to hear such things said before so many people.

However, Pauline coolly continued, "Proof? Didn't you think it peculiar that you hadn't seen any signs of the men you hired to attack my friends, and that those same friends are here with me? That's right, your hunters have been captured and are being questioned by the palace guard. Or, perhaps I should say, they *were* being questioned. They've already confessed everything, and right about now, the guards from the capital are probably headed this way…"

"Wh…"

Upon seeing his reaction, the crowd knew at once: *Everything the girl said is true.*

Pauline had purposely linked the crimes of the far past to that of the present, in the closely held hope that as long as there were witnesses to the present events, those of the past might be proved just as easily.

The president, meanwhile, finally realized that by remaining speechless, he had sealed his own fate. However, it was already too late. The recognition of his guilt had begun to spread throughout the crowd. There was no choice but for him to quash this by force. As long as he could root out the main offender in all this ruckus, he could deal with all the residual effects later, somehow or other. He had connections just for circumstances like these. He'd paid bribes just for circumstances like these.

"Seize the ones spreading these hideous rumors!" he shouted as he signaled to his guards, falling back.

The sign he had given was one that he had used many times before: *Kill them.*

The five bodyguards gave small nods and stepped forward. Four of them drew their swords, while one stood just a little behind them, brandishing a staff.

"Oh, so they intend to kill us to silence us! The man has as good as acknowledged his sin! Since they have drawn their blades to slay us, we haven't a choice! To battle we must rise! We act now in self-defense!"

As Mile shouted this long-winded explanation of her actions, she drew her sword. The other three drew their weapons in turn. Reina and Pauline had already begun preparing their spells.

The bodyguards forwent any sort of needless shouts, such as, "Die, you wretches!" or, "Prepare yourselves, knaves!" Instead, wordlessly and immediately, they launched their attack. Unnecessary chatter was reserved for third-rate killers or worse, and these men appeared to be second-rate fighters at the very least. Reina and Theresa had heard that these men did not possess guild certification, but this certainly was not for lack of ability. There must be some other reason at hand.

As the battle began, Reina and Pauline concentrated all their energy on the enemy mage. As they were unaware of their enemy's capabilities, this was a standard precautionary measure. Moreover, this was the first time they were able to take full advantage of their absolute faith in Mile and Mavis's ability to completely shield them from the four swordsmen at the front. After all, if you were set upon by your enemy's forward guard while keeping all your concentration on the backline, you would be killed for certain.

The two had finished their spells now, their proverbial fingers on the trigger, waiting to speak the final, simple words that would release the attacks. And then the swordsmen moved their way.

Each of the four men aimed for one of the four girls. They intended to render the girls defenseless in one blow, with their mage as a backup precaution. Clearly, they were vastly underestimating the rage, swordsmanship, magical attack power, and casting speed of these young ladies.

Nonetheless, Mavis and Mile handily took on two of them apiece, stopping the ones who had aimed for the backline fighters as well as their own opponents. They swung upward to block the attacks coming their way, then back down to disarm the ones headed for the backline, stopping the men in their tracks. In the over half a year that they had spent together, they had practiced together a fair bit. This level of synchronized movement was no sweat for the party.

Seeing this, the enemy mage panicked, and released the trigger on the spell he had prepared, letting it fly toward Mavis. It was an icicle javelin.

As they were fighting in close quarters, it was crucial that he select a spell that would not affect anyone but his intended target. Thus, a spell like this was ideal. Furthermore, because it carried its own innate kinetic energy, the icicle could easily pierce through any magical protection that might be enacted.

However, in this case, it was the wrong move.

Even if the enemy mages were kept in check, aiming at the frontline fighters, rather than the mages, left them completely free to attack.

If these were your average, garden-variety novice hunters that the men were facing, this likely wouldn't have been a problem. For a magic-user who was confident in his skills, who had plenty of experience in combat and specialized bodyguard work, it would not be difficult to defend himself against the spells of novice magic-users even after they had already been let off. However, while Reina and Pauline were certainly "novices," one might only call them that while mentally appending "somewhat out of the ordinary."

"Earth Shield!"

"Icicle Javelin!"

Both of their spells were set into action, the icy spear that had been flying Mavis's way crashing into the wall of earth that had suddenly risen from the ground, and the blunt end of another ice javelin flying toward the enemy mage.

By the time the icicle spear—or rather, the blunt icicle rod—struck the enemy mage in the gut and knocked him to the ground, the four enemy swordsmen were all rolling on the ground. The crowd cheered in a frenzy, while the president went very pale.

Just as Pauline moved to try to question the man again, a voice came from behind her.

"Well, well, what's all this commotion about?"

The girls turned to see a hunter, who looked to be in his thirties, standing by. Judging by the sword sheathed at his waist, he was a frontline fighter. He had wily good looks that gave the impression that he would have been quite popular with the ladies back in his day, but he had a quiet demeanor and seemed to have aged gracefully. The few blades of stubble that remained unshaven from his cheeks lent him a rugged, pleasant look.

He was a veteran hunter, one who had worked his way up from the bottom. This was something you rarely saw.

Seeing this man, the hope of salvation appeared in the president's eyes. This look told Mile everything.

I bet he's going to say something like, "Master, please help me!"...

"Master, please help me!"

Yep, there it is.

"You girls look like hunters, but what's going on here?" the man called Master asked. He did not seem as intent on obeying his employer's orders as on ascertaining the circumstances of the situation.

And interestingly, he had not asked the question of his employer. Did he not trust the man? Or did he merely think it would be faster to inquire of his opponents themselves?

"We're apprehending a criminal."

"A criminal, you say?"

"That's right. This man hired robbers to kill this girl's father, then stole his business using forged documents. Later, he illegally hired a group of hunters to murder us—citizens of the royal capital—which is an act of treason," Reina explained.

Hearing this, the man turned to the president, who was shaking his head wildly, and asked, "Is this true?"

"Sh-she's lying! This is all slander!"

"Well, sometime in the next few days a guard wagon should be arriving from the capital, so you'll see soon enough. What would you like to do until then?" Reina asked the hunter, casually ignoring the president's desperate denial.

"Unlike those goons writhing around there, I was hired officially through the guild. Therefore, if you were all government officials or soldiers—or, if you were under the orders of an employer or the Crown, I wouldn't do anything. Since that doesn't seem to be the case, I have no choice but to keep guarding the man I'm contracted to. You're all hunters, so you understand, don't you?"

"I guess it can't be helped. However, since it's four against one, would you like to take this opportunity to surrender?"

"I can't do that. I'm a B-rank hunter. If I surrendered to a group of four rookies, my reputation would be ruined, and I can't allow that. In any case, I can't exactly see myself losing."

"I see... Well then, let's do this." Reina sighed, moving to brandish her staff.

Just then, Mile interjected from beside her, "Reina! This is a real match!"

"Huh???"

The other three, as usual, were stunned at Mile's strange words.

"This isn't a story tale! No matter how much we fight in the name of justice, bullying a weakling in front of all these people wouldn't feel right! Plus, it wouldn't be any fun at all for our spectators to watch!"

Seeing how the other three nodded silently in agreement, the crowd suddenly understood.

"Gotcha. Well then..."

"Wait! Wait wait waaait! What on earth do you mean 'in the name of justice,' and 'bullying a weakling'?! What does that mean? Do you think I'm the problem? Are you saying I'm a 'weakling'?!"

"Huh? You aren't?" Mile asked, clearly perplexed.

The hunter roared, "Of course I'm not!!! I already told you, didn't I?! I took this bodyguard job officially through the guild! If you all were working officially, through the appropriate channels, I would just shut up and hand him over. However, all I know is that you're a bunch of random assailants acting independently on a grudge. So, I have to follow through on the job I was hired to do and defend him! Furthermore, all of my companions are off in other towns on business. I took this job on independently just to kill some time, but I'm actually the leader of a B-rank party. My individual rank is close to an A-rank! Do you understand? I'm not lying, and I'm certainly not a weakling!"

"No, the way you have to insist on that just makes you seem even weaker..." Mile said suspiciously.

"I'm NOT!!!" the B-rank hunter screamed, red in the face.

"Well now, it seems like this crowd is really heating up, so..."

"You did that on purpose!"

"Your opponent now shall be Mile, the average magical knight beauty..."

"Where?"

"Huh?" Mile, intending to ignore the hunter's complaints and continue her spiel, let out a small sound of confusion.

"I'm asking, where is this 'beauty' who I'm supposed to be fighting?"

The hunter looked around theatrically, a faint smirk upon his face.

You jerk...

Mile sighed. It was her own fault for getting too into it and slipping that 'beauty' comment in there. However, there were plenty of people in this world who would refer to themselves as something like the "beautiful knight" or "brilliant magical beauty"... weren't there? Even when it came from something like the "Headless Killer-Beauty Incident," you still got from it that she was a beauty, regardless of the fact that she was headless, right? That was the sort of thing Mile had been going for.

It was the kind of declaration everyone made! You couldn't

just jump right into battle! Was this his revenge for making fun of him?!

At the thought, Mile was grinding her teeth internally.

She would harness this rage, and...

"I'll do it."

"Huh???"

"This should be my fight," Pauline said, taking a step forward, while the other three looked on perplexed.

"Pauline...?"

"It's fine. Despite how I may look, I too am a member of the Crimson Vo—"

"EH-HEH-HEH-HEM!!!"

Mile, Reina, and Mavis all let out a loud and rather forced-sounding cough, interrupting Pauline's words.

Indeed, they had already decided ahead of time that this job was not one being undertaken by the "Crimson Vow," but rather by "Pauline and her delightful companions." They didn't want word getting around that the Crimson Vow had been involved in an operation that resided in such a grey area. This was not a real job, but rather a member's individual undertaking.

Pauline swiftly recalled this and tried to change around her words to cover for her mistake.

"...I too am thirsty for blood, as a member of the Order of the Crimson Blood..."

The other three were stunned at the overcorrection.

The crowd recoiled.

"J-just what kind of party are you all?"

The other hunter was taken aback as well.

"Today has nothing to do with our party. We aren't here together as party members—they came here of their own accord to aid me in a personal battle. They're just my friends... no, they're my best friends!"

The other girls realized something: Pauline's words were suddenly much simpler than her usual manner of speech. Someone who had never met her before would scarcely notice, but for her friends, who had known her for so long, it was clear. Furthermore, they understood what this meant.

"My name is Pauline. I have risked everything to take vengeance upon my father's foe. And as thanks to the friends who have put their lives and their futures in my hands for the sake of my personal vengeance..."

Pauline was not speaking to her opponent. She was reciting words that she had rehearsed in advance. As she spoke, all the resources of her brain were focused on a different task.

"Go!"

As Pauline raised her staff, the hunter gripped the handle of his sword to draw it.

"Owwwwwww!!!"

The hunter screamed, pulling his hand from the handle. His palm was dripping, red with blood. When he looked down to the still-sheathed sword, he saw that the handle was suddenly covered in thorns.

"Wh-wha...?"

He reeled for a moment, but anyone who could truly be

caught off guard by such a simple thing could never be called a B-rank hunter.

"Damn it! You're a shadow-caster?! And you cast a high-level spell silently in your head, while still speaking normally?!"

As he spoke, he quickly glanced to his backup shortsword, glad to see that nothing was sprouting from that one. He swiftly gripped the handle of the shortsword and drew it.

"Hooooooooot!!!"

And with as much force as he had drawn it, he flung the shortsword forward.

"Secret technique, 'Heat Blade!'"

Pauline shouted the name of her technique (read: spell) with a satisfied look.

Indeed, as the hunter had guessed, this was shadow-casting: a high-level technique by which one secretly cast a spell without an incantation while talking about something else and pretending not to be doing anything magical. Naturally, this was difficult to achieve while speaking to one's opponent normally, so Pauline could only do it while mechanically reciting words that she had prepared ahead of time. Even so, it was an impressive feat.

Incidentally, the "Heat Blade" spell was a reference to the weapon used by a giant golem in one of Mile's bedtime stories, though she had it a bit backwards as to which part got hot—the blade or the handle. As Mile heard the name that Pauline gave it, she thought to herself, *Shouldn't she be calling this "Heat Grip" instead?*

"D-damn it! Well, at least I can still use my fists."

As he spoke, the hunter tried to throw a punch Pauline's way, but just then, he fell to his knees on the ground.

"Uh... huh? What? Why am... I...?"

And just like that, he collapsed on the ground.

"I never said that the handle of your sword was the only thing I had raised the temperature of. By slowly raising the temperature of your body bit by bit, it seems you've fallen right to pieces as well..."

"Gaaaaaah! Water! Someone, please dump some water on his head! He's gonna diiie!"

At Mile's desperate cry, several of the nearby spectators rushed over to draw water from the emergency reservoirs in front of the shop and douse the man with buckets. If she had thought about it, this would have been much quicker for Mile to do with magic, but she was too aghast for this to occur to her. When, after a short while, the thought *did* cross her mind, she hurriedly used some cooling and healing magic on him.

Yet it was unclear whether healing magic could restore one's mind and memories to normal after something so traumatic, so she was rather concerned. This hunter was just trying to perform the duty he had been hired to do, after all. He wasn't a particularly bad guy.

In other words, they were the ones, in this case, who would be the villains in the eyes of the law.

"Wh-what...?"

As his final lifeline was severed, the president fell into despair.

However, fate smiled on him once more.

"Clear the road!"

Several riders on horseback and a single carriage approached, with several dozen foot soldiers proceeding some distance behind them.

"Bwahaha, you idiots! I can't believe you fell for all that stalling! The lord and his soldiers are here. It's the end for you! You better get ready!"

Reina, Mavis, and Pauline were floored.

Huh? they thought. *Really? What's going to happen now? Will we be all right?*

Mile, meanwhile, looked completely unconcerned.

It's all going according to plan...

"What is the meaning of this? Explain yourselves!"

"...And you are?" Mile asked of the man who had just stepped down from the carriage.

One of the soldiers, climbing down from his horse, answered in the man's stead.

"Insolent child! This man is the lord of these lands, his Excellency, Viscount Boardman!"

The president leapt in. "Your Excellency, these scoundrels have falsely accused and attacked me!"

"What? False accusations, you say?"

Mile, of course, chimed in to answer this. "Ah, yes! This man hired thieves to murder the owner of this shop, then took control of it using forged documents! Whoever approved these obviously fake papers must have been an accomplice of his as well, so we'd like to see them brought in together and executed! I wonder who around here would do such a wicked thing? Their superiors clearly must be investigated as well!"

As Mile spoke in a booming voice, everyone in the crowd grimaced.

"Wh-what are you shouting about?!" The lord tried to silence Mile in a panic, but she had already finished all that she had set out to say.

"Yes, we beg you, your Excellency—please apprehend this criminal!" This time Reina jumped in, shouting just as loudly.

"Sh-shut up, shut up, shut up! You wretches are causing a public unrest in my city! You're the ones who should be arrested!" The lord shouted back at them, conscious of the crowd around him.

"Oh? Now isn't this strange? How could you decide which of us is in the wrong without conducting a proper investigation? It's almost like something an official who would approve falsified documents would do, passing a judgment without an investigation, in spite of public protests. How very peculiar... Wait—could it be...?"

This time it was Pauline, whose ponderings grew bolder and bolder.

"D-didn't I tell you all to shut up?! You lot, seize them immediately!"

"I can't let you do that."

From out of the crowd, a woman stepped forward.

"Who are you?!"

"My name is Theresa. I'm a representative of the capital branch of the hunters' guild."

"How is this the business of some little girl from the guild?!"

"Yes, well, that merchant is a criminal who ordered the murder of these young hunters, who are citizens of the capital, so I've come here to follow up on that incident. Those girls there are the wronged party, and as recently as a few minutes ago, that man once again ordered them to be killed by those men rolling on the ground there. I cannot allow someone who appears to be in cahoots with these men, such as you, your Excellency, to take custody of these girls."

"Wha...?"

Theresa ignored the lord, and turned to the president.

"Outside of individuals caught in the act and other wanted criminals, the hunters' guild does not have the authority to apprehend those who are not members of the guild. However, you directed your underlings to kill a group of guild members. The guild therefore recognizes that act as a clear attack on the guild itself. Following this, it has been officially deemed that, from here on out, no requests to the guild shall be accepted from your company, your business partners, or anyone else who may associate with you. This shall be the case in any branch, in any country. No bodyguards, no caravan escorts, and no orders of materials.

"Furthermore, your involvement in the attempted murder of our guild members has already been reported to the city guard in the capital. What you've done is an offense against citizens of the capital, and thereby an offense against His Majesty himself, and so, regardless of your status as the constituent of another lord, the capital city guard has the authority to apprehend you. I believe the guards charged with that duty have already departed the capital, so they should be arriving very soon.

"Thus concludes my statement from the hunters' guild, capital branch."

"Wh...?"

The president and the lord were both stunned into silence.

The president had, just earlier, heard from Pauline about these guards from the capital, but he had yet to think anything of them. He had simply planned to shut the girls up, choose an appropriate merchant as a scapegoat, and assert, "He faked his identity to try and sully my name!" As always, he would wait for the lord's underlings to capture the man, torture him, then claim that he had confessed everything before killing himself. For the president, it would all be just as it had been so many times before...

Furthermore, even if the capital guards were able to collect the appropriate evidence and witnesses, he presumed that they would not be able to lay a finger on him, the citizen of another lord's lands—no matter if they were from the king's jurisdiction. No matter if they had evidence, witnesses, or testimony from criminals. The lord could attest to his innocence, after all.

Yet the guild was a problem.

The guild was not bound to the orders of any noble, nor even the Crown.

Furthermore, the guild chose whether or not to accept jobs purely at its own discretion, and beyond that, the guild was not even duty-bound to produce proof of wrongdoings in order to refuse an enemy service. The guild merely had to declare, "This person is our enemy," and a hunter would never work for them again. It was as simple as that, and no one was granted the right to protest it.

On top of this, it would not only be his shop affected by this ban, but also anyone who did business with his shop. This would mean the end for him.

Escorts for their caravans. Orders of supplies and goods. Hunters would refuse to have anything to do with anyone who associated with him. For a merchant, such a wound could prove fatal.

For his business partners, the means to avoid such a fate would be simple: They would merely need to cut all ties with the Beckett Company. And so, who in their right mind would possibly continue to do business with him after that?

Besides, he wouldn't be able to send out wagons with goods from his shop, nor order any new materials gathered.

He was ruined.

"Y-your Excellency," the president pleaded desperately. "You must apprehend these fiends and execute them! There's no way such a young girl could be a representative of the guild! They're trying to deceive us!"

If the girl from the guild was dealt with, the president would have time to select a scapegoat to throw the soldiers from the capital off his trail and avoid punishment from the guild.

The lord had the same thought. It certainly was peculiar that such an important task would be left up to some fifteen or sixteen-year-old rookie. Furthermore, it would be a problem to allow this commotion to go on any longer. They had to hurry and apprehend everyone, select some thug to take the fall, and prepare the scapegoat to be handed over to the capital guards.

If they did not, the president of the Beckett Company would be seized and hauled away by those same guards, and if he began to flap his gums while being questioned, then the lord would be put in a sticky position, too. To date, he had granted the Beckett Company a number of "advantages," which in turn saw a number of returns come his way. Put simply, all it would take was a single breath for his entire house of cards to crumble.

Moreover, this group of young ladies made quite an attractive set. Their bodies were... well, they were still somewhat lacking for his tastes, but they would do.

As the lord pondered this, his foot soldiers finally arrived, and he issued his command with a smirk:

"Seize those girls! But don't hurt them *too* much."

Even if they were hunters, they were still a group of young girls between ten and seventeen or eighteen years of age. There was nothing that they could possibly do against a group of over sixty soldiers.

And so the soldiers drew their swords and began to advance on the girls, menacingly.

Ka-blam!

The lid was blown off.

"There you have it, they're approaching with their swords drawn: a clear declaration of attack. We've just been granted the grounds for some justified self-defense!"

"Huh????"

The lord, as well as the crowd around him, raised their voices in confusion. They had never heard of such a term as "grounds for justified self-defense."

In any case, this granted the Crimson Vow the right to launch a counterattack on anyone who showed even the slightest hint of trying to harm them. They could look further into the circumstances once their opponents were felled. If they did not do so, then they would never survive, no matter how many lives they had.

In a world like this one, even the slightest show of malice, such as brandishing a weapon, was sufficient grounds for at least a little retaliation. Really, strictly seeking out a "grounds for justified self-defense" as one might on modern day Earth was nothing more than a means of satisfying Mile's sensibilities.

"Pauline, Reina, if you would."

Mile was wiped for the time being, and of course it would be impossible for even Mavis to fight this many soldiers head-on, so now, it was up to the other two.

From the beginning, this had been Pauline's fight, and Reina, whose father had similarly, been killed by thieves, had her own small stake in this, too. It would be dangerous not to let the two of them let off a little steam.

There were no magic-users in the soldiers' ranks.

There were few people around who could use combat magic of any sort, but mages who also had the tactical sense and level of ability to utilize combat magic in organized warfare were a rare breed indeed, and they were always well-salaried. It wasn't as though they lived in the lap of luxury, but their pay certainly amounted to that of several average soldiers combined.

The shop employee who had been dispatched to send word to the viscount had assumed Mile was a sword-wielder, and had reported that there were only two young rookie mages amongst the group. So, it was deemed that even if they did have mages in their midst, a group of rookie hunters would be helpless against a band of soldiers many times their number, and the lord elected not to dispatch the scant number of mages within the regional troops against a few young girls.

In other words, there was no one to stand up to the pair.

"Flare!"

The spell Reina let off was but a simple thing, a flame that would only graze an enemy, not explode or pierce or anything like that. Put simply, she was holding back. However...

"Gaaaaaaaaaaaaaaaaah!!"

This momentary flame had almost no effect on the soldiers' weapons or the parts of them that were covered by armor. However, their exposed skin and hair was not so lucky.

Their skin was all right. It was red on the surface and stung badly, but in medical terms, they had received only a first-degree burn. In a week or two, they would be right as rain, without even aches or scars.

Their hair, however, was singed. To a crisp.

Ignoring the flailing soldiers, Pauline now turned to another group, and let off a spell of her own.

"Ultra Hot Mist!"

"Eeeeeeeeeeeeeeeeeek!!"

A red mist rained down on the soldiers.

Once again, the "hot" used here did not mean thermal heat, but rather, spiciness. This was the mist version of the "Waterball: Ultra Hot" spell she had used before, when capturing the robbers.

"Eughaaaaaaah!!"

Unfortunately, it seemed that a portion of the mist had drifted onto the soldiers whose scalps Reina had already burned with magic. A scream the likes of which had never been heard in this world rang out.

"Wh-wha...?"

These young girls, of whom they had thought so little, had rendered nearly a quarter of the troops incapable of fighting in an instant. The lord was shocked. However, they were still fighting these enemy mages at point-blank range. Both of them had just finished casting, so it would take time for them to incant their next spells.

"Now! Before they finish casting their next spells!!" the viscount screamed, but Mile and Mavis had each already taken a step forward.

When it came to magic-users, it was not so strange to find someone of formidable skill, regardless of their age. However, when it came to the sword, this was not the case.

In the world of swordsmanship, the difference between someone of 45 years and someone of 50 was little, but the difference between 15 and 20 years old was an insurmountable wall. Such was the way of the weapon. Facing seasoned soldiers, a little girl of around ten and a young lady—who was older, but likely not even twenty—could easily be kicked aside, allowing for the mages' capture.

So thought the viscount, and thus, he felt relief, until suddenly a voice came from the crowd.

"Could you wait a moment?!"

Naturally, there was not a soldier around who would halt in the middle of a skirmish just because the voice of someone they didn't know asked them to. Several of the men swung at Mile and Mavis and were just as quickly blocked. The brief time it bought them was long enough for Reina and Pauline to complete their spells.

"Firebomb!"

"Slippery!"

Reina's fire magic—whose power and scope she had initially held back, in light of their surrounding environment—exploded. Immediately after this, Pauline let off her original spell, "Slippery," to halt that same fire's spread.

Several of the soldiers were blown away by the explosion, and those remaining fell into a great panic.

"E-everything's slippery! I can't grip my sword!"

The fearsome magic of "Slippery!"

How fortunate that there were no female soldiers present.

"Now then! Didn't I tell you to wait?!"

While the battle was put momentarily on hold, the owner of the voice that had called out before emerged from a gap in the crowd.

No matter how you looked at the man, it was clear he was a noble, and he was flanked by several knights, positioned around him like guards.

"Viscount Boardman, pray tell what it is you intend to do to my daughter."

"F-Father!" Mavis shouted. "And Third Brother...and First Brother..."

Indeed, Doting Daddy and the SisCons had just made their stage debut.

Since the morning following his first encounter with Mavis in the capital, Ewan had penned letters to their father every day, collecting the details he learned. One of these letters had even been written the day the plan to travel to Viscount Boardman's lands was made.

Each one, he sent by dragon mail.

Of course, dragon mail did not actually go by dragon. It was merely an express relay system, where horses and messengers were changed out at every station, so that a letter seemed to travel as though on a dragon's wings. After all, one could not put a price on assuring Mavis's safety.

Naturally, upon receiving Ewan's information, their father was indignant with rage.

"Someone tried to a-a-attack my dearest daughter, who is the spitting image of my beloved wife in her younger days...?!"

Not an hour after he received the letter, their father had set out toward the viscount's lands, along with six of his subordinates and his eldest son, who entrusted all his official duties to his next-youngest brother.

"Wh... C-Count Austien? Why has the Count himself suddenly appeared in my capital, without sending even a messenger...?"

Viscount Boardman apparently knew the face of Count Austien, who was not only an influential nobleman, but also a powerful player in military circles. Not yet grasping the situation at hand, he was incredibly confused.

"That girl there, Mavis, is my beloved daughter. Now then, might you care to offer an explanation as to why you are attempting to protect the offender who had my daughter attacked in the capital? Depending on what you say, this may not end well for you," said Count Austien to Viscount Boardman. His face twisted in loathing, and he tried to mask the way that his arms trembled in rage. "I—no—we, the entire Austien family, shall assume the responsibility of sending the man who appears to be your ally—the man who attempted to bring harm upon Mavis von Austien, our family's crown jewel—straight to the depths of Hell..."

Viscount Boardman was white as a sheet.

A lord could do as he pleased with his own citizens. He could threaten them and increase their taxes and kill them or their friends or families—anyone who did not follow his commands.

Many of the hunters, as well as the employees of the local guild branch, were citizens of his lands, too. There was not an idiot around who did not know that if they made an enemy of their lord, then a harsh fate awaited not only them but everyone they associated with.

However, the Count was a problem.

The fact that the Count held a higher station was a problem enough in itself, but the Austien family also had great influence over the Crown and other noble families, and furthermore, they were renowned for their militaristic bent. While their regional troops did not greatly outnumber that of other lords' territories, their strength was widely acknowledged.

If such a noble were to level his power and hatred at the Viscount, rally the aid of other influential nobles, and perhaps even involve the Crown... he would not stand a chance.

"Y-your daughter? Whatever could you be talking about? I came out here merely because I heard that man over there, who happens to be a merchant in my city, was being attacked. In any event, this is a problem for *my* territory. You may be a count, but you have no right to meddle in my affairs!"

The viscount tried desperately to gloss over the incident, but Count Austien was not ready to abandon this battle so easily.

"Oho! Well then, I suppose there is no reason a viscount should be meddling in my affairs either—I, who came all the way here because I heard that my daughter and her companions, young girls who are all citizens of the capital, were being attacked. If my family's only daughter, as well as citizens of the capital, a

place under the king's direct rule, are involved, then this is a problem for me and His Majesty."

"What frivolous chatter is this? It would be one thing if you
were His Majesty himself, but for a noble to be butting into
another noble's affairs—even if you *are* a count—is simply—"

"If you require His Majesty's seal as proof, then will this do?"

"What?"

Count Austien and Viscount Boardman both turned in surprise at the voice that came suddenly from beside them. They
saw a man in his mid-thirties, who looked like a knight, standing
there. A sword was fastened to his waist.

"My apologies for cutting in. I am Santos, of the second division of the royal guards. Recently, His Majesty received a missive
from the guild master of the capital branch of the hunters' guild,
stating that some personages under His Majesty's own watch had
come under attack. Moreover, the letter explained that those self-
same individuals were now undertaking an investigation into the
situation on their own behalf. I am the one who was directed
by His Majesty to confirm the aforementioned circumstances. I
come as the forbearer of an approaching unit that will apprehend
and transport the wrongdoers. As this is a matter concerning an
offense against His Majesty's people, and ergo, well within His
Majesty's jurisdiction, I have been granted the authority to apprehend the offenders in His Majesty's name.

"Count Austien, you are a faithful retainer of His Majesty.
Furthermore, these young women of the Crimson Vo... ahem, the
Order of the Crimson Blood, received half a year of *tuition-free*

education at the Hunters' Prep School and are associates of the capital branch of the hunters' guild. In the name of His Majesty, I request that you confirm the identity of the mastermind behind these offenses, as well as all those who have interfered in this investigation."

"Wh...?"

Viscount Boardman was speechless. The crowd's gaze shot back and forth in bewilderment as they followed every new sally in this ping-pong match.

Though the girls of the Crimson Vow had considered the possibility that Mavis's family might get involved, even they had never imagined that the king himself might take an interest in their affairs.

The viscount was sweating bullets. If he handled this poorly, it could spell doom for him. He thought desperately and reached a conclusion.

"I-I suppose, in that case," he announced, "I have little choice. Until the guards arrive to apprehend him, I shall deal with that merchant myself."

The merchant, whose expression had been utterly grim, appeared relieved. Perhaps he thought that the viscount was coming to his rescue.

However, at that very moment, Pauline called out in a flat voice, "What are you looking so happy for? Doesn't that just mean he's going to murder you to shut you up and then, when the guards arrive, tell them you killed yourself because you realized no escape was possible? That way you can't cause any trouble for him..."

The president went pale once again, his knees knocking and teeth chattering.

"Wh-what are you saying? You have no basis for..."

"If that is the case, then I shall be the one to handle that merchant."

The viscount glared at Santos, the knight of the royal guard, who had interrupted him.

At this rate, it was certain that the president would be taken to the capital and questioned, encouraged to spill everything he knew. There was no way that this man could stand up to a palace interrogator. And in any case, he had no reason to put himself through that much to protect the viscount. In fact, there was a relatively high probability that he would pin all sorts of wrongdoings on the viscount, once his gums got flapping.

Even if he was the rightful head of a noble family, they were still a lower-ranking clan. And if all of his past wrongdoings were to come to light, the king might seize his estate, or place him under house arrest and set up his son or some other relative to rule in his place.

This was bad. This was very very very very bad!

"All right now, what tomfoolery is this?! Am I to believe that His Majesty would take an interest in such unimportant little girls as these?! Or that this rookie hunter is truly the honorable Count's daughter? If you hope to deceive me, you are going to have to be a little more convincing than that! These miscreants have used a noble's name in vain and sullied the reputation of His Majesty—kill them!"

Kill them. That was his solution. As long as all relevant parties were eliminated, he could make some excuse for it later on.

They had attacked him suddenly, unprovoked.

They had demanded bribes and sullied His Majesty's name.

They had colluded with the merchant and conspired to overtake his lands. The fellow from the royal guard was in on it as well.

As long as everyone was dead, he could say whatever he wanted. He could do whatever he liked.

Viscount Boardman had no choice but to believe this.

Given how poorly everything was going, he had no real reason to believe this plan might work, and yet he had no other option.

On the viscount's command, the relatively few remaining soldiers, along with the knights that had accompanied him from the start, brandished their swords.

Mile thought, *This is the last ten minutes of the episode, isn't it...?*

And Pauline thought, *Why did he put so much emphasis on "received half a year of* tuition-free *education at the Hunters' Prep School"? Does that mean that they're going to start working us for free now? What a miser! The king is so cheap!*

Didn't I Say
to Make My Abilities
Average in the
——— Next Life?!

CHAPTER 23 |

A New Battle

AFTER THOSE with the most severe wounds dropped out, fifty-one units remained in Viscount Boardman's army, nine with minor injuries. Fifty-one versus the twelve of Pauline's forces.

The viscount himself did not count Pauline, Reina, or Theresa among Pauline's numbers. Judging by the strong showing from the Count's forces, the magic-users would not be a part of this fight. This battle was going to be decided with swords.

Santos, of the royal guards, joined their forces as well, of his own accord.

Still, speaking purely in terms of numbers, the viscount's forces outstripped Pauline's more than four-fold. If one analyzed the situation in terms of Lanchester's laws, the odds of their winning were indescribably low.

To start, situations where a very small number could beat back an overwhelming force were incredibly rare. Because they were so rare, any successful cases were widely heralded through-out the land. In other words, it was easy to prove that such things scarcely ever happened in reality.

When such aspirational situations did come about, it was because one side had weapons that were phenomenally stronger than those of their opponents, a plan was in place ahead of time, or some other such advantage was at play.

In this case, they had no special plan, their weapons were the same, and they were squaring off, face-to-face, with a group more than four times the number of their own troops. Not only was this not within the bounds of common sense, it was sheer madness.

However, there were those among them who shattered the limits of so-called common sense on a regular basis.

Indeed, just as a girl by the name of Kurihara Misato had shat-tered the balance of heaven and earth so very long ago.

"Graaaaaaaaaaaaaaah!"

Taking the lead, Count Austien charged forward into the en-emy lines with a mighty roar. Following him, the count's two sons and his subordinate knights rushed into the fray.

Santos proceeded behind them, while Mile and Mavis, hav-ing allowed the others to take the vanguard, casually followed after them in turn.

The mages stood by as spectators, but they had their spells prepared in advance. They were certain that the others would be fine, but it was better to be ready, on the off chance that they needed assistance. It was not a competition, after all. They would let off their spells when the moment came. Certainly, it was by their own choosing that the mages were not yet participating in this fight—not because of some promise to the enemy, or an obligation to honor the Count's desires to settle this battle with swords alone.

If it seemed that their friends or allies were about to take a loss, they would attack without hesitation. Just as they always did.

And then, the count's forces and the viscount's forces clashed.

A number of the viscount's soldiers circled around from the sides, hoping to entrap the count's forces; however, this maneuver was in vain. The count's forces had already broken into the enemy's front lines, and were pushing through to the other side.

One after another, the viscount's forces were blown away, as the count charged forth, magnificently wielding a sword in each hand. His two sons and his knights—along with Santos of the royal guard—were not to be shown up by the count's ferocity, and swatted here and there, sending their enemies flying. The count's fighters blasted through the enemy's front lines, then turned about to face the soldiers once again.

The viscount's soldiers were startled at this sudden turnabout. They had been the ones attempting to come at their enemy from behind, and now, they hurriedly tried to launch a counterattack, only to be pounced upon, almost casually, by Mile and Mavis.

They were suddenly pinned in place, trapped between the count's group and the duo of Mile and Mavis.

As Mavis matched blades with an enemy, she was stunned

by her opponent's skill and strength. Unthinkingly uttered, she spoke aloud: "...Th-they're weak!"

Yes, the viscount's forces were incredibly weak.

Any lord worth his salt should have the military forces to defend his fiefdom—in the same way the king had the royal guard. This particular viscount should have had top-class soldiers within his ranks. They should have easily been able to wipe out the count's forces, as well as Mile and Mavis.

The viscount's forces should have been at least that good, shouldn't they?

So Mavis thought, but for the viscount's forces themselves, this was a cruel way of framing the narrative.

Indeed, it was not that the viscount's forces were all that weak—it was that the count's forces were too strong. That was all there was to it. And naturally, there was no way that Santos, of the royal guard, would be weaker than the soldiers belonging to some noble.

And then, there were Mile and Mavis...

On the one side, there were the soldiers belonging to the forces of a lesser noble. On the other, there were a martially renowned count and his sons, their personal knights, and a strong and virile knight of the royal guard, along with Mile and Mavis—who, of course, were an incomparable oddity. Honestly, they might as well have been a bunch of bullies.

And then, the battle was over.

The difference in the two forces' strength was overwhelming

enough that the victors had been able to hold back, ending the skirmish with no deaths and few serious injuries on the part of the losers—though their hearts were certainly shattered by such a decisive loss.

Holding back like this required that there be a tremendous difference in ability. If their abilities had been matched, then they couldn't have avoided fighting at full strength, and if that happened, then fatal injuries became almost inevitable. Yet with this refreshing difference in their strengths, that had not become necessary.

"Now then, might I persuade you to take a trip with me, Viscount?"

"Wh-what...? I have no reason to go along with this practical joke!" Startled by Santos's sudden words, the viscount sputtered a refusal.

"Up until a short while ago, the idea was that the members of the Order of the Crazy Broa... ahem, the Order of the *Crimson Blood* are operating independently, and not on anyone's orders. The testimony of the men who are imprisoned in the capital pertains only to this merchant. Neither testimony nor accusation has been officially levied at you, Lord Boardman. One could say that you only came to investigate a disturbance within your own territory and attempted to apprehend the perpetrators..."

Hearing this, the viscount looked as though he had suddenly understood the gist of the situation.

"Hm, that's a royal guard for you. How incredibly astute!"

Santos, however, was not finished speaking.

"That *was* the idea. But now, Viscount, you are a rebel who has ordered your subordinates to kill not only the Count and his party, but also an agent of the master of the capital guild branch—as well as myself: a direct, authorized representative of His Majesty, the king. In other words, you are a traitor to your country. Even if you are a noble, I cannot overlook such a serious crime."

"Wh...?"

"You seem to have suffered a lapse in judgment. Well, I don't deny that *had* you been able to kill everyone here, there was a possibility that you might have been able to take back control of this situation. However, I believe it would take an exceptional amount of time and money for you to amass a strong enough army to make that happen. Now then, Count, if you would..."

Count Austien nodded at Santos' request and directed his subordinates to apprehend Viscount Boardman, who was pale and quivering. He no longer had the will to resist, and silently allowed them to bind him.

"I guess it's over, then," said Mile.

"So it is."

"Yeah..."

Reina and Mavis nodded in reply.

Pauline stared at the ground, silent.

Vengeance was now complete. It had been two and half years since her father had been murdered and everything stolen away, and the entirety of her life since then had been dedicated to the pursuit of vengeance. Now, they had won a complete—truly unimaginable—victory, and felled a black-hearted lord in the process. She would never have thought all this would be possible.

Thanks to her companions—her friends—her dream had come true.

"Pauline..."

Noticing how Pauline's shoulders trembled, Mile called out to her, but Reina gently held her back.

And as Pauline looked down at the ground beneath her feet, dark drops began to appear.

"Now then, while the viscount is restrained, let us gather some evidence. We must confirm whether the viscount's wife, son, relatives, or associates were accomplices to his crimes, mustn't we?" Count Austien proposed.

"Yes, that is correct," Santos agreed.

The results of this investigation would have an enormous effect on determining the fate of the Boardman family assets. On the one hand, they might be dismantled, but on the other, it was possible that one of the viscount's children or relatives would be instated as the head of the family in order to continue the noble line. Even if he had a legitimate heir, if any of that heir's associates turned out to be rotten, then the entire upper ranks would need to be replaced. And that was in addition to rooting out any associated merchants.

Along with his two sons and his guards, the count started to turn toward the viscount's estate, but stopped, and turned to Mavis. "The guard wagon from the capital will be arriving in two days' time. We will hand over the criminals then, and three days after, we shall return to our estate. Enjoy these final days with your friends."

"Huh...?"

Mavis looked on, bewildered, hardly comprehending what she had just been told.

"This shop will most likely be returned to the girl's family. And then, in the time to come, her family will need to conserve their strength to protect the place—the beloved shop that her father left behind. In other words, your days of playing 'Mavis, the adventuring hero' are through. And furthermore, Mavis, you must complete the bridal training lessons that you abandoned when you ran off!"

"That is *completely* UNNECESSARY!!!" Mavis, Ewan, and their older brother all shouted in unison.

"Mavis has no need to prepare herself for marriage!"

"That's right! Mavis will always be by our—"

"No, that's not it..."

It was not because she wished to remain single for the rest of her life that Mavis had objected to the Count's plan, which meant that she also had to protest at her brothers' interjections.

"In any case, who knows when danger such as the one that befell you here might come upon you again? This is the last time that I will tolerate your little games. If you want to play at being a knight, then I might be willing to let you train—now and then—around our estate. Basic self-defense is required, after all, of the wife of a noble, for the sake of both you and your children.

"Well, we shall discuss the details of this tomorrow. For now, enjoy the day with your friends."

With these words, the count collected his sons and his underlings, then departed.

Once the count's party was gone, the Crimson Vow turned their backs on the crowd, which was still abuzz with chatter, and returned to their inn.

Santos and Theresa had joined the Count, heading for the viscount's estate. Naturally, this was part of their duties.

"............"

This was someone's future they were talking about—someone who was their precious companion, and furthermore, the daughter of a powerful noble. It was not a topic of conversation they could just shoot their mouths off about.

Yet keeping silent about it would not see anything settled, and Mile was the first to set the gears in motion.

"So, Mavis, what are you going to do?"

"Refuse, of course!! I still haven't accomplished anything at all! Am I just supposed to give up everything and go live my life in some cage?!"

Mavis was half in tears.

Pauline, who should have been happy now that her family's problems were solved, felt responsible. She hung her head in silence at the notion that her joy had come at the cost of Mavis's strife.

Reina's mind was on the reality of the situation: if both

Pauline and Mavis left, the Crimson Vow would be no more. She hung her head too, her expression dark.

Even if she and Mile were to recruit new members, they would never be equal to their classmates, the allies who fought and learned alongside them, the "allies bound at the soul, sworn to each other in eternal friendship." They could no longer call themselves the Crimson Vow. They would have to change their name, and start out again as a new party.

Plus, if that happened, there was a chance that Mile might not even come along.

They were a party of classmates—of roommates—so of course, she had joined them without any objections. If it was Reina alone, and Mile suddenly saw her as nothing more than "someone who just happened to be my roommate, out of a class of forty," then that was far too weak a reason for Mile to stay with her.

Plus, mightn't any new members covet Mile's abilities? Or, wouldn't Mile start getting invitations from higher-ranking parties? Wouldn't the Roaring Mithrils have her join them without a second thought? For Mile, that would be a far better...

Yet Mavis, the daughter of a noble family, had a life of her own, and certain duties to fulfill as someone born into a noble household. Hers was not the sort of problem that Reina could simply overpower with her own concerns.

When she thought about it that way, there was not a thing that Reina could say.

And so, silence fell upon them once more...

"Well then, let's just turn Mavis's family away!"

"Huh?"

Mavis, Reina, and Pauline all gaped at Mile's sudden, unexpected proposal.

"What? I mean, none of us wants Mavis to return to her home, right? Um, am I wrong? Umm... Anyone who thinks it would be better if Mavis stayed with the Crimson Vow, raise your hand!"

Ping! Ping! Ping!

All of their hands, including Mile's, shot straight up.

They all turned to look at each other's faces.

"Then it's settled."

As she said so, Mile's face lit up with a wicked grin.

Pauline smiled too. Before, she had been wallowing in her own sense of guilt for bringing this situation about by drawing her friend's into her own family's problems. But really, she realized, all they had to do was drive Mavis's father away. It was a simple matter, wasn't it?

Even as she thought to herself, *Shouldn't I object to this?* Reina's eyes sparkled.

"B-but how?! My father won't listen to anything anyone has to say..."

Mile grinned wide and replied, "There's a saying in my home country: *Know thy enemy, and know thyself, and in a hundred battles thou shalt never know fear...*"

It was the first time they had ever heard this saying, but all of them were experienced in battle. They could easily fill in the blanks.

"We know a lot about you, Mavis. And about your family as well..."

"Ah!"

Reina and Pauline both understood.

Only Mavis still stared blankly, obviously in the dark.

It seemed she did not realize how many times she had told them tales of her family in the over half a year that they had been together.

Indeed, Mile, Reina, and Pauline all knew quite a bit about Mavis's family. Perhaps more than anyone but the members of the family themselves.

"What? You'd like for me to train with you, Father? No, I'll have to pass. That won't help me improve myself any—"

"Wh-what?"

The next morning, the count returned, proposing once more to take Mavis back home with him. Mavis, however, refused his offer with a grimace, leaving the count wide-eyed.

"Wh-what are you saying?"

"Well, it's just as I said... You're nowhere near my master's level, Father."

"Wh...?"

Before her father's expression could morph into anger, the look on his face was one of utter shock.

Her two brothers and the other knights all looked on in bewilderment.

Count Austien was an accomplished individual, renowned

throughout the land for his martial prowess. There was no teacher of swordsmanship anywhere in the vicinity who could hope to best him. Therefore, if Mavis wished to grow stronger, it only made sense that he would be the one to train her. He had offered to as a bribe, and yet this was her reply.

Once he had recovered from his surprise, the count, who assumed that Mavis was only spewing nonsense out of desperation, chuckled internally. Now, he knew he had a way to bring his stubborn daughter back home peacefully. If he could show Mavis just how weak her so-called master was, and prove that she hadn't really grown all that strong, then the grounds on which she objected to his plan would be completely dashed. He didn't want Mavis to be angry or to hate him. If possible, he wanted his daughter to consent to returning home of her own accord, so he felt he had been tossed a lifeline.

"Oho! Well then, you must have quite an illustrious master. If they're really so strong, I should like to face them in one-on-one combat. If this person is truly stronger than I am, and you can prove to me that you have been earnestly following their teachings, then I will have no objection to you continuing with your training. However, if this is all just bluster, then I hope that you will quietly..."

"Understood! If you lose, Father—and, hmm, if I can win against First Brother—then we'll quit this talk of my returning home, and you'll let me live however I choose! And everyone gathered here can serve as witnesses to that fact!"

"Wh...?"

The count, his two sons, and the attendant knights once again appeared to be utterly taken aback at Mavis's declaration. A satisfied grin had spread across her face.

The count, who should have been pleased with the way the discussion of Mavis's return home was proceeding, had a bad feeling about all this. Perhaps it was his intuition as a tactical genius...

"No! If that happens, then I shall invite this master to reside with us..."

Even if it seemed cowardly, or made their loved ones hate them, it was the job of family to take precautionary measures in order to keep their relatives out of danger, no matter how faint that possibility of danger might be.

"No. My master is not one to be tied down to a single household's whims. You're only saying this because then I would naturally come along as well. Or, Father, could it be that you are not confident that you'll win?"

"All right... Have it your way! When shall we hold the match?"

"Tomorrow evening, after we have handed over the viscount and the merchant. In this town's arena."

"What? Will your master be able to make it here in time? Well, that's fine. I accept. Tomorrow evening. You had better enjoy this final evening with your companions as best you can."

He had given in to Mavis's provocation. Though he was no longer entirely confident in his own victory, the count was not truly shaken. He did not know who this person was that he would face, but there was *almost* no way he could possibly lose to some no-name teacher who would spend their time on a rookie hunter pupil. That much he was sure of.

And, on top of that, there was no way that Mavis could win against his eldest son. Even if miracles did exist in this world, they never happened one right after the other. That much he believed.

"Mile, are you sure this is gonna be alright?"

The moment the count departed, Mavis's face, which had been shining with confidence, morphed instantly into an expression of unease.

"That all depends on you, Mavis. Now then, let's go!"

And so, the girls headed to the town arena.

Any reasonably sized town had one. Obviously, it was nothing compared to the one in the capital—just a bit of dirt surrounded by spectators' booths—but it was a requisite facility for a population which had very few entertainments.

And so there, Mile's crash course began.

"That's all wrong! There, you have to smirk and then say, 'Do you really think that one such as I required special training to acquire such a simple move?'! Once more, from the top!"

"……"

The other two were stunned into silence.

The guard contingent that arrived just after noon the following day had only been informed that they would be transporting the merchant, and so they were few in number, with only one two-horse wagon, a driver, and three guards in total. No thief would be foolish enough to attack a wagon transporting criminals, and their chief likely could not spare more men than that.

Normally, this group would have been plenty, but now that there was a noble to be transported as well, it was nowhere near enough. Furthermore, now that a noble had been apprehended, this would require a lot more attention from the higher-ups. Still, once the count explained the situation to the head of the transporting soldiers, and offered to accompany them to the capital as well, the group appeared relieved.

Perhaps he could also accompany Mavis home via the capital—or else he could entrust that duty to his sons, and have them take her directly back to the estate. As he pondered whether it might be a cleaner break from her friends for Mavis to leave directly from here, time marched by, and soon, the time for the trial match with Mavis's party had arrived.

The count called to his sons and his attendants, and they all headed for the arena on the outskirts of town.

"Wh-what is this...?"

The count's party arrived to find a massive crowd, so big that they wondered whether the entire town had gathered there. Food stalls and carts and roaming peddlers shouted over one another, hawking their wares.

"Ah, Count Austien, please allow me to show you to the waiting area!" said Pauline, rushing up to greet them.

"Wh-what is the meaning of all this...?" the count demanded.

"Well, these townspeople are starved for entertainment, and we thought this would be a great opportunity for the local merchants to do a bit of advertising, so we put this together... Is that going to be a problem for you?"

None of this was a lie. Indeed, it was just as Pauline said. However, there were also other reasons for this setup.

First off, the prideful count was not the sort of person to break a promise. That was the conclusion they had reached from analyzing over half a year's worth of stories involving the man. However, no one knew what her older brothers might do when it came to protecting Mavis. For that reason—to assure that their agreement would not be broken—a large assembly of witnesses had been gathered.

Additionally, they had established a contract with the local merchants' guild to collect twenty percent of the profits from the food stalls and merchandise carts. After all, it was going to take a lot of money to rebuild the reclaimed shop.

The count grasped this much from Pauline's initial explanation. To rebuild a shop whose name had been dragged through the dirt, it was crucial to let everyone know that they were now under new management. That was an indisputable fact. Plus, it was difficult to spread information very quickly, so there was no one who would pass up an opportunity as promising as this one.

"Where is Mavis?"

"Ah, even if this is just a mock battle, she said, it's not good for the opponents to interact before the fight. She's waiting over on the opposite side."

"Hm, that's a very mature way to think about it..."

The count made a peculiar face, which was almost endearing.

"The other side has already completed their preparations. So as soon as you are ready, your lordship, we will proceed with the match between Mavis's master and yourself."

"Understood," the count replied, and began his preparations.

"Thank you for your patience, everyone! What we present to you now is a battle for freedom, between the young lady hunter who helped to deliver this town from the wicked merchant, and her father, who wishes to drag her home against her will and force her into preparations for an arranged marriage!"

"Wooooooooooooooo!!"

"Wait a minuuute!!"

Just then, a voice rose up from somewhere in the crowd.

Pauline heard the random cry of protest, but ignored it, continuing her patter.

"The conditions for victory on the young hunter's side are that her own master must win a fight against her father, and she must win against her older brother! You should know that her father is a renowned master of the sword, and her brother is also a skilled swordsman, from the first division of a count's own knights. What a foolish, one-sided bout this is sure to be!"

"Heeey!!!"

Pauline was more than aware that someone was raising an objection, but she had an important job to do, so she chose not to concern herself with interruptions. Taking care not to let either their family nor given names slip, she continued.

"The first match will be the young hunter's father versus her master! Now then, Father, please step forward!"

It was a rather harsh introduction, but he had to proceed. To accept a loss by default would be even worse. Count Austien stepped out onto the arena's field with a dour expression.

"And now, if his opponent, the young lady's master, would please step forward!"

At the call, a figure appeared on the opposite end of the field from the count.

The moment they saw this person, the chattering from the crowd was subsumed, and a hush fell over the arena.

It was a woman, silver-haired and with the stature of a child.

She was the young lady hunter's master, so it was not peculiar that she should be a swordswoman herself.

There were plenty of people who were small even as adults, and if she were an elf or a dwarf, it would not be strange for her appearance to diverge from her age. Considering it from that angle, she was not all that bizarre. Indeed, there was nothing unusual about this whatsoever.

Or at least, there wouldn't have been, had she not been wearing a mask to obscure her appearance.

"My name is Evening-Gown Mask!"

"What kind of a name is thaaaaaaaaaaat?!" the crowd roared.

In the first place, this woman was not wearing an evening gown at all, but standard hunters' garb. Then again, that wasn't really that much of an issue.

"Wh-what a bizarre... Are you really Mavis's master?!"

"And what if I am? You are just a foolish man who cannot recognize my pupil's abilities..."

"Wh-what exactly is there to recognize? I am well aware that that girl has above average ability when it comes to the sword. However, that says nothing in and of itself! I'm sure you're aware that, among all swordsmen, half of them have abilities below the average, while the other half have abilities above the average. One will either be above or below—that is but a matter of chance. There's nothing special about that, is there? I have no intention of allowing her to pursue a path of mortal danger on that basis alone! She should live a life of happiness, as a noble's daughter and a noble's wife..."

For some reason, Evening-Gown Mask made a rather displeased face upon hearing the word "average" bandied about so many times. Enough that it was visible even from behind the mask.

"You fool..."

"Wh-what?!"

The count was enraged, believing that she belittled his feelings for his daughter.

"You're rather fond of pickled cabbage, aren't you? And you always tried to force Mavis to eat it as well, did you not?"

"Huh? H-how did you know..."

The count felt himself trembling at this strange accusation.

"Did you know?! That Mavis actually hated it? That pickled cabbage that you love so much?!"

"Wh-what did you say?! Y-you're lying!"

"It's no lie. You need to realize that the thing you believe will make Mavis happy may be something that will bring Mavis herself no joy whatsoever. What a fool you are."

"Sh-shut up! You're lying! That couldn't be..."

"In that case, why does Mavis wish to remain with me and not return home with you?"

"Sh...sh-shut your mouth! I just have to show Mavis how weak you are, and then her eyes will open! Come!" the count said, drawing his sword.

The mysterious Evening-Gown Mask drew her weapon as well, and rushed toward him.

The count stepped quickly and brought his sword down upon his shorter opponent's head. It was just like splitting bamboo. A young woman like this, he assumed, could not block such a blow from her disadvantaged position.

On the one hand, this was an overly showy move. Yet, he thought, it was just right for showing off their difference in power. But Evening-Gown Mask did not attempt to dodge or deflect the blow, instead blocking the attack head-on with her practice sword.

"Grrrrrrngh..."

The count, who thought that he could easily overwhelm his tiny opponent, was shocked at the strength of this woman, who should have had difficulty blocking with any sort of force from such an inconvenient stance. So he pushed harder.

5 seconds, 10 seconds, 15 seconds...

The count's face was turning red and beads of sweat were forming on his brow, but his sword showed no signs of budging.

After a bit more time had passed...

"Pah!"

Mi—Evening-Gown Mask let out a shout, and the count's sword was forced back. Flustered, the count stepped back in retreat.

"Tch... Are you a dwarf? Or perhaps, a halfling...?"

Judging from the disconnect between her physical strength and her appearance, the count determined that his opponent could not possibly be purely human. And yet...

"Hm? But I'm just a completely ordinary, *average*, normal human girl."

THAT'S A LIIIIIIIIEEEE!!!

Well, at the very least, the last part of that statement might be true—that is, the "human girl" part.

However, the beginning of it was certainly a lie. An absolute lie! If this woman was not herself aware that she was lying, then perhaps she should go and review her language skills.

So thought the crowd, as one.

"Now then, let's get this started for real..."

She was not going to use magic during this match. It would be meaningless if she did not win with her sword skills alone.

Mi—Evening-Gown Mask thought to herself, *This should be just as fun as fighting Gren.*

This time, Evening-Gown Mask—*Mile* was the first one to make a move. It was a high-speed assault.

In an instant, she closed the distance between them and swiftly drove the practice sword toward her opponent's left flank. The count caught this blow with his own sword and struck back to fling her away. Mile's sword was up, so she swung it down at the count's chest.

What followed was a fierce volley.

This was not a reckless match where she could run around in circles, as in the battle with Gren. The count was a knight to the very end and chose a straightforward, head-on tactic, so Mile met him on the same terms.

There was little movement. Instead, it was a vigorous, static duel. One might assume that for a hunter, who made it a point to move around a great deal in combat, this might make things more difficult. Yet this had no impact on Mile. As hunters went, her swordsmanship was rather crude in the first place, so it made no difference what style of battle she was involved in.

Speed and power. That was what Mile had going for her. Nothing else mattered.

As the match dragged on and on, the count gradually began to grow impatient.

This was due, in part, to his partner's incredibly crude technique.

A person with a reasonable amount of skill could hardly ever win against a truly superior swordsperson. The swordsperson would surpass them in skill, speed, judgment, and the ability to read their opponent's movements. They could not be beaten.

However, an amateur moved in erratic ways. They made decisions that were not based in common sense, and they chose techniques that no person in their right mind would ever attempt. Because their speed and technique would still be inferior, their chances of victory were low. However, there was always the possibility of them striking an unexpected blow, which made them exhausting opponents for a veteran, who could not read their moves ahead of time.

This was an opponent who had speed and strength surpassing most experts, but the moves of an amateur.

This was dangerous. This was an incredibly dangerous opponent.

Her continued attacks were powerful and quick and completely unpredictable, and a moment's lapse in judgment could lead to a fatal blow. In order to carry on, he needed to concentrate with every bit of his will, and this was making the count incredibly exhausted.

Normally, such an amateur would quickly fall victim to a single blow, and it would all be over. In this case, though, no matter how many times he swung, none of the swings seemed to be connecting. They were evaded, or blocked, or deflected, and every action thereafter was met by another counterblow.

It was not as though things were not going well on the count's side; rather, it was the way the battle went on and on, without an end in sight. By degrees, the count grew more fatigued, his impatience beginning to swell.

At this rate, we'll come out evenly matched... Wait, is that true? Is this woman truly even using all of her power? If she can handle my attacks so nonchalantly and at such speed, does that mean that she's capable of even quicker attacks? She isn't showing even a fragment of impatience or fatigue.

C-could it be that she's toying with—That's impossible! There's no way that could happen!

In his irritation and weariness, the count's blade became unsteady, creating an opening.

Clack!

The lower part of his blade was struck, and the count stared, dumbfounded, as he dropped his sword.

It was not that the sword had been knocked away. He had been struck with blows of the same speed and weight up before now. No, he had dropped his sword. His sword had been *dropped*.

The crowd swelled, and a few broken cheers rang out.

What a disgrace for a knight. What humiliation.

His face was flushed, and his arms would not stop trembling.

"Please hurry and pick that up."

"Wh...?"

She should have raised a cheer of victory and declared her win, but...

There were limits to how long he could be toyed with.

Normally, he would demand that he be taken seriously, kick his practice sword away, and leave—but he could not do that this time.

The life of his precious daughter was on the line in this fight. He simply could not allow her to continue to live the dangerous life of a hunter. No matter what.

He did not doubt that his son would win, but he could not shut his eyes to the thousand or even ten-thousand-in-one chance that his daughter's life might continue to be put in danger. No matter how he had to humiliate himself in front of his subordinates, in front of this crowd—if there was even the slightest chance that he could still prevail, then he could not surrender this match.

And so, the count picked up his sword, and once more took his stance.

Thirty minutes later, Count Austien was on the ground, on his hands and knees.

He had reached his limit. He no longer had the strength to stand, or even to grip his sword.

It was a complete loss. There was no other word for it.

"Would you say that we can call this my win?" Mile asked, to confirm.

The count nodded silently in reply.

As Mile returned to her waiting area, and the count's men jumped forth from theirs to lend him their shoulders, the crowd erupted into applause and cheers.

Not a single person there was laughing at the count.

The count was strong. So much so that it was unclear whether a B-rank, or even an A-rank hunter, would be able to win against him. He had merely faced a vexing opponent. That was all.

They applauded him freely and vigorously, and yet the count's face was still twisted.

He held no hatred or disdain for his opponent. On the contrary, he was filled with admiration that such strength could be carried in such a small frame. Based on her technique, he could only assume that she had likely received formal instruction for but a short period of time, but that *strength*! That power could only have come from endless self-study and training. Truly, it was worthy of praise.

The count's rage was directed only at his own shortcomings—self-hatred for the fact that he had not been able to ensure his daughter's safety by his own hand.

When the count finally made it back to the waiting area, he said to his son, who stood, confident, "You must win. Don't ever drop your guard."

"Yes, sir!"

And so Waylon von Austien, the eldest son of the Austien family, stepped forth.

For the sake of his beloved sister, he would harden his heart, and face that dear sister herself in battle.

Waylon had regrets.

After three boys, a daughter had finally been born to the Austien family: Mavis.

Their parents and grandparents doted on her, but her three brothers doted on her all the more. She was raised as the princess of the Austien family, wanting for nothing, and spent her days watching her brothers practice at swords, until she declared that she wished to do so as well.

Thinking that she would never be on her own, without anyone to protect her, she was offered only cursory instruction, but she proved an unexpectedly serious and patient student with a fair amount of talent. Her three brothers were shocked. Furthermore, they loathed the idea of their adorable sister being attacked by some man, and thought she should at least have some capacity for self-defense. So, her brothers took the time to give her a bit of instruction in between their own lessons.

When she came to Waylon, saying, "Big Brother, I want to practice with you!" he could not possibly turn her away. As was his privilege as the eldest brother, they practiced many things together, just the two of them.

It was not until much later that he found out that Mavis was also going to her other brothers as well, so she was actually receiving three times the instruction than he had imagined.

The way that she had watched him and his brothers at their promotion ceremony, her eyes sparkling with admiration, had made the joy of becoming a knight all the sweeter. But they had assumed that the look in her eyes was directed toward them.

Who among them would guess that her admiration was for the profession of knighthood itself—that her heart was already filled with dreams of becoming a knight herself one day?

He had failed. If they had realized this problem sooner, they might have been able to direct Mavis's interest toward other things. At the very least, they might have been able to stop her from running away from home.

However, this time, he would not fail.

He would bring Mavis back home, no matter what. He swore it on his name, as the eldest son of the Austien family.

"Lend me your heart, First Brother."

The siblings faced one another in the middle of the arena.

"To have a match like this after eight whole months... However, I won't hold back today. I'll take care not to injure you, but it still might hurt a bit. This is a punishment for your childish behavior. Learn some self-restraint!"

Mavis smiled wryly at her eldest brother's words.

"First Brother, I'm not a child anymore. I'm Mavis, the leader of the Crimson Vow, a C-rank hunting party. Bear witness to this power of mine!"

Declaring this, Mavis drew her practice sword. Waylon drew his in turn.

"Now, we fight!" they shouted in unison.

Suddenly, Waylon stepped forward.

It might seem a bit childish, but the situation was what it was. His precious sister's future—no, her life itself—was on the line. This was not the time to hold back or play around. In order to avoid making a mistake or running the risk of scarring her adorable face, he swung to strike her in the side.

Shing!

"Is something troubling you, First Brother?"

Mavis should not have been able to block a full-powered attack of his.

At the very least, the Mavis of eight months ago would not have been able to defend herself against an attack that was even seventy or eighty percent as fast as this.

Cling cling cling!

"I-Impossible..."

There were few even among his subordinate knights who

would have been able to defend themselves against those three incredibly serious, deadly swings.

Yet she had flicked them away as though they were nothing.

"This can't be..." Waylon muttered in disbelief.

"First Brother, did you forget that I've spent weeks away training and growing stronger with someone other than you?" Mavis replied, mysteriously. "And that there are people who are far more tempered, faster, and stronger than you, my dear brother?"

"Wh...?"

And then Mavis proceeded to land the *coup de grâce*.

"First Brother, I'm sure it's been said that Father's age means he's past his prime. Physically, you are now the strongest in our lands. But in truth, Brother, even excluding Father, you're only the second strongest."

"What? Then who would you say is the strongest?"

Mavis pulled her left hand from her sword, extended her index finger, and pointed to her own face.

"Huh..?"

Waylon was stunned speechless.

No matter how intense their special practice had been, there was no way that Mavis could have gotten that much stronger in just one night.

Indeed Mile, thinking that it would be difficult for Mavis to win against her brother using honest means, had used their preparations the day before to access her forbidden, top-secret grimoire. She had long ago decided to restrict herself from making use of this resource unless there was no other option.

The nanomachines.

Reluctantly, Mile had called upon them to answer a variety of questions, such as why Mavis couldn't use magic.

The nanomachines, as though they were thrilled to be called upon again after so long, cheerfully replied.

OH? BUT SHE CAN USE IT.

Wh-what did you saaaaay?!

THERE ARE A NUMBER OF REASONS WHY SOMEONE MAY APPEAR UNABLE TO USE MAGIC. IN THE CASE OF LADY MAVIS, THIS IS DUE TO HER HAVING ONLY A FRACTURED POWER TO EXTERNALLY RADIATE THOUGHT PULSES. I.E. THERE IS A MALFUNCTION IN THE EXTERNAL ACTUALIZATION OF HER IMPULSES. THERE ARE SEEMINGLY MANY IN HER FAMILY WHO FALL UNDER THIS CATEGORY, SO IT MAY BE GENETIC...

In that case, doesn't it mean that she can't *use magic?!*

NO, WE MERELY SAID THAT SHE HAS "FRACTURED POWER TO EXTERNALLY RADIATE THOUGHT PULSES," SO—

You're saying that she can radiate them internally?

THAT IS CORRECT. DID YOU NOT YET GRASP THIS, DESPITE YOUR CLEAR INTELLIGENCE?

Sh-shut up!

The result of Mile's questioning of the nanomachines was something along the following lines:

The reason that Mavis's pulse emission was weak was that the part of her that radiated the pulses—a part equivalent to an antenna on a radio—was malfunctioning. Therefore, she could not transmit her intentions externally, and ergo, could not use magic.

However, even without an antenna, the signals were still flowing throughout her mental circuitry. Even if they were weak, the thought pulses were still inside her.

Which meant, Mile concluded, that if there were nanomachines *inside* of her, they would react...

NORMALLY, WE NANOMACHINES DO NOT RESIDE WITHIN THE BODIES OF ANY LIVING CREATURE... IT IS UNPLEASANT.

Somehow, this made sense. Moreover, the directive given by the nanomachines' creators to maintain a fixed density throughout the world did not appear to apply to the insides of living creatures.

HOWEVER, THERE ARE MANY CASES WHERE NANOMACHINES DO EXIST IN SUCH ENVIRONMENTS. ONE SUCH CASE IS WHEN MAGIC IS INVOLVED.

Indeed, at times it was necessary for nanomachines to enter the bodies of living creatures in order to enact the effects of spells, such as when using healing magic. Still, they exited the body as soon as their duty was complete. Moreover, since Mavis was unable to perform any spells that would compel them to enter her body in the first place, this point was moot.

Incidentally, the nanomachines had a weak response rate when it came to spells aimed at the destruction, rather than healing, of the flesh. Plus, because it took a bit of time for them to enter the body, these effects materialized a tick slower than those of healing spells. Furthermore, because it took so long to actualize these effects, it was likely the owner of that body might notice something abnormal and be distressed by their symptoms. Then, that thought would take priority, and the original effects would be canceled. The thought that flowed to the nanomachines most directly, from a point-blank range, would naturally be prioritized. Humans thought of this phenomenon as "magical resistance."

However, attacks like these could still be utilized in some cases. When, for example, Pauline faced the B-rank hunter, it didn't matter if it took some time for the effects to come about, especially when the target was not cognizant of any abnormality. Then, there was the case of someone with magical power great enough to interfere with someone else's body unimpeded by their resistance.

ONE OTHER CONSIDERATION IS "NATURAL ENTRY," WHEN A NANOMACHINE ENTERS A CREATURE'S BODY THROUGH NATURAL MEANS, SUCH AS BREATHING, EATING, OR DRINKING.

IN THESE CASES, THE NANOMACHINES IMMEDIATELY EXIT THE BODY, BUT IF THERE IS A SUFFICIENT DENSITY OF NANOMACHINES IN THE VICINITY, THEN A STANDARD CONCENTRATION OF NANOMACHINES WILL REMAIN WITHIN THE LUNGS, VIA THE ORAL CAVITY.

IF THOSE NANOMACHINES WERE TO RECEIVE A DIRECT PULSE TRANSMISSION, THE RESULTS WOULD BE LIMITED BECAUSE THEIR NUMBERS WOULD BE FEW, HOWEVER...

They would still react, wouldn't they?

And so, Mile thought—about Mavis, who could not utilize the nanomachines externally, but could still somehow draw upon the scant number that might exist inside. And, she thought about a simple means of strengthening Mavis, who wished to be a knight.

Indeed, there was no other option.

She would have to use body-fortification magic.

The moment Pauline got wind of the idea to turn the mock battle into an event, with a portion of the vendors' profits going to the merchants' guild, she rushed out immediately, presumably to speak with the heads of each local guild branch. Worried, Reina followed along with her.

Only Mile and Mavis remained in the arena.

All things considered, compared to Reina and Pauline's power leveling, Mavis had received relatively few of Mile's blessings.

There *was* the "Godspeed Blade," of course. However, that was the fruit of Mavis doggedly forging herself in battle after battle against Mile, and it would be a disservice to Mavis to consider that in the same vein as power leveling. Rather, that had been the natural result of Mavis's excruciating, persistent efforts over the course of half a year of being excluded from her friends' magical training.

Even with these gains, it was not as though her abilities had improved as much as Reina's and Pauline's, who had seen rapid growth after Mile had "thought of a few tricks for them." In and of itself, the power of Reina's fire magic and Pauline's healing magic was at a B-rank, perhaps even nearly an A-rank. Factoring in their knowledge, experience, and technique, as well as speed, physical ability, and their overall potential as hunters, they were in the upper echelons of a C-rank, at the very least.

By contrast, Mavis's swordsmanship was only at the level of an upper C-rank or a lesser B-rank.

Even if she called her technique the "Godspeed Blade," the speed produced was nowhere near what the name implied. While it was accurate to estimate that her speed was 1.4 times what it had been previously, that did not mean it was all that great to begin with. Even if she had grown faster, it would still not far surpass that of a soldier or knight who practiced every day.

Thus, she could face several opponents at once if they were at the level of your average bandit; however, soldiers, knights, and other more sophisticated enemies might prove a bit more intense. Except, of course, when those enemies' shoes were filled with pebbles, or the soles had been cut into a disadvantageous slant.

Even if she were facing only a single enemy, if that enemy were a skilled combatant, then victory could prove difficult.

And so, Mile decided to lend a helping hand to Mavis, who had been worrying herself sick over her insufficient strength.

After Reina and Pauline had left, and only the two of them remained on the arena grounds, Mile finally spoke up. "Um, so, Mavis... You absolutely need to win tomorrow, yes?"

"Huh? Um, yes. That's why we're doing special training right now, isn't it?" Mavis looked suspicious, wondering why Mile was asking such a thing at a time like this.

"Well, you see, the truth is... There *is* a way that you might be able to win."

"What?! Seriously?! What is it? You have to tell me!"

Mavis was already deeply invested, but Mile's reply was timid. "Well, it's a means of body fortification, but I don't know if it would suit the pride of someone like yourself, aiming to be a knight, Mavis..."

"I don't care! That doesn't matter to me at all! If it helps me push through as hopeless a situation as this, I can swallow my pride a bit! Now, hurry up and teach me! What do I have to do?"

This was a bit of an anti-climax for Mile, who had been certain that Mavis would refuse, declaring something like "A real battle is one thing, but in a practice match that's just cowardly!" Even in this world, there were plenty of suitable aphorisms for such a situation—sayings along the lines of "To make an omelet, you have to break some eggs," or "The ends justify the means," or "That was then, and this is now."

And so, Mile explained to Mavis how the body fortification would work.

She got the feeling that if she told Mavis, "You can use magic, too," it would become a whole different issue. So instead, she decided to describe it as "a secret technique of physical strengthening," in which one could control one's flesh through sheer willpower. That way, it would be easier for Mavis to accept her strength as an ability obtained through her own training and discipline.

Mavis watched Mile intently, her eyes sparkling, and drank it all in.

After the lecture was through, it was time for some practical applications: modulating one's strength, balancing one's power, and calculating one's speed.

Again and again, Mavis failed to connect with her own senses and tumbled, her body covered in scratches and bruises. Each time, Mile healed her with magic.

It was not until it was beginning to grow dark that Reina and Pauline returned from speaking with both the guilds.

There, they found Mavis, beaming with a confident, satisfied grin.

"Wh-what a ridiculous thing to say..."

Waylon, who had been momentarily stunned speechless, burst out laughing.

Certainly, he had been shocked at the way that Mavis handled his attacks earlier.

However, up until eight months ago, he had been a part of Mavis's training for many years. Waylon was completely aware of her power and abilities, and while, for a young woman, she was nothing to scoff at, she definitely was not at the level where she could have surpassed him a matter of mere months.

Though he truly did not hold back against her, the power he used was not the same that he would employ on the battlefield, when his life depended on it. This was his beloved little sister Mavis. There was no mistaking that his power and speed had been blunted, if only unintentionally. Mavis had simply happened to avoid one of his attacks, and now, she was overestimating her own abilities, bluffing just to get him riled up. This was Waylon's assessment.

"If you're going to overestimate your own abilities, then you really *aren't* suited to be out on your own. At this rate, you'll lose your life in short order! It's time to make you understand that!"

With those words, Waylon launched another attack. This time, it was an all-out, three-point offensive, with his true full speed and weight behind it.

Clingcling-cliiiiiing!

"Wh...?"

Not only Waylon, but also the spectators, and the count, who stood in the waiting area along with Ewan and the other knights, all gasped, their eyes wide.

It was a perfect block. She had completely blocked his three-point attack. No, she had goaded him into it. You might even say he had asked for it.

A great shout rose up from the stands.

Waylon was a strong and fairly handsome young man, but for some reason, the great majority of the cheers coming from the young ladies in the audience were directed toward Mavis.

"Impossible..."

Even though he was experiencing it himself, Waylon could not believe this was real.

If he were to believe it, his own common sense, as well as his confidence, would desert him.

He could not, at any cost, allow himself to believe that this was happening. That his own younger sister might be surpassing him...

Meanwhile, Mavis's heart was soaring higher than it ever had.

Her three older brothers were not so formidable that they could be thought of as equivalent to the royal guard or, say, an S-rank hunter. However, they were still top-notch among the count's regional forces, well deserving of the designation of first-class knights.

The foremost of all of them was her eldest brother, Waylon.

And she was fighting seriously against that same brother. There was no way that her heart wouldn't be dancing!

However, Mavis still knew that she had to assess herself rationally.

She knew that this wasn't really her true ability.

As time went on, she would be less and less able to stand up to her better trained and more experienced brother and his sword.

She had to settle this match before her brother could become accustomed to her speed and skills, and begin to challenge them. If she was to win this match, there was no other way.

"This time, allow me to begin," said Mavis, taking her sword in her left hand. "Secret technique! Earthen tidal wave, Urban Splash!"

The first step of this technique, Urban Splash, was to scoop up earth with one's sword, sending a splash of dirt flying into the opponent's face to startle them. In that moment came the second blow.

It was a special technique that could only be used in urban areas, not in forests or fields that might be covered in grass, or contain obstacles like fallen trees. The sword was held underhand so that it could scoop up earth with a natural movement, and so that one could follow through in the same motion with a swing toward one's opponent.

Naturally, the one to name it had been Mile, an avid reader of shounen manga in her past life.

"Tch!"

As might be expected of the foremost fighter in the region, Waylon evaded the tip of the sword, which only grazed him lightly. Even so, he only narrowly missed the splash of dirt and the blow that followed after it.

"D-did you really think that a c-clever little trick like that would work on me?!"

In fact, it was in fact a fairly dangerous move, and Waylon was shaking quite a bit.

"Ah!" said Mavis. "Of course you, First Brother, would be able to avoid the hero's special technique, Urban Splash. However, how will you fare against a move that was formulated to fell any manner of superior beast that may appear on the hunting grounds?"

With that taunt, Mavis launched another special attack.

"Sworn sword of the hunting grounds, Excalibur!"

"Whooooooaaaaa!"

Waylon somehow blocked her attack with his sword, but he winced at the force behind it, which was far greater than he could have imagined.

Even if the power that Mavis could produce was nothing to scoff at, she was a girl of noble birth, and her strength still had its limits. Or at least, that was how it should have been. However, the strength of that attack just now was...

He could not let his surprise show on his face. It would show weakness and get his opponent even more riled up. He had to maintain a calm expression.

"Hmph! Is that all? Nothing else in your bag of tricks?"

Waylon spoke with feigned coolness, but Mavis, who had something else up her sleeve, looked even cooler.

"First Brother, I beseech you not to belittle me. Do you really think that one such as I would need to undergo special training for a finishing move as feeble as that?"

"Wh-what?"

"True Godspeed Blade! 1.4 speeeeed!!"

"W-whoooooooooooooaaaa!!!"

The match was no longer an exchange of one-shots, but a continuous, tumultuous volley.

Striking, blocking, stepping hard, flying back and forth.

This was her First Brother, who she so admired. A person whose skill as a knight was at such a lofty level she could never hope to even approach it.

Now, in an all-out fight against that big brother—well, he was losing steam, and his movements growing sloppy. Against that big brother, she was excelling.

She really might win this!

She was, of course, aiming to win. But honestly, she might actually win! Against her eldest brother!

Mavis's heart was on fire, her soul alight.

She was all out of special techniques. She had used everything they had practiced the night before in her two previous moves.

That said, this "True Godspeed Blade" could probably be thought of as Mavis's real secret power.

All the practice that Mavis had put in during her six months at the prep school—and even since then—was now paying off. No matter how much the nanomachines increased her synaptic reactions or temporarily tautened the sinews of her muscles, if her existing abilities were not sufficient to handle it, she might suffer muscle ruptures and bone fractures as her body destroyed itself. However, thanks to all of her training, Mavis possessed a body that could withstand such rigors, even if it was only for a few minutes at a time.

Meanwhile, Waylon's offensive strength was waning. He had to remain vigilant, on the lookout for other secret techniques, in case Mavis was bluffing. Even in perfect form, anticipating each of her moves, he had only barely blocked the last two special attacks. If she tried to perform some other big move, she might launch a third attack in the moment that it took Waylon to guard against her. He couldn't afford to be careless here.

Mavis's attack speed was abnormally fast. It took everything Waylon had just to block her volleys, leaving him unable to launch his own counterstrikes. Just like his father before him, Waylon began to grow extremely impatient.

Mavis's brothers could not use magic. By contrast, though Mavis herself did not realize it, thinking that she was only strengthening her body "by her own willpower," she was using body-strengthening magic in this very moment. Her fatigue dissipated; her stamina increased. Yet as a young man, tempered by long years of training, Waylon's base abilities were still far beyond Mavis's. While Waylon's combat abilities were declining gradually as his fatigue increased, Mavis was going to hit her limit all at once. Thanks to Mile, who had consulted with the nanomachines, Mavis herself knew this. Thus, she knew she had a very brief window in which her plan could work.

Indeed, while she did not let it show upon her face, Mavis was even more frantic than Waylon in this moment.

Once she reached her limit, it would all be over—and that limit was approaching fast.

Slightly, ever so slightly, Waylon's reaction speed was beginning to decline.

Yet at the same time, perhaps because he was starting to grow accustomed to Mavis's speed and moves, and finding ways to fight against them, the force of his attacks was starting to increase again. Now that he was focused on the battle, his hesitation was gone, so his experience was truly beginning to show.

Mavis was gradually being pushed back, her body beginning to approach its limits.

She did not know whether she would hear a warning sound or sign from within her when those limits were hit.

There was no more time.

With this thought, Mavis decided it was time to unleash her final attack, which she had hoped to avoid using, if she could. Her final, special technique, which Pauline had thought up, and whose efficacy against her elder brother had been guaranteed by Reina and Mile. If she did not make use of it now, it would all be over.

For the sake of her own future, Mavis summoned all the strength of her soul and launched her final attack.

"I hate you, Big Brother! Please don't talk to me ever again!"

"Huh...?"

Waylon froze, dumbfounded, looking as though he had been overcome by a deep despair.

Smack!

For Mavis, landing a blow on Waylon, who was standing stock-still, was simple.

"Wh..."

The audience was incredulous.

"What was thaaaaaaaaaaaaaaaaaaaaaaat?!?!"

They were vexed.

The count, Waylon, and Ewan were all incredibly vexed.

However, in front of this many witnesses, there was not a thing they could do. They could not possibly allow the common folk to see a group of nobles—knights, no less—breaking a promise without batting an eye. Furthermore, Theresa, a representative of the capital branch of the guild, and Santos, a guard who spoke on the king's behalf, were on Mavis's side. Their hands were well and truly tied.

Hanging their heads, the Austien family and their underlings plodded out of the arena, powerless.

As Mile saw the Austiens off, she glanced to the side to see Pauline standing nearby, her face dark.

"Oh! Pauline, what's the matter?"

Pauline wailed in despair.

"If only we'd had more time! If only we'd had *more time*, we could have made more money off of this match! So much more! I want to go back to yesterday! If only we could go back to yesterday!!"

Just then, a strong breeze blew past them, carrying the smell of flowers to Mile's nostrils.

Back on Earth, this smell would have been that of lavender blossoms.

Mile patted her fist against her palm in recognition.

"Aha! It's 'The Girl Who Leapt Through Money'!"

CHAPTER 24

A Triumphant Return

"**Y**ou did it, Mavis!" Reina cheered.

"Congratulations!" Pauline continued. "Now you're free until the day your marriage prospects run out entirely!"

"Ugh..."

For some reason, Mavis did not seem entirely thrilled.

"This is all thanks to you guys, especially Mile. Thanks to that special technique, True Godspeed Blade, I was able to stand up to my eldest brother in combat, if only for a short while. And now—and now!—once again, I get to chase...my...my dreams...!"

She began to sob so hard her words were lost.

"Mavis..."

This was Mavis, who was always so collected, who could grin and bear anything that might come their way.

Reina, whose emotions were wild and volatile; Pauline, who had a dark side; and Mile, always naive, watched gently over

Mavis, who had always watched over them, as her whole body trembled with sobs.

After some time, when Mavis finally calmed down, the four started back to their lodgings to celebrate Mavis's victory.

When they returned to the inn, someone was standing outside the front door: a woman in her thirties, with a kind, soft appearance, but eyes that betrayed a strong will. She stood with a boy around ten years old.

"Pauline!"

"Mother! Alan!"

It was Pauline's mother and younger brother.

Given her status as the lover of the apprehended merchant, Pauline's mother had been questioned in order to ascertain whether she was an accomplice to his crimes. So that they could not conspire to corroborate each other's stories, anyone connected to the case, including the shop's employees, had been isolated and kept under observation, and because they were all interrogated one at a time, it had taken some time before any of them could be released.

Theresa and Santos, who were both aware of the circumstances, were involved in the actual questioning, so no one was terribly worried. But now, they would be free and clear. After that, Pauline's mother could act as the provisional manager of their shop until the process to officially hand the rights back over to the family was completed.

Though she conducted herself with a strong heart, Pauline was still a fifteen-year-old girl. Even if one might be considered an adult at fifteen, life had been incredibly harsh for Pauline until now. So much so that, if she did not bury her true kindness and gentleness in shadowy depths and cloak herself in a dark shield, she would never have been able to bear it...

However, those days were over as well.

Leaving Pauline to sob into her mother's arms, Mile and the others headed into the inn.

"So, what're we gonna do?" wondered Mavis.

"I wonder what we should do...." Reina mused.

"Whatever shall we do?" pondered Mile.

A few minutes earlier, once Pauline had calmed down, she had come in with her family and offered them her thanks. Then, she told them that she would be spending the night at her mother's home, and she, her mother, and her brother departed.

"Now that our business here is finished, I was thinking that we should head straight back to the capital," Mavis ventured. "But..."

For Mavis, who had certainly made a splash in this town, their stay had been a bit too intense.

In just the short journey between the arena and their inn, there had been hordes of hunters and throngs of young girls flitting about her. It would be impossible for her to walk around this area much longer. Besides, it would only be a matter of time before people came around petitioning her to introduce them to her master, saying things like, "Who exactly *is* Evening-Gown

Mask?" and "She has to teach me!" and "No, she needs to join *my* party!"

"It doesn't seem like we have much choice..."

"You're right."

Reina and Mile were of the same mind and agreed to leave the following day, at the first morning bell.

At dinner, they relayed their intentions to Theresa and Santos, as well as the innkeeper. Thankfully, Theresa replied, "Well then, I'll go and find us a carriage." Santos, of course, would be leaving the day after along with the guard wagon, so he would not be coming along with them. It would be rather unfair to make a coachman who had just arrived that day leave without even one day's rest. Plus, traveling with the count's party would be less than comfortable, so on the whole, Theresa's offer was much appreciated.

After dinner, the three continued to discuss their plans for what would come next.

"If Pauline ends up staying here, it's going to be hard running things with just the three of us. Should we recruit a new member?"

"I don't think we have much choice. Thankfully, Mile is pretty much all-powerful, so we have a pretty wide field to recruit from... Which profession would it be best for us to look for?"

As Mavis noted, the pool of candidates *was* incredibly wide.

If Mile fought as a backline mage or slingshot user, them they could recruit a frontline fighter, or, if they recruited a mid- or backline archer or another mage, Mile could continue to act as a frontline fighter, as she had thus far. Since Mile could use healing and utility magic too, they didn't even need to worry about getting someone with the same magical talents as Pauline.

Mile: the wild card of their deck.

Still, they were all a bit concerned.

Would someone who knew of Mile's usefulness—no, her *talents*—become blinded by greed?

Would someone who learned the abilities of these supposed novices and realized the differences between the trio and themselves be crushed or start thinking strange thoughts?

Could they simply teach Mile's "magic improvement tips" to someone whose true character they didn't even know?

They couldn't teach that person their secrets and then have them leave.

"Hmm..."

The three of them thought deeply.

Just then, Mile piped up.

"Um, what do you think of asking around among our former classmates?"

"Oh..."

Indeed, many of their classmates from the Hunters' Prep School still lived within the capital. Because their class had been gathered from all over the country, most of them had returned to their hometowns after graduation. This was only natural, as they had left their families and friends behind. Even as a matter of national policy, no one would think of locking the graduates up within the capital, preferring to distribute promising young hunters equally throughout the country instead.

Yet for the most part, those who were originally from the capital, as well as those who did not have anyone to care for in other regions, had remained in the city.

When one spends half a year in a group of just forty people, one tends to get well acquainted with the rest of the group. The girls knew a lot about their classmates, and likewise, those classmates knew quite a lot about their group. This, of course, included the fact of Mile's mental shortcomings, such as they were...

Of course, there were some individuals that they wouldn't want to team up with. However, excluding those, it wouldn't be so bad to reach out to some members of their class. That way, they could truthfully remain "a party of fellow classmates."

Indeed, now and then, they saw some of these classmates around the guildhall and elsewhere. Yet unlike the Crimson Vow, who had recklessly gone it alone with a party of only novices, those classmates had mainly entered into parties comprised of more veteran hunters. That said, it seemed there were many of these cases where the veterans were of the mind that they were "helping newbies to become full-fledged hunters," and treated them mainly as apprentices. Thus, those newbies' shares of the profits were considerably lower.

Those veterans had likely been in the same position as the newbies in their younger days, so this was not a particularly cruel move. That was simply the way that such parties were devised.

Still, if the Crimson Vow were to reach out to any of their classmates who were in such a situation, it was possible that said classmates would be happy to join them. They might not be the most interesting choice, but perhaps it would be better than feeling overlooked.

"I'm a little worried," said Mile. "In our party, there isn't anyone besides Pauline who has a good sense for money and commerce and negotiating. With someone around who had the calculating heart of a merchant, there was no fear of us getting swindled, but now..."

"Ah!" Just then, the face of a certain person floated through all of their minds.

It was the face of a ten-year-old girl, who was fairly adorable, yet also calculating, and even callous. In the boobs department, too, she would be a suitable replacement for Pauline—at least, in a few years' time.

"No, no, no! Absolutely not!!!" That was the group's consensus.

At any rate, that girl had no combat ability, and she was already employed—at her family's inn.

The three appeared calm as they discussed Pauline's departure, but on the inside, they were by no means unworried.

The half a year at the Hunters' Prep School.

The exciting and harrowing days spent afterwards, as fledgling hunters.

In the dorm or in the inn, the four of them always roomed together.

There was Mavis, the only daughter of a noble house, who was raised having little contact with those outside of her own family.

There was Reina, an orphan, who never knew her own

mother and whose father, her sole blood relative—along with the Crimson Lightning, the hunters who she traveled with—had all been taken from her.

There was Mile, who, in her previous life, had no one who she could call a friend, and even in this life, had been separated from the very first group of friends she ever made.

And then, there was Pauline, who'd been living her life like a wounded beast.

They were all starving.

They all wanted. For friends. For companions.

And then they found each other: allies bound at the soul, the Crimson Vow.

It was the four of them.

They were true companions.

If they lost one of them, they could replenish their numbers with another.

But it wasn't that sort of equation.

They knew this. Yet none of the three could bring themselves to say it.

Pauline had her own life, and her own happiness.

Her desperate wish had finally come true, and she had achieved her foremost aim: to live together with her family, and protect, along with her mother and brother, the shop that her late father built.

This was just the same as Mavis aiming to be a knight, and Mile seeking a normal happiness in life—important goals, which they would never give up on, which no one could stand in the way of.

And so, after a time, as the words hung in the air without anyone working up the nerve to speak them, they all slipped into bed, and the conversation ended, unfinished.

The next morning, the three girls collected their things from the inn and headed to the guildhall along with Theresa.

The carriage that Theresa had arranged for them was not a passenger coach or a hired cart, but a merchant's cargo wagon... laden with cargo.

"Our schedule didn't line up with the passenger coaches, and hired wagons are too expensive. Thankfully, the Order of the Crimson Blood can work as guards, and one of the local merchants waiting to depart jumped at the chance of an escort."

Gathering a number of merchants together in a caravan saved money on fees and bolstered overall security. There was no one who would pass up the chance to employ (and pay the rate of) a group of four hunters who possessed the escorting power of a group of ten—and who could, moreover, leave immediately. The townspeople had seen for themselves that the group's sole swordswoman possessed the strength of several C-rank hunters on her own, and judged that, by extension, any party affiliated with this swordswoman and her master would be comprised of no ordinary individuals... Of course, these assumptions were correct.

Furthermore, if there were currently bandit spies sneaking around the town, they would be loath to attack this group. That much was certain.

Theresa felt strange about accepting any jobs on the group's behalf, so she had only made a verbal agreement with the merchants the night before, leaving the duty of formally accepting the job to Mavis. Therefore, they needed to swing by the guildhall.

Since Theresa herself was a guild employee, it was important for her to do everything by the books.

Once the job acceptance paperwork was properly finished, the group proceeded to the merchants' guild, where their employers were waiting.

When they arrived, they found three wagons assembled in the guild's established waiting area. Beside them were three merchants, engaged in conversation. They all appeared to be small-time merchants, each with only one wagon apiece.

Naturally, these modest business owners could not afford to hire drivers and would be in charge of driving their wagons themselves.

"Looks like those are the ones. Well then, let's hurry up and introduce ourselves. We can continue our conversation about finding Pauline's replacement after we depart..."

Snap!

"Huh?"

Grindgrindgrindgrind...

"O-ow, owwwwww!"

She was not truly in agony, but Mile cried out, unsettled by the phantom—or was it only emotional?—pain.

"What is this talk about 'Pauline's replacement,' huh?!"

Mile whipped around to see Pauline, the veins bulging in her forehead.

"Why were you trying to leave without me?!"

Trembling at Pauline's face of pure rage, Mile could only stare, her mouth opening and closing but no sound emerging.

Mavis, thankfully, tossed her a lifeline.

"B-but, Pauline, we thought you were going to be rebuilding the shop along with your mother and brother..."

Pauline replied with a sour expression. "My mother managed the shop alongside my father. As long as she's there, they'll be fine. There are older employees who stayed behind and held things together for my mother's sake, and those who quit will probably come back. Plus, since I'm the one who reclaimed the shop, having me stick around would actually cause a lot of problems. We'd be bound to get people rushing in to say ridiculous things and offering sneaky marriage proposals..."

"Whoa."

The life of a merchant was, the other three thought, a frightening one.

"In any case, it's better for everyone if I'm not there. My little brother is officially the successor, but his position would be weakened if I stuck around. I won't be near them, but if any evildoers try to lay a hand upon my family or the shop, I can be the mysterious long-lost daughter who appears—along with her plucky friends. That's enough for me."

"........."

Whether Pauline was mincing words, or whether all this was

true, they could not be certain. However, it didn't really matter either way.

Pauline was still sulking a bit, her cheeks puffed out.

But then, Mile flung her arms around her, burying her face into Pauline's chest, and her pout began to waver.

"Nn..."

Tears formed in the corners of Pauline's eyes and slowly began to flow, marking her cheeks. She wrapped both arms around Mile's back and squeezed her tight.

"Uuh, wuh, wahh..."

A relieved, happy grin spread across Mavis's face.

Mile pulled away from Pauline's chest, grinning wide, the trails of tears still wet upon her cheeks.

Even Reina, unable to fully conceal her joy, looked on with a peculiar expression, her smile shining in her eyes.

"Now then, we had better get going. I don't think the Crimson Vow will be splitting up for a while yet," Reina said.

They all let out a cheer.

"Yeah!!!"

As soon as they received confirmation of their wages, per the job request, the merchant caravan began to move. Yet just as they were setting off, before they had even made it past the city limits, Count Austien and his two sons came rushing up, breathless.

"W-wait, please wait, Mavis!"

The four girls grimaced, sensing that trouble was once again on the horizon.

The merchants could not possibly ignore the count calling to them, so they stopped the wagons. With little choice now, the Crimson Vow hopped down to face the men.

"What is it, Father? I thought we had concluded our discussion..."

"Oh, yes. I fully acknowledge that. I don't want to acknowledge it, and I don't want to let you go, but I know I must. I won't try and complain about it now. But there's something else I'd like to talk to you about. Please, won't you formally introduce me to your master?"

"Huh?"

"Your honorable master is incredibly strong. However, I don't believe she has been formally instructed in technique, so there is little form to complement her immense physical ability. It's regrettable—indeed, it's painful to see! I was hoping to formally invite her into our household, so that we might facilitate a mutual exchange of skills...

"My thought was that I could instruct her in technique, and that in turn, your master could impart upon me the means by which I might attain such a superior physical form. That way, we could both become leagues stronger than we are now! Your master claims to be purely human. If that is the case, then might she still be young? If she were to wed a member of our family, then the future of the Austien line would be secure! Wouldn't it be splendid for you and your master to become kin? What do you think? It's a splendid idea, is it not? Now please, let me know how I might contact her!"

"Please, Mavis!"

"All we want is to be introduced!"

Waylon and Ewan bowed their heads as well. Certainly, the figure of this so-called "Master" suited the tastes of the men of the Austien line.

"Wh...?"

The Crimson Vow were stunned.

To tell the truth, they understood what the count was saying. But whether or not they thought it permissible was another matter.

From the count's point of view, this proposal was not strange at all. In fact, this line of thought was only natural for the head of a militaristic clan.

What Mavis and the others were startled about was something else entirely.

Have they seriously not figured out who "Evening-Gown Mask" is with Mile standing right in front of them?!?!?!

Her mask from the match hadn't even been enhanced with any sort of identity-obscuring magic.

Mile thought, *I-Is this "the will of the world"? The "compelling forces" and "pre-established harmony" that (the so-called) God was talking about?!*

Of course, this was not truly the case.

They were simply incredibly dense.

That was all there was to it.

Mavis managed to wave off the count's request, telling her father to "Ask me about it the next time we meet."

After that, the merchant caravan returned to the capital, largely without incident.

Well, at the very least, they weren't *attacked*. If there were any trade routes that were attacked that frequently, anyway, no one would ever use them. And if a certain route did get that way, then commerce would grind to a halt, and the king or lords would send out a large-scale extermination force.

Normally, so as not to obstruct commerce, bandits aimed only for stupid merchants who were too cheap to invest in an escort, or weak targets that the king or lords would have no interest in. Normally.

Within the wagon, Mile and Mavis received a lecture from Reina.

"There is something that I need to say to the two of you..."

While the two of them wondered what this something might be, Reina continued.

"I'm sorry, but pickled cabbage is delicious! Especially when you eat it with boiled sausage!"

It was a completely frivolous topic.

"Or, when eaten as a snack along with ale..."

Why was she so invested in this pickled cabbage?

Not wanting to cross-examine their friend, Mile and Mavis sat quietly, listening respectfully to Reina's sermon.

Their return to the guildhall also passed with little incident.

Theresa would be handling the report to the guild. As a result, there was no need for the Crimson Vow to do anything. All they had to do was receive the job completion approval for their escort job and collect their pay.

Theresa sneakily tried to collect pay for the job as well, but she was told that her portion would go to the guild master "because she was still on guild business." Needless to say, she was quite vexed...

"We're back!!"

As always, Mile called out when they entered the inn.

However, Lenny did not greet them in return with a cheerful voice, as she usually did.

Thinking this peculiar, Mile looked to the counter, only to see that no one was sitting there.

"Hm, I wonder if she's in the bathroom?" Mile pondered, tilting her head.

Just then, the sound of pounding feet came from further within the inn, and Lenny came flying out.

"M-M-M-M-M-Miss Miiiiiiiiiile!!"

Lenny flung her arms around her, letting out a sob.

"Wh-what's wrong?!" Mile asked, startled.

Lenny explained through her tears.

She was at the end of her rope, and it was all thanks to the baths.

After the Crimson Vow had left the capital, Lenny went to seek out a mage on behalf of her busy parents.

Even if, proportionally speaking, magic-users were relatively rare, this was still the capital. About one in ten people was good enough at magic for it to be useful in their work, and about one in every few dozen skilled enough to earn a full-time living. With a population as large as that of the capital, there should be a fair number of such people around. Furthermore, many magic-users came from their home regions to live in the capital, meaning that there was an even greater abundance of talented workers, many of whom could be found around the local shops and factories, and at the hunters' guild.

There was no need for them to worry about maintaining a reserve of magic when they were safe in the capital, particularly if they were a hunter. Even if they had stored away any magical energy just in case of an emergency, they should have no problem using most of it up by dinnertime or so. If they slept, it would all be replenished by the next morning, so it should have been well worth helping Lenny just to earn a little pocket money for booze and snacks.

At least, that should have been the case, and indeed, there were tons of people willing to take on the job.

However, this was where the troubles began.

The amount of water that your average mage could produce was very little.

Seeing how easily Mile had always been able to do it, Lenny had assumed that producing hot water with magic was rather simple, but in truth, it was quite a chore.

When one attempted to produce water with magic, unless another means was specified, the nanomachines in the area that the magic—or rather, the thought pulse—reached had to condense the water particles from the air. Until the temperature reached freezing, the water could not be completely extracted and would automatically be cut off at a moderate level. Therefore, people whose thought pulses had a short reaction range would not be able to produce very much water.

To obtain a larger supply, water had to be transported from a different place, typically by aerial means.

The distance of the water source also factored into this. If it was transported from the ocean, then the salt would have to be removed before it could be transferred. For particularly large amounts, this was not an instantaneous transfer, and the transmission formation would need to be maintained over a long period. Unless one gave extremely concrete instructions, the strength of the thought pulse and powers of visualization required to persuade the nanomachines to properly arrange this shot way up.

Therefore, for all but the most accomplished magicians, the amount of water produced would be limited to what was in the air in the immediate vicinity, which is to say, not very much. Once that water was removed from the air, subsequent attempts to draw water would prove fruitless, until the air currents moved to bring in new air that was full of moisture.

In other words, executing the magic necessary to draw out large amounts of water was quite difficult, and your garden-variety mage could produce only a little. That was the sum of things.

In fact, a simple way to gauge a magic-user's abilities was simply to ask, "How much water can you produce, how many times can you do so in a row, and, how long does it take before you can draw water again?"

In conclusion, if one could only draw water from the air

around oneself, it would be impossible to draw enough water to fill up an entire bath in one go. Plus, it would take some time for the moisture in the air to replenish itself, by which point the mage's power would have dissipated. As the amount of mages the inn had to employ increased, the cost of the free food and drink they provided them had ballooned.

In response to this, the matron of the establishment had handed a hellish decree to her daughter.

"Let the magicians focus on using their powers for heating the water alone. As for retrieving it, Lenny, you can go draw it from the well..."

"I'm dying! I'm definitely going to die! Please, Miss Mile! You have to do something!!!"

"Ah..."

As far as Lenny was concerned, the fact that the bathtub was large was a curse. Filling it even halfway probably required countless trips back and forth to the well. Plus, it was not only the baths, but the reservoirs above as well, and filling them with water was quite difficult.

If things continued this way, in half a year, Lenny's body would be strong enough for her to become a splendid hunter...

No, no, no, no, no!

The Crimson Vow all shook their heads in unison.

They truly were four peas in a pod.

For now, as a temporary countermeasure, they would partition off the baths.

One part of the large tub was sectioned off into a portion about the size of two of the bathtubs in an average Japanese household. When Mile and the others were not present, only this side would be used. It would still require a great amount of water to fill it, but considerably less compared to all the trips Lenny had been making up until then. That, combined with a little help from the magic-users, should make Lenny's job a great deal easier.

"Th-thank you so much! Honestly, I really thought I was going to die!!"

The problem behind her ordeal had not been entirely solved, but at least when the Crimson Vow was present, she wouldn't need to worry about it. Lenny looked greatly relieved— even more when Pauline tossed her another lifeline.

"It isn't very efficient to use you for such a menial task when you can do so many other things around the inn, is it, Lenny? Wouldn't it be better for you to continue your job as a receptionist and hire some orphan children to carry the water from the well? Orphans will work for cheap, and as long as they can earn enough money to buy food, then they're happy, aren't they? Hiring mages to produce the water must be a lot more expensive."

Hearing this, a glimmer formed in Lenny's eyes.

"M-my Goddess..."

And so, thanks to the black-hearted goddess, Lenny was saved from a life of pain—and a future as a beefy macho man.

"Now, that just leaves Mile..." Reina muttered suddenly, after a short rest in their room.

"Yeah," said Mavis.

"You're right..." Pauline agreed.

"Huh?"

Mile stared blankly.

"I'm saying that now that the troubles with Pauline and Mavis's households are settled, that just leaves your folks, Mile. Pauline and Mavis's situations were resolved in part thanks to you, so now it's only right for the two of them to do something to help with your situation, don't you think?"

"Yes!" said Pauline.

"Yeah, of course!" Mavis agreed.

However, Mile did not appear pleased.

"Oh... But, I'm being sought after by the king and princess back in my home country, you know? And if they say I have to take a husband, in order to continue my family's line, I'll have to give up being a hunter..."

"Well then, if you're sure... Let's take a break for a few days, and after that, we can start our next job!"

"Good idea. I hope we can find something fun this time!"

"That sounds good! Let's pick something worthwhile—not something basic like goblin hunting!"

Somehow, it seemed that their previous topic had been thrown completely by the wayside.

Interludes

1. A Difficult Town to Live In

IN A CERTAIN TOWN, a man who had been swindled out of his money was being comforted by his friends.

"Do you plan on just lying here and crying yourself to sleep?" his friend asked.

"Of course not!" the man answered. "I'm still in pauling right now, but even I have crimsonian friends at my side. Soon enough, I'll make a pauline-about happen!"

In this town, thanks to one particular incident, a number of special idiomatic phrases had come into use.

"Pauling": *n., adj.* lying in wait, devising; or, plotting a counterattack.

"Crimsonian": *adj.* merciless, and with an inhuman level of supporting strength.

"Pauline-about": *n.* a disproportionate retribution.

This town was an incredibly difficult place for anyone named Pauline to live...

────────────── *2. Ambition* ──────────────

"**N**OW THEN, please carry the water from this well to both the bathtubs and the water supply up top that I showed you before."

At little Lenny's directions, the six orphans before her nodded dutifully.

After much trouble, Lenny had finally convinced her parents, who were beginning to grow concerned about how long the counter had gone unattended, to let her bring on some orphans for when the Crimson Vow was out of town.

The pay was low, but for children who were guild hopefuls—particularly those who lacked the funds for regular meals—the job was a godsend. The job was not dangerous, it would strengthen their bodies, it went on for several days, and they would earn enough money to eat for a few days after it was over. Plus, even once their tasks were done, they could return at the next opportunity, and there was the possibility that more clients would start hiring orphans for similar tasks in the future.

And so, the orphans paid even Lenny, who was barely older than they were, the full respect due a client.

Their pay was calculated not by the hour, but by the task. In other words, they were paid once all the work was done. It didn't matter if it took them one hour or ten—the pay was all the same. Thus, several of the orphans had gathered, in order to finish the task as quickly as possible. They figured this would make their client the happiest, and anyway, the leader of their group had decided it would be too difficult for a single child to try and do the entire job alone.

Besides, completing the job was not their only aim.

"All right, everybody got that?"

After Lenny completed her explanation and left, one of the orphans, a boy of around eight or nine, who appeared to be the oldest among them, issued a reminder to the group.

"Big brother Veil's—and subsequently, our—benefactor is staying at this inn. It pretty much goes without saying that he's still head over heels for her, right?"

The other five nodded.

Somehow or the other, it would appear that these orphans were the children looked after by Veil, the boy who Mile used as her "sacrificial lamb" at the graduation exam.

Again and again, Veil had impressed upon the orphans that all their good fortune was thanks to a girl named Mile, and that, should anything ever happen to him, they ought to pay the favor back to her in his stead. Though he never explicitly shared his true feelings for her, they were obvious enough that even the youngest of the orphans, who were no more than four or five years old, could easily figure out how he felt.

"If we run into our benefactor, let's take a break and talk to her. We need to try and find out her interests, hobbies, and things like that. And then, we need to tell her how great our manager is—and then mention Veil's name. And then we say something like, 'What?! You know big brother Veil?!' so we can arrange a reunion. We can't mess this up. Got it?!"

"Yeah!!!!!"

Three days later...

"This is weird... We've tried working at all different times, but we've never run into her..."

On a break, the boy who served as their leader pondered this conundrum, just as Lenny came around.

"Hm? What's the matter?" she asked.

The boy hesitated for a bit, then ventured, "Um, I'd heard that there was an all-girl hunting party that was lodging here long-term, but we haven't run into them at all..."

"Oh, you must be talking about Miss Mile's group!" Lenny answered, offering the boys a smile and an explanation. "When those ladies are here, they fill the baths for us using magic. So the only time that we hire you all is when the ladies are away from the capital on business. In other words, you'll never encounter that party while doing this job."

Lenny had relatively few chances to speak with children her age or younger, so rather than using the formal patterns she usually employed while speaking to adults, she took a more relaxed, childlike tone. In fact, it seemed that she had purposely come by when the orphans were taking a break, just so that she could talk with them. However...

"Whaaaaaaaaaaaaaat?!?!"

The orphan boys fell to their knees in the dirt, despair upon their faces. They did not seem to be enjoying this conversation at all.

"N-no way... All of our hopes... All of our big plans..."

"Our dreams of establishing the party Griffon's End, and training everyone into first-class hunters, under the guidance of Veil and our benefactor..."

Apparently, these orphans had all heard Veil's tales of Mile from their days at the prep school.

"Hm? Huh?"

Lenny only gaped at them, not understanding what was going on in the least...

<hr/>

3. All-Purpose Mage

"**O**H, IT'S REINA!"

As the members of the Crimson Vow were looking over the job request board one day, a voice called to them from behind. When they turned to look, they saw Fran, one of their classmates from the prep school, along with the three members of the Flaming Wolves, who had been their allies in that fateful escort mission.

Reina greeted them mildly. "Well, if it isn't Fran and the Flaming Wolves. It's been a while."

"Oh, Fran, have you joined up with the Flaming Wolves?" Mile asked with interest.

"Eheheh, that's correct. As you know, initially, I was in a party of our classmates, but they all turned out to be somewhat unreliable. For someone starting out, it's a lot safer to have the guidance of people with more experience. I'll be able to advance much quicker this way!"

Fran's chestnut hair was cut in a short bob, from under which shone big, round brown eyes. Fran was incredibly cute—small in stature, but bright and full of energy—and had been very popular at the prep school. Additionally, Fran was a mage by profession, something that the Flaming Wolves were sorely lacking. Fran's magical skills covered a relatively wide and useful range, from combat to healing magic.

"I'm only a newbie, but they're taking really good care of me. I'm so happy right now!"

"Really? That's wonderful!"

It was probably a bother for the party that Fran had left, but that couldn't be helped. All of this was voluntary, so everyone had to pick the path that was best for them.

After they stood and talked for a while, the Flaming Wolves' job acceptance paperwork was completed, and the groups parted. Just before they left, their leader, Brett, hung back, leaning in toward the Crimson Vow.

"Honestly, I've really got to thank you all. Thanks to that incident, our names got around, and we gained a lot more credibility. Now, with little Fran with us, our party has more balance... If we could get just one more mage to join, our group would be complete, but at this rate, I'm confident that it'll happen soon. The only problem we have now is figuring out which one of us three is going to get to date Fran first and smother all these sparks that are flying, you know? Ha ha ha!"

"............"

With that, Brett departed, leaving the four to watch him go, their expressions inscrutable.

"Ah... I wonder if those boys know..."

"From the way he was talking, I'm guessing that's a 'no.'"

"I'm thinking they don't. I'd bet a gold piece on it."

"Oh, me too! I'll wager ten gold on that."

"In that case, it isn't even a wager!"

The all-purpose mage, Fran. A graduate of the Hunters' Prep School's twelfth class.

With soft chestnut hair and big, round eyes.

A short and slender, but bright and energetic, adorable youth.

The third son of a poor farming family, or so they had heard. Indeed, the third *son*.

The four girls of the Crimson Vow prayed for happiness for Brett, Chuck, and Daryl in their next lives.

Didn't I Say
to Make My Abilities
Average in the
Next Life?!

CHAPTER 25 |

The Wonder Trio, Secret Hunters

THE CAPITAL OF THE KINGDOM OF BRANDEL is a city that is home to two academies: Ardleigh and Eckland.

On the evening of a rest day, in one part of that city, three girls were walking together.

"I wonder if she's doing well..."

"I'm sure she's fine. Wasn't it you, Miss Marcela, who once said, 'Even if a dragon stepped on her, she would never break'?"

"That's right! In fact, I bet she's somewhere this very minute, saying, 'I wonder how Marcela and the girls are doing...'"

"Perhaps so... No, I'm sure of it!"

It had been eight months since that fateful day. Marcela, Monika, and Aureana were now third-year students.

After graduation, Marcela would be returning to her home to begin her training in domestic skills; likewise, Monika would go home to help out with her family's business, while also searching for a potential husband. Aureana, who had received a scholarship, would have to take up work in a public office in order to repay her debts. They had only one year left to lead their carefree student lives.

They were walking down a fairly narrow avenue, some distance from the city center. Though this was by no means some derelict, untraveled lane, it was not long before the three girls found their path impeded by two men. Marcela quickly glanced behind them, to see two more men standing there.

They were surrounded.

"Can I help you with something?" asked Marcela, betraying not a hint of fear.

Monika and Aureana could do no such thing. They clung to each other, clearly frightened.

"What? We just thought you gals might like to come have a good time with us."

"If you wish to court any of us, you may send your representatives to make a formal introduction and properly petition our fathers."

"Wh...?"

Naturally, she was not being serious. There was no way that some rogue or disgraced hunter would petition to make the formal acquaintance of the daughter of a noble. Marcela was different from Adele. Totally different.

"D-don't screw with us, you little... Just come with us already! There's someone who can make good use of you!"

As he shouted, the man reached toward Marcela.

"Ignite!"

"Oww!"

Aureana let off one of her spells, which were weak in power but still useful in everyday life. The spell, normally used for lighting a fire, singed the man's outstretched arms.

"Y-you little bitch! Y'know, they told us that we only had to bring 'em the noble's daughter! They said it didn't matter if the commoners were dead or alive! You can regret that little trick of yers in hell!"

The man pulled his hands back and drew his sword.

"Diiiiiiiiiiiiiiiiie!!"

As he swung down his sword, Aureana's life flashed before her eyes. Just then, Monika thrust herself between Aureana and the blade.

"Wha...?!"

The man panicked as the noble girl, who he had been instructed to deliver unharmed, had stepped in front of his blade. Hurriedly, he tried to stop his swing, but it was too late. There was an unfortunate sound, and a dull *ka-shunk!*

However, the sword had not sunk into the noble girl's body. What the sword had struck was the mass of ice that had suddenly appeared in front of her.

"Wha...?"

"Ignite."

Before the man could react, Aureana whispered the word stoically. Violently, the man's hair flared up.

"Gaaaaaaaaaaaaaaaaaaaaaaahhh!!"

As the man flailed around, trying to extinguish the flame atop his head, Aureana stared at him with cold eyes. She was angry. Incredibly angry.

"Water Ball!"

A volleyball-sized sphere of water appeared at the behest of Monika's spell, which was truncated to only the name. It flew into the face of the other man, who was standing ahead of them, and stopped there.

"Ugh! Guhbluhbluhbluh!"

Naturally, the man, who had inadvertently sucked air into his windpipe, swung his head violently to try and remove the sphere, but the water would not budge. No matter how he tried to flick it off with his hands, or run around to shake it away, the globe would not leave his head, and eventually his movements began to grow sluggish.

In the instant that Aureana's spell drove the man away, Marcela turned around and began a spell aimed at the men behind her. Just like Monika and Aureana, she only needed to say the spell's name. Of course, they did not truly need to say anything at all, but when they had the time to, saying the spell's name made it that much more efficient.

"Fire Shot!"

Two flame bullets shot out, aimed for the right shoulders of the two men standing behind them. They dropped their swords and fell, rolling. Marcela had plenty of room, it seemed, to properly aim her attack.

In the two years since the girls had first received magic lessons from Adele, they had by no means been playing around. They had spent a year and two months of that time with Adele. For the eight months after, it had been just the three of them. Still, for the sake of their futures, their research and efforts had continued.

The three girls, who were quite bright, had continued to research the principles of magic that Adele had taught them, negating their initial lack of magical power. Of course, they had not been expecting to suddenly be swung at by men who aimed to take them captive. Yet though their situation was dangerous, they could not falter: if they went easy on fiends as weak as these, they could easily be captured.

"Now then, perhaps you might tell me who it was that hired you..."

As she stood, grinding her foot into the rogue, he wailed that they had been misled, that they hadn't been warned that Marcela was a remarkable mage, but just told to expect some stupid noble schoolgirl. They hadn't known that even her commoner companions could use magic.

In the midst of these complaints, some nearby hunters finally came running.

Apparently, the men would be turned over to an expert for further questioning.

Later, they headed to the hunters' guild to explain what had happened. Along the way, Aureana, who was wearing an unusually displeased expression, suddenly turned to Marcela.

"What was that all about, Miss Marcela?!"

"Oh? What do you mean?"

"When that man tried to attack me! Why would you do something so dangerous? Are you not afraid to die?! Your life is worth so much more than—"

"Miss Aureana," Marcela interrupted. "Of course I am afraid of death. However, compared to the fear of losing you before my very eyes, doing nothing to stop it, and having to live with that regret for the rest of my life... the fear of death is nothing."

Marcela smiled as she spoke, but Aureana was indignant.

"Please don't toy with me! Are you saying that it means nothing if *I* have to watch *you* die before my very eyes—just to protect me?! There is nothing more frightening than that! Would you have me carry that weight on my shoulders for the rest of *my* life?!"

"Ah..."

With her own grave oversight pointed out to her, Marcela froze, her mouth agape.

"I-I understand now..."

"In that case, I pray that you will not do anything like that ever again!"

Marcela shook her head back and forth. "I cannot promise that."

"Wh-why not?!"

Marcela, perplexed at why the other girl would ask a question with such an obvious answer, furrowed her brow as she replied. "Because you are my dear friend, and I am who I am—the girl Marcela."

"......"

No matter what she said, it was hopeless. Aureana was certain of at least that much.

There was nothing to be done for ft. She looked at Marcela, a splendid noble girl, suddenly overcome by a sense of honor and gratitude...

"That is about the sum of it."

In the guild master's office, on the second floor of the hunters' guild's headquarters, the three girls explained what had happened.

The guild master was sitting not at his desk, but at the table situated in front of it. His back was to his desk and the three girls were in a row facing him. A clerk, who also served as his secretary, sat diagonally behind him.

"Hmm. If some fiend were to get their hands on Lady Marcela, who is a fond associate of the third princess... Might they have had some particular aim in mind? Did they wish to curry your favor? Or perhaps hold you hostage? Well, we'll have our experts investigate something along those lines. Honestly, though, to challenge three mage hunters so forcefully, even if you're only D-ranks, they really must not have done their research..."

"Ahaha..."

Indeed, the three girls were now D-rank hunters.

By hooking Monika and Aureana into her "Adele Simulator" by means of a "connection system," Marcela was able to form a "Super Adele Simulator," in order to predict Adele's actions. The results of their predictions were something along the lines of the following:

Where might she be?
    She was still in the country: 6% chance
    She had fled the country: 94% chance
What might she be doing now?
    Hiding out somewhere deep in the woods   5% chance
    Living undercover in some noble household: 4% chance
Working...
    as a live-in maid: 7% chance
    at a shop in some town: 9% chance
    as a hunter: 69% chance
    Other: 6% chance

And so, just in case it might help them, the three had decided to register as hunters.

Their goal was to reach a C-rank by the time they graduated. Or, at the very least, a D-rank.

By the time they graduated, they knew, Adele would definitely be a C-rank. It was unlikely, too, that she would become a B-rank or higher. Even if she had the opportunity to do so, she would want to remain at a C-rank, where she would stand out less. This much they were confident of.

Blessedly, thanks to the knowledge that Adele had imparted to them, Marcela had the magical strength of a standard mage, Monika had that of about the lowest level of mage, and Aureana had half that still. And, thanks to the fact that they could cast in their heads—which was not the so-called "silent casting" of this world, but rather Adele's special brand of "directly visualizing the intended effect, without saying an incantation at all"—they could work magic at a miraculous speed.

Of course, in order to conceal their special talents, they purposefully took a bit of time with their workings, telling people that they learned how to cast quickly inside their heads by "practicing so hard we were vomiting blood."

In any event, thanks to this efficient means of casting, the three of them could produce a force far greater than what one might expect, given their apparent magical strength. Indeed, their practical magical power exceeded that of the average mage. Because of this, when they registered with the guild, they were able to utilize the skip system to start out at a D-rank.

Naturally, they kept all of this a secret from their families.

The girls did not truly have any intention of living their lives as hunters.

They merely thought that, should they encounter Adele again someday, being registered with the guild would leave their own field of options just a little bit wider.

Besides, once they had the qualifications of a C-rank hunter, there was nothing that could stand in their way. When it came to seeking a spouse, there would be no greater proof of their magical ability than to say, "As a mage, I possess the qualifications of a C-rank hunter."

No, they had no intention of living as hunters, but at least for the time being, they figured that they might be able to arm themselves with the general knowledge and skills of such, so they temporarily joined up with other novice parties to collect herbs, as well as hunting jackalopes, goblins, and the like.

And, of course, they never turned down invitations from parties of F to D-rank boys who might ask the girls to join up with them. Not even once.

The girls typically did not take on harvesting or extermination jobs, making them a rather unique party. Still, as D-rank hunters, they took on most other recommended tasks...

Such as escort missions.

They were not guarding merchants or anything like that. It was true that, normally, a C-rank party would be requested for those jobs, but students such as the Wonder Trio would not be able to take on jobs that would take them away over a long period.

Instead, the Wonder Trio was frequently requested to escort young girls, just for the day.

When the daughter of a noble or wealthy merchant could not go out because of concerns for her security, the three of them would escort her, secretly acting as guards in the guise of sisters, friends, or attendants.

Because they appeared to be merely a group of lovely preteen girls, they could stay with girls in the restroom or the bath, and even when they were sleeping. They had no need to carry weapons and could fend off a surprise attack of even several attackers—at the very least, stalling for time until help could arrive.

There were always normal guards nearby, so fending off attackers for even a short amount of time was enough, and these girls, who performed their guard duties with certainty, were incredibly treasured.

They took these jobs not only on their days off, but on weekdays as well, in which case they convinced the school to give them a pass, regarding this duty as a permissible alternative to their attending class. Luckily for them, there were those influential enough at the academy who were happy to allow this.

Furthermore, they were almost never attacked, so the girls ranked up A-grade after A-grade on their job completion reports.

As they did not often do much rummaging around on the guild's first floor, there were many hunters who did not even know of the girls, and even when they saw them around now and then, seeing them only in uniforms, without any sort of other protection, they assumed they were clients, guests of the guild master, or the friends of family of some guild employee who had come for a visit—nothing more.

Thus, they were the guild's secret weapon, a group of guard specialists formed eight months ago, the lovely uniform-clad girl hunters of the Wonder Trio.

As they reached a break in the conversation, the guild master took up a cup of the black tea that had been set on the table before them, and the girls picked up their cups as well.

Silently sipping her tea, Marcela's eyes drifted to the guild master's desk behind him, on top of which sat several items.

For some time she had been acutely aware of the four objects positioned there. They looked rather like dolls and seemed very out of place atop the desk of a guild master.

When Marcela took a closer look, she realized that they were indeed dolls, in the shape of young girls.

The four of them were each adorned with light armor, like something a hunter would wear. Two of them outfitted with swords, the other two with something like mages' staves. They looked very much like an all-girls' hunting party.

Perhaps they were thinking of using these dolls of young girl hunters to popularize the image of hunters and recruit more young folk?

One of the girls was a tall swordswoman, with her hair painted a golden color. Another was a mage, with brown hair and a large bust. The third of them was a short, childlike mage with red hair.

And the final one had silver hair, with a cute and amiable countenance, as well as a rather pleasant, vacant look about her...

Pffffffffffffffffffffffft!!!

Marcela spat. All the tea that was in her mouth was propelled directly onto the guild master, who sat before her.

Startled at the enormous spray, Monika and Aureana, who had their cups to their mouths and had just sipped in the bulk of their tea as well, followed Marcela's gaze, and...

Pfffffffffft!

The secretary, who had been seated behind the guild master,

pulled a handkerchief from her pocket and rushed over to him, but the guild master waved her off gently with his left hand.

After wiping his face with his own handkerchief, he carefully refolded it and placed it back into his breast pocket. He did not notice the clerk's chilly gaze.

"W-we're so sorry!"

The three girls apologized hurriedly—in such a way that their gazes never so much as flicked toward the desk.

They wanted desperately to ask about the dolls, but if they let on that they had such a strong interest in them, there would definitely be an investigation on the horizon.

His Majesty, the king, had not given up on searching for Adele. The girls were not so foolish as to think that he would. They were different from Adele! Different!

And so, they left the guild. On the way home...

"It seems like she's doing well."

"So she is a hunter after all."

"And she's already standing out..."

The girls could not keep a straight face.

"Pft..."

"Aha..."

"Ahahahahahaha!"

Passersby glanced suspiciously at the three girls, who had all suddenly burst out laughing, but the girls' laughter continued to ring out.

"...And that is all for the actions of Lady Marcela and company for today." So spoke the man who had been assigned the duty of watching over the three girls, secretly guarding them from the shadows. He had made his report to an audience of the king; the first prince, Adalbert; the third princess, Morena; and the second prince, Vince; along with the prime minister and the chief guard, Bergl.

"Why did you not step in to help when Miss Aureana and Miss Marcela were in danger?!" Morena shouted angrily, having heard his full recounting.

"Ah, well, I never thought that they would actually be faced with injury or..."

"Just *what* did you think that guard duty entailed?"

"......"

"Never mind. Leave us."

"Yes, sir..."

After the guard had left, the king said to Morena, "I'll pick a new one."

"Next time, please actually pick someone reliable!"

"Of course."

The guard had watched over the girls since before the time they were attacked, up until they reached the guild. Of course, he could not enter the guildhall with them, so he only watched over them on their way back to the dormitory, and then, once that

duty was finished, returned to the palace. Listening in on the girls'
conversation in the guise of a passerby, he had only heard as far as
Aureana and Marcela's quarrel.

"As for the mastermind of this operation..."

"Understood! I'll handle it, don't you worry!"

"Hm. But..."

The king was mildly fearful for Morena, who worried so
deeply for Marcela and the others.

Just then, the first prince, Adalbert, spoke up. "She stood in
the way of an incoming blade, all for the sake of a commoner...
And then acted as though it were no large feat at all. What a truly
interesting person..."

"Miss Marcela is a wonderful girl! She's strong—and cute too..."
Just like Adalbert, Vince seemed extremely interested in Marcela.

"Wh...?"

The king, the prime minister, and the others, who had been
wondering which of the two boys they would set up with Adele
once they found her, were completely lost for words at the sight
of this sudden interest from not only Adalbert—who had never
shown any interest whatsoever in the noble girls who always
flocked around him—but also from Vince.

Morena, of course, could only think, *Between Miss Adele and
Miss Morena, I wonder which shall become my elder sister-in-law,
and which the younger...*

Dreaming of that lovely future, a pleasant smile crept across
her face.

CHAPTER 26 |

A New Request

"**N**OW THEN, I wonder if there are any interesting jobs here..."

The Crimson Vow looked over the job request board, uttering words that would surely draw the ire of any low-ranking hunters struggling to make a living, if they overheard.

The last job they had done was a personal matter, and they weren't hurting for money, so this time, they wanted, for a change of pace, to pick a job that was interesting or unusual—not the kind of minor work you did by rote.

However, they had to take care not to let any parties who *were* hurting for money overhear them saying such a haughty thing. Inevitably they would be chewed out, in a "Just who do you think you are?" sort of way. To put it in terms of the idioms Mile knew from her past life, they were being so boastful that, "Even Gandhi would run up and slap them."

Thankfully, no one nearby seemed to find fault with their comments, and simply ignored them, continuing to browse the board themselves.

"Oh, this one..."

At Mile's words, the other three felt a sense of déjà vu.

Indeed, it reminded them very much of the time they had found the posting for the rock lizard hunting job...

On the advertisement that Mile pointed to was written the following:

Wyvern Hunting. Reward: 30 gold pieces.

"This is the ooooooooooooooooone!!!"

Among draconic types, wyverns were in the class of what were called pseudo-dragons.

Unlike the so-called elder dragons, which were at the apex of that taxonomy, and then the more standard dragon varieties such as earth and water dragons beneath them, pseudo-dragons, while still dragons, were vastly inferior in rank.

To defeat even a normal dragon—even below the class of elder dragons—one would need to dispatch at least tens, or more likely hundreds of fighters for the sake of safety and certainty. Even then, felling the dragon was not a done deal.

A serious extermination effort would need to include several spirited dragoons and employ a fairly complex ballista. It had to have a "primary force," as well as a "secondary" force, proportionate in size.

In a nutshell, while pseudo-dragons still carried the name

"dragon," they were, as the tag "pseudo" implied, significantly inferior creatures. In other words, they were weak. So much so that even a team of only six to eight hunters, with the right formation and technique, could fell one.

Of course, whether or not a group of that size could fell one without taking any injuries was another matter entirely...

As a result of that—and because they did still have the classification of "dragon" attached to them, the pay for hunting pseudo-dragons was quite good.

With just a few people in a party, the probability of grave injury or death could be fairly high, and naturally, the more fighters who were included, the more expenses added up, with the pay-per-person falling accordingly.

Furthermore, materials from such a hunt would sell at a fairly good price. Not only was the work interesting; when it was done, one could then say, "I felled a dragon."

This was the first time that the Crimson Vow had laid eyes upon a wyvern-hunting request.

This region was not especially close to where wyverns dwelled, so if they let this chance slip by them, who knew when they might have another chance to take advantage of such an opportunity?

They absolutely could not let this one pass them by.

"I really would advise against..."

At the clerk's words, the girls once again felt a sense of déjà vu.

Yes, indeed, this was *just* like the time when they tried to take on the rock lizard hunting request...

"Come on, have we not proved our skills to you already?!"

"Even if you claim—"

Undeterred by Reina's haughtiness, the clerk tried to explain.

"First of all, to hunt a wyvern, you need to pull it out of the air, down onto the ground. In order to do that, not only do you have to have the power to bring it down, you need to be fast, have a lot of stamina, and have ranged attacks that can strike upward at a long distance. If the majority of your party cannot fulfill these conditions, then you must give up on this job."

"We have three mages, all of whom can use strong attack spells! We're fine!"

Ignoring Reina's retorts, the receptionist continued.

"Furthermore, even if you manage to land a good deal of damage upon it, the wyvern will run."

"Wh...?"

The four were stunned. The clerk explained further.

"Wyverns aren't the type to keep fighting stubbornly until the end. If they feel they're outnumbered or outclassed, they fly away at top speed. After that, they will remain in their nests. Then, once some time passes, they will emerge, but even then, they won't return to the location where they were attacked for a very long time. Most wyverns have very wide territories.

"Plus, the wyverns will remember any human who harmed them. Even if they encounter them in an entirely different place, they won't approach any hunter who faced them with malice ever again. And furthermore..."

"Furthermore?"

"A wyvern's hunting ground covers an area of dozens of kilometers in every direction. Where, in all that space, do you intend to find one?"

"Uh..."

The Crimson Vow all stood slack-jawed.

"You're facing an opponent who can fly through the air at top speeds, with an immense territory amidst which you can't know when or where they will appear. Once you finally encounter one after ages of lying in wait, *then* the battle can begin. After your allies have been killed or sustained grave injuries, just when you think you've got it on the ropes, then the wyvern runs away. And after that, it will never come near you ever again.

"You'd fight for days in vain, sustain casualties, and fail to complete your assigned task, meaning that you don't get paid, and also have to pay the job-failure fee. Then, there would be medical bills for your party members, and you'd have to deal with the bereaved families of the fallen... Please think carefully about why this job is still here, even when the pay is relatively good. If you don't, you may not have a very long life before you."

"............"

The four were stunned even further into silence, but the clerk was not yet finished.

"As far as dragon classifications go, it's true that wyverns are still considered to be pseudo-dragons. If a well-composed party with the right compatibility battles one head-on at full power from the outset, then a wyvern isn't such a fearsome foe. Indeed, for a party with sufficient power and experience, winning in and of itself would not be all that difficult. However, what is difficult is snagging the opportunity to fight against a wyvern in earnest, and often, when you finally get one, it will run just when it looks like the fight is in the bag. A wyvern is a troublesome foe of a very specific ilk.

"This is a job that is practically blacklisted, probably posted by some desperate client who couldn't get anyone from their local guild branch or the surrounding ones to take it. Neither their local lord nor the Crown would help them, so they came here to the capital branch, thinking that among all of the hunters on our roster, there would be someone just foolish or starved enough to take it.

"We have a name for jobs like this, ones that are likely to result in your allies' blood flowing like rivers, where the cons far outweigh the pros... A 'red mark.' Jobs like these are only for stupid beginners and heroes."

As she finally wrapped up her explanation, the Crimson Vow looked at one another.

They nodded as one, and then Reina replied for them all.

"We've been waiting for something like this. We'll accept this 'red mark' job!"

"Wha...?! Did you not hear a word I just said? What in the world are you thinking?"

"My, my! Isn't it your job to allow us to accept jobs?"

"Gngh..."

At Reina's prodding, rage began to simmer up within the clerk, but then she remembered her place, swallowing her words.

"Wh-why exactly do you want to take this job?!"

"Does it really seem so strange to you? You just said so your-self, didn't you?"

"What?"

The clerk tilted her head in confusion, so Reina elucidated: "It's. Because. We're. A. Bunch. Of. Stupid. Beginners... *And* we're heroes!"

Ignoring the clerk, who was utterly speechless, Mile shouted from beside her, "Wait a minute, Reina! How come when you said 'stupid,' you were looking at *me*?!"

And so, in the end, the Crimson Vow accepted the wyvern-hunting job.

As much as the clerk might be able to advise them, she was in no position to refuse a legitimate job acceptance based on her own misgivings, as long as the party in question met the appro-priate qualifications. If she had justifiable reasons to refuse them, or prior approval from upper management, it would be one thing, but this incident did not fall under either of those scenarios.

And so with a heavy heart, the clerk, who was quite fond of the Crimson Vow, processed their request.

"All right! First, let's stop by the guild."

They were five days' walk from the capital. Having arrived in the town from which the wyvern-hunting request was originally issued, the regional capital of Helmont, the Crimson Vow headed to the local guild branch. They explained to the clerk there that they were the ones who had taken on the job, and, after a short wait, they were directed up to the guild master's second-floor office.

"So you all are the hunters from the capital who accepted the wyvern-hunting job…?"

As the girls entered the office, the guild master greeted them with a despondent, almost angry expression.

"I take it you accepted this job knowing full well what wyvern hunting entails…? Did any of the staff at the capital branch properly explain this task to you?"

The girls were somewhat annoyed that the middle-aged guild master had started the conversation this way the very moment they entered the room, without even a greeting. However, there was no particular ill intent behind his words. He probably was merely concerned about these rookie girls doing something so dangerous, so they ignored his tone and continued to listen.

"If I send hunters from the capital off to a pointless death, my reputation will take a huge hit. Worse, if I let four cute young girls get killed, everyone's going to start talking about me."

"…………"

Apparently, the only one he was worried about was himself.

"We are a C-rank hunting party, the Crimson Vow, who have accepted the wyvern-hunting job from the capital guild branch."

As Mavis was still too stunned by the guild master's words to reply, Reina took the lead.

Compared to her fellow party member, she had a much lower boiling point; however, she was also well aware of the impression her appearance gave. Based on her looks, she knew, people tended not to take her seriously on first meeting her. This particular problem did not anger her.

Or really, that was not fair to say. It was just that she was accustomed to it. That was all.

Besides, this time, Mile was with them. Telling herself that Mile's presence must be the reason the guild master was looking down on them, Reina's spirits remained high.

"What? The Crimson Vow, you say?"

The guild master seemed a bit shocked at the introduction.

"You are the ones who..."

It seemed that he had heard rumors of them. Maybe it was about the mock battle at the graduation exam, or about the bandit-slaying, or the wicked merchant... No, actually, that last incident had been handled by the mysterious party, the "Order of the Crimson Blood," so that couldn't be it... Anyway, he could have heard about them anywhere.

As far as the merchant incident went, anyway, it would still be some time before rumors about them made it from Talwess to the capital, and then from the capital out into the other regions. Public officials and nobles were one thing, but it took much longer for rumors to reach the ears of the common folk.

"Um, I don't know what you are insinuating. But, yes, we are the Crimson Vow."

This time, Mavis was the one to reply. At least for now, she was the party leader. Even though it was easy to forget about that now and then...

"I have heard rumors of you. About the strength of your mages and the skill of your swordswoman... If you're the ones facing the wyvern, then perhaps there is a chance that you might be able to strike it down and land the finishing blow once it has fallen. However, I'm not confident that you'll be able to land enough damage to strike down the wyvern in the first place. Don't you think this might be a pointless venture? Not only might you get hurt, but you'll have to pay the penalty fee..."

"Even so," Mile interjected, "we've already accepted the job!"

The guild master grimaced, knowing this to be the case.

Finally, recognizing that they were no ordinary rookie hunters, he explained to them the details of the job.

They had already heard the gist of the assignment from the staff at the capital branch, but what had been written on the job-request ticket was a simplified summary to begin with. Moreover, there was new information that had come to light since the job was posted, and there were a number of small details to inquire after.

Usually, this sort of briefing would be the clerk's job, but in this case, it was an important request, one that had been recirculated all the way from here in Helmont to the capital branch. In short, because the Crimson Vow had been dispatched from the capital to handle a job request at the Helmont branch, this task became the guild master's personal responsibility.

That said, it was still generally the case that after a brief discussion with the guild master, a clerk would go over the finer details. Yet in this situation, it seemed that the guild master had taken a personal interest in the Crimson Vow, making this an exceptional instance where he himself would explain everything in detail.

Because the contents of this request were of a rather formidable nature, the guild master explained it all to them frankly, holding nothing back. Throughout, the expressions of the Crimson Vow were impassive...

"So, let's get this sorted."

After leaving the guild behind, the girls headed to an inn and booked a four-person room, then began their team meeting. As always, Reina was the moderator.

"First of all, our client is the local lord. However, the lord is only paying the reward. He gave the guild free reign to handle the details, so we don't need to worry about arrangements. There won't be any need for us to meet with the client, either."

This much they had heard from the guild master.

It seemed that this lord had no interest in meeting with such lowly creatures as hunters.

This was completely normal. Indeed, times when nobles actually took time to meet with hunters—such as when Count Amroth, the presiding lord from the bandit incident, had met the Crimson Vow—were few and far between.

To tell the truth, all of the Crimson Vow were far more comfortable with it being this way. The only one who wouldn't be troubled by meeting with a noble was Mavis, who was, of course, accustomed to that sort of thing.

Even for Mile, her experience talking and dining with nobles outside of her family was more or less limited to the time they had spent with Count Amroth. Plus, now that her memories of her previous life had returned, talking with nobles made her very tense. While it would not be outwardly apparent to most, Mile was a bit tense to begin with. Of course, when she was at the academy, she was comfortably conversing normally with a noble classmate, but that was another matter entirely.

"The wyvern has been active across roughly thirty percent of this region. The wyvern's active area has also included about half of the neighboring region, but that's a largely uninhabited area, so most of the casualties have actually been from this region. Likely, the lord of that region did nothing about it because they figured it would be handled by the people over here. Honestly, I would do the same in that lord's shoes. It's stupid to waste your soldiers and resources on a pointless task," said Reina.

The other three nodded in agreement. Of course, they had all heard this information from the guild master, but it was important to review everything aloud as a group like this. It would eliminate any miscommunications and make certain that they were all on the same page, smoothing out the proceedings going forward.

"And so, the problem is this."

With these words, Reina spread the copied materials that they had received from the guild master out across the table.

It was a crude map of this region and the next, with notes marking the towns that the wyvern had attacked, the other places it had been sighted, and the dates and times of these incidents.

The marks were, for the most part, concentrated within a particular radius. This much was fine. This much was completely normal. However...

"How weird..."

"Yeah, that's a little unnatural."

"It's a little different from what we heard in the capital about wyverns' usual habits..."

Just as Pauline, Mavis, and Mile had all noted, this wyvern's territory appeared to be in a slightly—no, an *incredibly*—strange location.

First off, compared to your average wyvern, the apparent scope of this one's territory was very small. Normally, they hunted across a far wider area. And since wyverns rarely appeared in this area to begin with, it could hardly be the result of a turf war or something similar.

Next, there was the fact that the reported sightings of the wyvern formed a perfect circle.

Now, that they formed a circle was not all that strange in and of itself. However, the circle that they formed, in this case, was too perfect. Normally, the dots would be a bit more scattered, the sort of shape that was vaguely, mostly a circle. *This* was far too much like an actual geometric shape.

Yet the clincher was the times and dates of the appearances. They were precise.

This wyvern appeared systematically in the same key locations at excessively punctual intervals.

The wyvern had chosen when and where to appear as though

it had a comprehensive knowledge of the human calendar and the different days of the week.

This was, of course, suspicious. Indubitably so.

However, the wyvern itself was not the only thing that the Crimson Vow found suspicious here.

"Naturally, other hunters have found this strange as well, and countless parties have accepted this job. And yet, they've all ended up with casualties and zero results. There's just a string of red marks. Of course, that isn't *so* strange. We could come up with plenty of reasons why that might happen—the hunters weren't skilled enough, or the wyvern was too strong, things like that. However, if it is relatively easy to encounter..."

"Then," Pauline muttered, "shouldn't the regional forces have been deployed?"

Indeed, the primary reason that local armies were not usually deployed for wyvern hunting was that wyverns were relatively difficult to locate. Mobilizing a great number of soldiers for many days required a lot of money. If one were to embark on such an operation fruitlessly, the army's entire budget could be wasted.

An opponent with an incredibly low encounter rate was not one that a lord would be interested in taking on.

However, if there was a relatively high chance that one would be able to encounter the wyvern, that should be a different story.

Defeating the wyvern would put a stop to further casualties in the region, provide good battle practice for the soldiers, strengthen one's reputation amongst the other lords, raise one's standing in the eyes of the Crown, and improve the general morale of the populace. With these aims in mind, it would be worthwhile to spare both a bit of the budget and even a few casualties.

Even if the wyvern escaped after they shot it down, it likely would not appear in that town again, so it would effectively be driven away—another appealing outcome.

If the wyvern was making such regular appearances, why hadn't the troops been dispatched?

"There must be some reason why they haven't sent the army out..." said Mavis.

Mile continued: "Or they did send them out, and they were already defeated. And now, they're just covering that up?"

Silence fell across the room.

The next morning, the four gathered up their things and left the inn, headed for a certain village.

Naturally, the place they were headed was where the wyvern was scheduled to appear tomorrow. There were no carriages that ran there, and it would take half a day to reach on foot, meaning that they would be arriving in the early afternoon.

The Crimson Vow had ridden in their client's wagons or in a passenger carriage many times, but in truth, this would count as a luxury for most hunters. Barring instances where they had a lot to carry, had injured or otherwise incapacitated party members, or some other limiting circumstance, hunters typically traveled on foot.

As they walked, the girls discussed their current job.

"What's the story with the lord, do you think?"

"Well, the pay is right. It just seems like, after countless parties were annihilated, there was no one left here to take the job. Eventually, it got transferred to the capital... But as long as we're involved, that won't happen again."

"Yeah. If he were scheming, then he would probably want to meet up with us. If you're trying to pull the wool over someone's eyes, it's important to meet them in the flesh. Conjecturing based only on assumptions is dangerous, but really, I don't think anything suspicious is happening here."

Pauline and Mavis agreed with Reina's assessment. Mile, who was rather removed from the thoughts and motivations of other people, merely nodded in agreement.

"Plus, there is a strong correlation between sending out more soldiers and registering more casualties, isn't there?"

"That's true."

"Indeed, if they took one-sided losses, without conquering or driving the thing away, then they couldn't possibly approve any more casualties. Losing multiple times would just cause them to lose face... By sending the job to the hunters' guild, all you lose out on is the payment for the job, and for a lord, it's much safer to say, 'I'll just pay the money, and have someone else take care of it for me.' They only have to pay for a success, so no matter how many times the mission fails, that's all they'll ever lose."

Leaving Mile in the dust, the other three continued their conversation.

"So then, this begs the question: If everything is normal, and the lord expects that the wyvern can be eliminated, then why hasn't it been eliminated yet? A wyvern is a dangerous opponent for a normal party, but any party who took on the job would have known at least that much, and only taken it if they felt they had a strong chance of succeeding. Right? As for the soldiers, even if they've specialized in fighting other humans, without much experience in beast-hunting, they're still combat professionals. I'm sure they would have done enough preliminary preparation and planning, most likely with a veteran hunter along to advise them. Which means..."

"Oh oh oh! There's a lot of the wyverns, or they're very strong!"

Now that they had finally come upon a topic she understood, Mile chimed in.

She had leapt in at the juiciest moment, but Reina could understand Mile's desire to contribute to the conversation when it finally came around to something that she understood. Gently, she acknowledged her.

"Well, something like that, yes..."

Such was the way of a leader... *not*. Mavis was the leader. Even if it was easy to forget that sometimes.

"Anyway, we must assume that our enemy is strong, and proceed with discretion. As Mile told us before, um, yes—'Life is a precious thing,'" said Reina.

The other three nodded.

"Will we really be all right? It's not that I don't believe in everyone's magic, but if you don't pull the wyvern down to the

ground, I won't have any way to lend you my strength in the battle, so..."

"It'll be fine! We'll figure it out somehow!"

For some reason, Mavis had a bad feeling about Mile's
confidence...

It was already well past noon when they reached their desti-
nation. They had taken their time as they walked, discussing not
only their job, but other frivolous things, and the journey had
stretched on longer than they expected.

The four of them planned to get to bed early that night in
preparation for the next day, so on arrival, they decided to go
straight into reconnaissance. After that, they would eat their fill
at lunch-slash-dinner and head straight to bed.

First, of course, they needed to find an inn. There was only
one inn in the village, so there weren't exactly a lot of choices.
They told the innkeepers that they did not need to have dinner
provided, and headed out to find an eatery or bar.

In a rural village like this, which was not even big enough to
have a guild branch or post office, the best places to gather information were at a bar, the village elder's house, and the marketplace.

However, in this case, as their job request had not come from
this particular village, they did not expect that the village elder
would have any pertinent information. Besides, they weren't
looking for any favors, so they decided to skip that step, at least
for now.

"Here's the place."

After walking around for a bit without finding anywhere that resembled an eatery, they heard from the passersby they asked that the village had but one saloon, which served food as well as drink. However, it wasn't very well marked...

This was the sort of little village that had very few visitors besides traveling peddlers, who already knew the place well, so there probably wasn't much need for signage.

Upon entering the building, the girls found ten or so villagers inside.

"Huh?"

The four made a noise of surprise, not expecting the place to be so crowded at such an odd hour. The villagers were just as surprised to see them.

"What? You girls... you're hunters, aren't you?"

"Yes. We've taken on the job of hunting the wyvern. We're a hunting party from the capital—the Crimson Vow," Mavis replied.

The villagers clamored.

"W-w-we're so grateful that you took on this job," one of the villagers started in a slightly troubled cadence, then continued mincingly, "but, well..."

This was not an unreasonable response. Within the radius of the wyvern's attacks, this village was the closest to the regional capital. In other words, most of the parties that had taken on this job had probably tried to use this village as an interception point, and perhaps the local troops had even used it as a temporary base.

This, of course, meant that the villagers knew the results of all these expeditions.

If they had known that the next hunting party to appear would be a group of four young girls, they would have been discouraged, or overtaken by fear. So, the girls did not feel too bad about surprising them.

"Please don't worry. We are already well aware of the circumstances. Three of us are mages, able to use strong attack magic, and the last is a strong swordswoman, able to defeat even a top knight. We will most definitely take down that wyvern! If you all can tell us everything that you know, our victory will be all the more certain!"

Hearing Pauline's forceful speech, the villagers raised a cheer of joy, and one after the other came to share what they knew.

It seemed that the reason that so many villagers had gathered while the sun was still high was not only for the food and drink, but also to discuss the wyvern that was due to strike again the next day. In fact, the only things atop the tables were pitchers of water and wooden cups.

As the girls suspected, the villagers reported that a number of parties, as well as a dozen or so soldiers from the regional militia, had taken stabs at felling the wyvern, but all of them had sustained grave casualties.

Though the wyvern naturally defended itself from people who attacked it, outside of that, it rarely harmed anyone, most often simply grabbing the cattle, horses, or sheep it had decided to hunt that day in its claws before flying away. As a result, there had been no casualties among the villagers to date.

Because of this, the villagers did not personally fear the

wyvern. However, having their livestock carried off at regular intervals meant that they could not make a living. For the village,
this was still a matter of life or death.

And so, they had devised two plans. The first was to take the
oldest, thinnest animal they had, and place it somewhere conspicuous in order to minimize the damages. The second was to chase
the wyvern away, in order to protect *all* of the livestock. However,
the first plan was not a long-term solution, as they would still be
losing more and more livestock, which would hurt the village in
the long run. And as for the second plan, if it went poorly, the
wyvern might decide to switch its prey from livestock to humans.
Whichever path they chose, it did not change the fact that the
village's prospects were looking dim.

"Hm? Cows and horses? Are wyverns really that big?"

Mile was utterly shocked.

Her surprise was not unreasonable. In order for birds to fly,
their bodies had to be as lightweight as possible. They simply
could not muster the power to fly while lifting something exceed-
ing their own body weight.

Though clearly wyverns were not birds, just how immense
would they have to be in order to fly carrying an entire cow...?

"What are you talking about? They taught us all about the standard monster sizes at prep school..." Reina groaned, exasperated.

Mile replied, "No, I do remember that much, but there are
different types, so... Anyway, I didn't think that they would be
big enough to fly away with a horse or cow! If they were a bird
attempting to carry prey that size, they would have to be..."

"But birds can't use magic."

"Huh?"

"I said, birds can't use magic, can they?"

"Magic...?"

"Dragons use magic to fly. Wyverns have large wings, so that's one matter, but do you think that something with a body as large as an elder dragon's could fly with their wings alone? Plus, things like dragon's fire would have to be magic, wouldn't they? Just how exactly did you think that all worked?"

"Maybe inside their bellies they have some kind of organ that works like a fire sac...?"

"Absolutely not!!!" the other three shouted in unison.

The villagers behind them nodded, too.

In her previous life, her father would have said something like, "They're awfully dis-organ-ized."

In that same life, Mile would have been ashamed by this ripe old dad joke, but thankfully, she had no friends back then, so he'd never had the chance to embarrass her in front of them.

That was perhaps the only benefit to not having any friends...

There was no doubt that there existed a subset of monsters that was capable of using magic, such as fire-breathing dragons and dire wolves that could leap with a force unimaginable on Earth. However, Mile had always simply assumed that those creatures were capable of such things because they lived in a fantasy world. She had never thought to question it very hard.

While yes, wyverns were still within the class of things that might reasonably be able to fly, it was an absolute mystery that elder dragons could do it, given their immense bodies and tiny wings.

In reality, these creatures surpassed humans in that, though they could not form the words with which to craft magic through complicated spells, they could merely "think intensely about their desired result" and make the same thing come about. And of course there were many that held immense magical power.

The (so-called) God had said of the nanomachines that "they react to the thoughts of living things and bring these desires into reality." Not just "humans," but "living things."

That was when Mile recalled the very first time she spoke to the nanomachines. They had told her, "INCLUDING HUMANS, THE AVERAGE CREATURE IS SET AT A BASIC LEVEL 1."

Returning to the conversation at hand, the Crimson Vow continued to listen to the villagers' stories about the wyvern.

Putting all of their stories in order, the situation was, in brief, as follows:

Starting about two and a half months ago, the wyvern had begun appearing once every twelve days, taking with it a single cow, horse, or sheep each time.

At first, everyone was too frightened to do anything, but after it showed that it was no threat to the humans, they began to grow a bit more optimistic, and on subsequent visits they mustered all their courage to try and protect their livestock. Still, every time they faced the angry wyvern, their determination evaporated.

Perhaps realizing that the villagers lacked the basic means by which to attack it in the first place, and could only huddle together to defend themselves as it chased them off, the creature did not launch any deadly attacks. Instead, it appeared to be toying with them.

At first, when they informed the area guild branch and the local lord about this, the lord appeared uninterested. However, once he heard that the wyvern was appearing at regular intervals, his attitude changed.

Indeed, if encountering the wyvern was a sure thing, he could secure important battle practice for his troops, increase his reputation as a lord, and make the strength of his army known across the land, all at relatively little cost.

Plus, protecting his lands from harm *was* a lord's duty, in the first place.

Unless a state of emergency had been declared, it was a policy that the guild could not issue its own job requests. In this case, as long as there had not been a request from the lord himself, there was, fundamentally, nothing they could do to act. They were not a charitable organization, and without anyone to pay the fee, no hunters would take on the job. It was not the guild, but rather, the lord or the Crown who was expected to be in charge of eliminating things like wyverns.

Unless there was an emergency, the guild acted only once a job had been filed. Such was the nature of things.

However, a rule of thumb also existed that indicated the guild should be informed of the appearance of a strong monster, for, if all the hunters within the region were to combine their forces, they could likely outdo even the regional army. It was with this in mind that the villagers contacted the guild.

The lord had dispatched an extermination force of eighteen soldiers, including combat mages, archers, and javelin throwers, who could bring the wyvern down to the ground, as well as lancers and swordsmen who could strike it once it was down.

Normally, excluding those who were A-rank or above, or perhaps the highest of B-ranks, your average soldier was stronger than a hunter with the equivalent years of experience. Therefore, this should have been more than enough soldiers to comprise an extermination force.

Even though they did not have a veteran hunter experienced in fighting wyverns along as an advisor, no one would complain about a team that strong being sent out to fight a single wyvern.

And so came the day of the wyvern's next attack.

The villagers were instructed to remain in their homes for safety's sake, and when they emerged, several hours later, what they saw was a bedraggled band of soldiers and a group of equally bedraggled mages, desperately using healing magic to patch up the more dire wounds.

The seriously wounded: six soldiers. The mildly wounded: five soldiers. MIA: a single cow.

About half of the seriously wounded were in such a state that the healing powers of these mages, who specialized in combat spells, would not cut it. Later, they would require multiple treatments from mages who specialized in healing. Of course, once they returned to the capital, there would be healing specialists who were in the lord's employ, mage hunters who specialized in healing magic, and clinics that served the common folk, as well as those healing mages who had stepped back from the front lines for the sake of aiding the elderly. Once they arrived in the capital, those soldiers would be fine.

Still, an enemy who they assumed could be dealt with easily had wiped out their extermination force.

Moreover, the wyvern had clearly been holding back, toying with them. If it hadn't, there was no way they could have escaped with zero deaths on their hands.

While their commander was flabbergasted that his soldiers had taken so many injuries, he judged that, while they had not defeated the wyvern, they had at least driven it away, saving the village from further injury. Thus, their duty was complete. He reported this to the villagers, and the news put a spring in everyone's step.

Even if the wyvern decided to use villages in other territories as its hunting ground, that would be a problem for that region to deal with, and no further concern of theirs. Or so their hearts told them.

The villagers were relieved. No longer would the wyvern bring despair to their doorstep.

And then, twelve days after the battle against the soldiers, the wyvern reappeared.

In other words, the wyvern clearly had no thoughts such as

"I lost" or "My opponent is a threat" running through its head. It had completely overlooked those weaklings who had come to harass it and flown home with its head held high and its prey in its clutches. It hadn't the slightest reason to avoid this prime hunting ground from here on out.

The villagers had made no special arrangements and watched in panic as the wyvern took the youngest, most valuable of their heifers. Once again, they hurried to inform the officials and the guild, but the lord's reaction was less than favorable, and so after that, one party at a time, the hunters began to appear.

They heard from the hunters that rather than sending out more troops, the lord had issued a request to the guild for the wyvern to be exterminated.

As far as the villagers were concerned, it did not matter *who* felled the wyvern. If the lord was willing to pay for someone else to do so, then they were all the more thankful for that.

However...

The first party. The second party. The third party.

One after another, the hunters failed.

They even heard tell that there were hunters who tried to face the wyvern at other locations as well, and that already, several other parties had been forced to retreat due to their injuries.

Fortunately, though there were many who had taken injuries, the villagers had yet to hear of anyone being killed, likely because, as always, the wyvern was only playing with them, holding back its true power. The wyvern could easily afford to do so, after all.

And then, just when it seemed that all the hunters nearby had been defeated, and none had appeared in the village for some time, the Crimson Vow had suddenly arrived.

"It's all more or less as we predicted. Nothing really stood out to me in any of their stories. Except for one thing..."

"Yeah, you're right. Everyone acted as they were equipped to, and handled themselves accordingly."

"Indeed. It's just that..."

The four came to the conclusion as one:

"The wyvern is way too strong and way too smart!"

Indeed, that was the only thing that was particularly strange.

"I guess it makes sense that the request didn't have the full details on it when it made it to the capital."

Yes, just as Reina implied, there had been no extra information written on the job request slip. After all, most of the "facts" were still confined to the realm of rumor, while the rest would have been inconvenient for the client to relate.

Lying on a request was strictly forbidden, and intentionally withholding crucial information was taboo as well.

In those cases, if the client meant anything malicious by their omission, the deposit would be seized, and they would face the penalty of increased deposits and handling fees for any requests filed in the future. Furthermore, if the client's omission put hunters in danger, they would be judged by a government official independent of the guild. In that case, it could become an incident of "attempted murder via willful negligence."

However, in this case, the fact that the request was to

"eliminate one wyvern," as well as the general danger of the situation, had not changed. The fact that the soldiers had been defeated and the hunters had failed amounted to nothing that required special disclosure. If the opponent was not actually a wyvern, or there were multiple wyverns, that would be another matter entirely.

But in this case, it was simply that the wyvern was strong, or perhaps that the soldiers and the hunters were weak. No one could know for certain, so they had no responsibility to go out of their way to include this information in their request.

Plus, if the hunters did any investigating, such things would be easy enough for them to confirm for themselves.

If everyone were to share prolific details of indeterminate veracity on their request forms, their job acceptances would grow scarce, and those who would take on such clients would have more than enough information to try and negotiate a rate increase.

If the lord had included a note about the systematic nature of the wyvern sightings, the number of takers for the job might have increased; however, if they did so, it would also have awakened suspicions, inviting questions which would be inconvenient to address, such as, "Why is it so systematic?" "Why doesn't the military handle it?"

"So, the question is... what should we do?"

"Normally, the only choice would be to face it head-on and bring it down."

"Yeah. There isn't really any other way..."

As Reina, Pauline, and Mavis had all suggested, even if the wyvern was a fairly intelligent creature, and even if there was something else at play, "exterminating the wyvern" was still the task that the Crimson Vow faced.

The Crimson Vow were neither royal spies nor official investigators. Without any special authority, they had no right to take on that sort of task.

The task they had accepted was simple: defeat the wyvern. That was all.

Later, they went back over the information that they had gathered from the villagers. However, since no one had been brave enough to peek around the battlegrounds where the soldiers and hunters faced the wyvern, and no one had been stupid enough to interrogate anyone who was injured and preparing to retreat to the capital as soon as they could, the particulars of the previous battles were unclear.

The local guild branch likely would have investigated all of this, but what the guild master would not have expected was the fact that there was nothing special to report.

They probably already knew that the wyvern was strong, but that much could be guessed from the failed hunters who came back with nothing more to report than the fact that their enemy had been a powerful one. If there had been something else to report, like the fact that there were three wyverns, or that this one could breathe fire and shoot laser beams from its eyes, then that would have been a different story...

Once their information-gathering mission had concluded, the Crimson Vow ate their lunch-slash-dinner at the saloon and retired to the inn.

Aside from Mavis and Pauline, who ate comparatively little, the villagers were agog to watch such small girls wolf down such large mountains of food. However, they *had* gone without lunch, and whenever a hunter could eat, she should always eat her fill. Particularly while they were in a completely safe place, where there was no worry of them cramping up from a full stomach.

Pauline and Mavis were a little embarrassed to be eating while the watching villagers were not, but Mile and Reina did not even appear to notice.

Reina would have written it off as nothing, since even while they were eating they were still on the job. As for Mile, she was merely hungry, and did not think anything of it at all.

Apparently, compared to her previous body, in this life Mile's body was not very fuel-efficient...

The following morning, a single cow was taken from the village to the top of a short hill, a little bit away from the village, then fastened in a clearing of trees.

Naturally, the Crimson Vow was there as well.

If the Crimson Vow were to stand alone atop a hill, that alone might have been enough to attract the wyvern's attention; however, on the off chance that the wyvern were to develop a taste for human flesh, it might become a problem. They could not deny the villagers' request to send a cow up as an offering as well.

Perhaps the villagers were considering the girls' safety. If a cow, which was far more appetizing than a human, was present, and if the girls handled themselves properly, then it wasn't impossible that the wyvern might simply grab the cow and fly right away. In that case, of course, they would not have succeeded with the extermination; however, compared to the possibility of the still-young girls becoming martyrs and seeing one or two of them dragged away by the wyvern, losing a single cow was nothing. So thought the kind-hearted villagers.

Once the cow was secured in the clearing, the villagers headed home, and the Crimson Vow waited silently for the wyvern to arrive.

Because their quarry was flying in from far off in the sky, it wouldn't have been a problem for them to speak in quiet voices, but as hunters, they were trained not to speak while waiting to ambush a target...

As it happened, they were not alone. A courageous youth, who was "incredibly fond of cute girls," was watching stealthily from behind a tree, waiting to run and alert the village the moment the wyvern flew away, should any of the girls sustain serious injury.

He was the sort of youth who, so far unsatisfied with the rough country girls of the village, would face any danger for the sake of a "pure and beautiful" young maiden. He was not bad-looking, and was often seen caring for children, but for some reason he had not been very popular with the women of the village.

Perhaps that was because the only children he took care of were always young girls...

Still, the youth thought, compared to someone who never looked after children at all, he was a far better catch, so he was hard-pressed to understand what was so unappealing about his behavior.

Mile was scanning the perimeter with her location magic, so naturally, she knew that the youth was there. However, she assumed that he was a witness sent as a representative of the village and had already considered the possibility that there might be a messenger present to send for relief. So, she ignored him.

In any case, even if he were to see something odd in the ensuing scene, people would merely assume that he was overexcited by seeing a wyvern extermination for the first time in his life, or that he was exaggerating what he had witnessed for the sake of spinning a yarn. No one was likely to believe him.

Unless a number of people corroborated his testimony—or the listener was particularly gullible—no one was likely to believe a ridiculous story of what some villager had supposedly witnessed. If it was something that affected their own lives, people might be inclined to do a bit of investigation before waving it off as a lie, but if it was something like, "I saw an incredible battle!" they were likely to just laugh and ignore it.

In other words, he was harmless. Not a threat. That was the sum of it.

"It's here!"

Of course, the first to spot the approaching wyvern was Mavis.

This was less a matter of her having a higher vantage point and wider field of vision because of her height, and more because of her innate abilities.

The other three looked in the direction that Mavis was pointing, and sure enough, there was a dark speck in the sky, growing larger by the second.

"Huh?"

Mile, whose abilities were even greater than those of Mavis, raised her voice in confusion.

"What's wrong?" Reina asked suspiciously.

"It looks like the wyvern is already holding something..."

When they looked more closely, they saw, sure enough, that the wyvern appeared to be clutching something that looked vaguely like a cow in its talons.

"That's weird... If it already got its prey somewhere else today, wouldn't it just pass by this village?" Reina muttered.

And yet, the wyvern continued to fly straight toward them.

Then, when it was very near to the hill, it dropped in altitude and disappeared beyond the grove.

"Huh...?"

The four were stunned at this unexpected maneuver, but they quickly collected themselves and began to prepare.

When the wyvern rose above the trees again, it was no longer gripping the cow-like object in its talons, but instead a log about 30 centimeters in diameter.

"It's coming!" said Reina.

"All right!!" the other three cheered.

It was not a particularly girlish battle cry, but they were hunters, after all.

It seemed that the wyvern had deemed the Crimson Vow to be a threat from the start.

Perhaps it could tell from their gear and weapons that they were not villagers, but of the ilk of those people who had launched attacks against it so many times before. It was in attack mode from the get-go.

In its talons it gripped a log, probably a fallen tree. The method that the wyvern had chosen to attack most effectively with this implement was a loft bombing attack.

Compared to a horizontal bombing, this method had a much higher rate of accuracy, and though it was a far greater burden on the body, if one could withstand it, the results were worthwhile.

A drop bombing attack of higher than a 30-degree angle, such as could be called dive bombing, would prove too difficult for a fleshy creature incapable of aerobraking, so the wyvern continued downward at a leisurely angle of less than 30 degrees, its large body accelerated by gravity and trembling violently against the pressure of the wind.

It would not need to pierce through any bulky shielding, so it did not require an immense amount of speed. On the contrary, the more slowly it descended, the more precisely it could aim at

an enemy that was running around until the very last moment—
and moreover, enjoy prolonging the fear it caused in its target for
as long as possible.

There was no time for the girls to duck into the trees to avoid
the attack.

Mile, judging from the fact that the wyvern was performing this trick so handily, deduced that this must be its preferred
method of attack, and shouted directions to the group.

Hearing this, the other three did as she said. Normally, she
was a bit of a scatterbrain, but when it came to magical abilities
and other such miscellaneous trivia, everyone happily followed
her lead. Even though they might poke fun at her for her sillier
moments, no one thought Mile was stupid.

She was merely sheltered, couldn't read a room, lacked common sense, was absentminded, made unthinkable mistakes, and
was much too soft-hearted.

Basically, she was what most people in the world would call
a fool.

The wyvern was fast approaching, but the four of them stood
unmoving.

Then, just as the wyvern appeared to enter the final stage of
its throwing attack, Mile shouted, "Run!"

As she had previously instructed them, they turned and ran
with all their might in the opposite direction to the approaching
wyvern.

Seeing this, the wyvern opened its beak, as if to grin.

Yes, its prey always ran. Then, the log would barrel forward, striking the running prey down from behind.

As long as it aimed a little ahead of its prey's current position, the log would either hit them or else land just a little behind, before rolling in their direction. That was what it had learned from its master, and it had seen the effectiveness of this method confirmed time and again in real life.

From behind the point where its prey was running straight forward... Now!

"About face!"

At that moment, Mile, who was coolly keeping watch over her shoulder, saw the practiced movement of the wyvern's claws and shouted.

The next moment, the four of them skidded to a halt and turned about, toward the wyvern, then ran at it at full tilt.

The log, which had already left the wyvern's grasp, sailed over their heads and behind them.

"Attack!"

At Mile's next signal, Reina and Pauline, who had been incanting as they ran, let their attack spells fly.

"Fire Bomb!"

"Water Bomb!"

Whoosh!

The wyvern, overcome with panic, twisted its body, barely managing to avoid the spells that came flying. The first one, and then the second...

"We did it."

Watching the wyvern desperately dodge the magic, then take a swift upward turn to return to a higher altitude, Mile crossed her arms, looking on proudly.

"What do you mean, 'We did it'?! It just got away! What do we do now?! I guess that did save us, at least…"

"It's fine. It still hasn't taken any damage, and it doesn't seem like the sort of opponent to run away just from that little attack."

As if it had heard Mile's reply, the wyvern did not flee, but rather began circling in the sky above them once it had attained a sufficient altitude.

And then, Reina's shout rang out. "Why is it that you can't read people at all, but you can read *monsters* just fine?!?!"

The wyvern continued circling at an altitude their spells could not reach, peering down at their party. Apparently, now that the hunters had avoided its special attack and nearly scored a direct hit with their combat spells, it was remaining vigilant.

However, it had no intention of shamelessly running back home, or abandoning this valuable feeding ground.

"This time, we have to let off a preemptive strike," Mile suddenly said.

Reina's response was reflexive. "Preemptive strike?"

"It means that we have to make the first move," Mile clarified.

"I know that much! What I was asking was, how do you expect us to attack an enemy that's so high up our spells won't reach it?! Guhuh, hff hff hff…"

Apparently, Reina had screamed her throat raw. A mage's windpipe was a valuable asset.

Next time, I'll make her some lozenges, thought Mile.

"Are you saying that *your* magic can reach it?" Reina asked, having recovered at least a little bit of her voice.

"Hmm. I don't know about all that, but if we can't reach it by attacking from the ground, then all we have to do is just get to somewhere where we *can* reach it," Mile answered. "Therefore, Reina, would you please start the incantation for an attack spell? Just before you let it off, I'm going to make you fly with magic. And then, please fire your spell directly at the wyvern. We only have one shot at this, so please use the strongest spell you have!"

"Huh? Wh-what do you mean, 'fly'? Wait a minute, just what are you..."

"Now! Hurry and start the spell! There's no time!"

"Huh? A-all right, then..."

Now was not the time to sit and chat. Knowing this in her heart, Reina decided to trust in Mile. Even if she was talking nonsense, Mile was still a fellow party member and a reliable friend who had saved them many times before. If she couldn't put her unconditional trust in her now, then what was their friendship for?!

Plus, she was rather interested in this alleged flying magic.

She was going to fly through the sky, free as a bird. Deep down, her heart was aflutter.

With this thought in mind, Reina began her spell. There was no choice here but to use her magnum opus, "Crimson Hellfire."

Reina began the incantation, and when she had reached the halfway point, Mile grabbed her around both sides from behind.

"Eep!"

Reina was startled at this sudden gesture, but she was still a pro hunter, so she did not allow the flow of her spell to be broken. This was surely a part of the procedure for the flying spell, so she ignored the tickling sensation.

"Here we go! Thunderbird No. 1, prepare for liftoff!"

With that announcement, Mile swung her around in a huge circle.

"Wh-hwa-whaaaaaa-whaaaaaaaaaaaaaaaat?!?!"

As Mile swung Reina with all her might, finally, Reina let out a scream.

"Swingby!"

The moment that Reina had amassed enough centripetal force, Mile launched her toward the wyvern, at full strength.

"Magical Fireblaster, Reina Gun!!!"

"Gaaaaaaaaaaaaaaaaaaaaaaaaaaaahhhh!!!"

The wyvern was trembling.

A human, which was not supposed to be able to fly, was flying in a direct line toward it. At considerable speed.

It was making a hideous expression and baring its fangs, letting out an awesome roar as it approached at high velocity. This was the one that launched the attack earlier. Oh no!!

Momentarily forgetting its wyvern pride, the creature dodged.

And yet, the human did not alter its course, soaring directly past.

Roaring all the way.

"Gaaaaaaaaaaaaaaaaaaaaaaaaaaaaaaaaaaaahhhh!!!"

"Reina, why didn't you hit it with your spell?!"

Mile pouted and complained, performing her next spell a bit grudgingly.

"Rising air currents! Give Reina a soft landing!"

As she said this, a whirlwind whipped up counterclockwise in the spot where Reina was expected to land, and a strong upward current rose... Apparently, they were somewhere in the northern hemisphere.

Whether the air had begun to move in an upward current because of the counterclockwise spiral, or whether the counterclockwise spiral had arisen because of the air current, was not certain, but at any rate, Reina was cushioned by the strong upward draft and made a successful safe landing.

"All right, Pauline, you're up next. Please don't you fail me, too!" Mile said, approaching, but Pauline thrust both arms out, refusing her with a dire expression.

"N-no! Absolutely noooot!!!"

Mile inched slowly nearer, and Pauline inched slowly away.

"The name of this attack is 'Flesh-Ravaging Halo, Pauline'!"

Inch, inch...

Inch, inch...

Inch, inch...

As she slowly closed in, sweat poured down Pauline's neck, when finally a voice of salvation rang out.

"I'll go next!"

Mile turned around to see Mavis, a broad smile on her face.

With Mile's attention redirected at Mavis, Pauline took the opportunity to escape.

She couldn't run away from the battleground, so she ran instead to check on Reina. When she arrived at Reina's landing spot, she saw that Reina appeared safe and was using some kind of magic.

"Reina, are you hurt? I've got my healing magic ready!"

It was not that Reina could not use healing spells herself, but Reina, who specialized in combat magic, was nowhere near as strong a healer as Pauline. Pauline was running toward her in a panic, but Reina stopped her frantically.

"St-stay back! You can't come over here!!!"

It was then that Pauline noticed. The spell that Reina had been using when Pauline approached, her face bright red, was the body and clothing cleaning magic that Mile had taught them so long ago.

"Oh......"

Pauline stopped in her tracks. Her expression was uncertain and delicate.

And then, Reina's scream rang out.

"Nooooooooooooooooooooooooooooooo!!!"

The wyvern, meanwhile, continued circling in the sky above, its heart pounding like a freight train.

It had been afraid. The face on that approaching human had been truly frightening. That in and of itself was terrifying.

It was the first time the wyvern had felt fear in a very long while.

And, just a little—just a *little*—it had wet itself. For a strong and proud wyvern, this was incredibly embarrassing.

It would have no choice but to defeat these humans, to wash itself of this disgrace.

So as not to violate its master's orders, it would not kill them, but it would send them fleeing in terror!

"Are you ready?"

"Yeah, ready whenever."

"Do you need to go to the bathroom? Have you prayed to your god? Is your heart ready?"

"Look, I said I'm ready whenever, didn't I? What in the world are you going on about, Mile?"

Mavis was jittery with anticipation.

She was going to fly.

She was going to soar through the great heavens above and strike down a wyvern, lord of the skies, on a battlefield far above the ground.

She was going to achieve something that no knight in existence had ever done before.

She was going to do it. Mavis was going to be the one. Look at her now, Father and Big Brothers!

Mile grabbed her gently beneath her arms. And then, she began a mysterious spell.

"Thunderbird No. 2, prepare for liftoff! Use your No. 1 weapon, the shortsword!"

Whoom.

Her body was being swung around.

Whoom whoom.

However, this was nothing for a body as strong as hers.

Whoom whoom whoom whoom whoom.

Just a little more...

"Swingby!"

She could hear Mile's voice. And then...

"Mavis Cutter!!!"

Ka-whoosh!

Mavis was soaring through the air.

With her sword held fast in both hands, poised at the ready, she was flying straight toward the wyvern.

"True Godspeed Blade, Second Form, Heaven Blade. Attack!"

Here comes anotheeeeeeer!!!

The wyvern was in a complete tizzy.

Naturally so. Yet again, a human, who should not have been able to fly, was now shooting directly toward it. The fear it felt before came roaring back.

However, this individual was not one of the humans who had fired a magical attack at it before.

Judging by its appearance, and based on the types of humans who had challenged the wyvern in battle before, this one was not the magic type, but the type that brandished an iron stick. In that case, this one was less formidable. As long as the wyvern took care not to let its wings be damaged, its body and tail could not be badly hurt.

The only choice it had was to drop down from above.

If it had considered this more fully, it would have realized that, unlike a magical attack, where a bit of distance was no object, if the wyvern just dodged a sword attack a little bit, it would be over. Probably, Mile had predicted that the wyvern would choose to attack head-on... Probably.

"Hiyaaaaaaaaaaahhh!!!"

Mavis swung her sword straight ahead at full strength, aiming for the wyvern's neck. However, the wyvern, predicting this all too well, twisted its body and swung its tail at full force toward... or rather, it tried to, but Mavis's attack was a lot quicker than it thought it would be!

The wyvern tried desperately to twist its body some more, keeping its neck away from the approaching sword. Quickly, quickly it had to strike the human with its tail!

Ka-shunk!

After a moment's clashing, both of the parties' bodies separated and flew apart.

"Gyaaaaaaaaaaaaaaaaaaaah!!!"

Mavis, seeing the tail approaching, had given up on aiming for the neck. The wyvern was hurt, its proud tail damaged by the redirected attack. It was stunned by the pain.

And then, Mavis, who had now begun her descent, looked down at the ground below.

Both of them screamed until their throats nearly burst.

"Oh... ah..."

The wyvern continued circling shakily in the sky, so once Mile had set up her upward draft cushioning magic to break Mavis's fall, she had nothing to do but go to check on Mavis, once she landed. For some reason, she was on her hands and knees in the grass, groaning.

"Oh no! Are you hurt somewhere?" Mile asked, worried.

Mavis weakly replied, "I-It's nothing. Just... please, please give me a moment..."

After a short while, Reina and Pauline reappeared.

Reina looked incredibly displeased, but for some reason, after she glanced at Mavis's lower half, she appeared all the more irritated. She stomped toward Mile.

Whack.

"Oww!"

Mile let out a cry as Reina suddenly jabbed her in the head with her staff.

Whack whack!

"Ow! That hurts! What are you doing, Reina?!"

Whap whack whack whack whack!

"St-stop! Please stop iiiiit!!!"

Whack whack whack whack whack whack whack whack whack!

"I-I was wrong! I apologize. Please stop it alreadyyyyyyyyyyy!!!"

Thanks to her naturally high stats, this attack did not truly hurt Mile, but seeing Reina's expression, feeling a sort of intellectual pain along the lines of "I'm pretty sure this should hurt," and recognizing the seriousness of Reina's anger from a vigorous attack that normally *should* hurt a great deal, Mile apologized profusely.

"Mile, do you really understand why I'm angry with you?"

"Of course!" Mile quickly replied. "I should have launched you more accurately, and at a much higher speed, so that the wyvern couldn't have dodg—ow! Owwwwwwwwwww!"

Whack whack whack whack whack whack whack whack whack!

"Hff hff hff hff..."

When Reina, Mavis, Mile, and Pauline—who, besides Pauline, were all exhausted for some reason—looked up into the sky, they saw that the wyvern, which had been unsteadily circling up until now, had begun to move more purposefully. It seemed it was preparing to do something else.

"Looks like this is Round Two..." Mile muttered.

The other three nodded.

The wyvern was shaken to realize that the wound it had received was deeper than predicted, but its tail had not been cut off, and it was far from a life-threatening injury. As yet, its movements were unhindered. As long as it left it alone, the wound would heal up soon enough.

However, while the blow to its body would heal naturally, the wound to its pride was not so easily mended. The wyvern would have to stitch up that gash itself. Indeed, by defeating its enemies.

It had never had to get serious against the enemies it had

faced so far. They were trifles, little things that it only needed to toy with. It had never needed to get down and dirty, and pull the ace from its sleeve.

However, *this* time... Finally, it had encountered a foe that would require it to summon its full strength.

The wyvern was rather pleased about this.

Now, playtime was over. It was time for a real battle.

It began its descent. Then, it began to inhale. It was time to launch a serious attack, against an opponent that the wyvern itself had deemed neither prey nor plaything, but a true enemy.

"A direct attack?"

"Yes!"

Seeing that the wyvern was going to launch a direct attack, using either its claws, its tail, or its teeth, everyone was thrilled, and Mavis was particularly delighted. She laughed out loud at this perfect chance, brandishing her sword.

However, seeing how the approaching wyvern had opened its mouth wide, Mile went pale.

I've seen something like this before! It was on an anime VHS that was in my father's library!

"Dodge!!!"

Seeing Mile leap and thrust Pauline, who stood beside her, out of the way, Mavis and Reina quickly moved as well. Just then...

Blam!

There was a sensation like the air trembling, and then the ground where the girls had been standing burst open.

After that, the wyvern quickly pulled its body up and ascended again.

"What?! A ranged attack?!"

"Dragon Breath? But I didn't see anything!"

"I-I've never heard of them having an ability like that!"

Mavis, Reina, and Pauline were all utterly awestruck, but Mile folded her arms and spoke with apparent comprehension.

"Of course..."

"Y-you knew about this, Mile?!" Mavis asked.

"The Stomach Flute Technique..."

The what?!?!

This ultrasonic barrage was probably a kind of Breath attack.

A wyvern using a Breath attack was an incredibly rare occurrence, but it was not entirely unheard of.

Though they may have been pseudo-dragons, they were still a variety of dragon, and masters of flight-assisting magic. Thus, a particularly intelligent creature might be able to learn a Breath technique by watching and imitating other dragon types. Such things had been observed many times in the past. That said, none of them had expected to bear witness to such a rare occurrence on this occasion.

They had already concluded that this was an abnormally intelligent specimen, so they should have anticipated the possibility. Yet there had been no reports of anything like it from the other hunters. If there had been, the guild master most certainly would have told them.

And so, it would be overly harsh to criticize the Crimson Vow, who could not have been expected to assume that the wyvern possessed the wisdom to conceal its strongest technique until the very end of the battle. There were scarcely any hunters who would ever assume such a thing...

"Wh-what was that 'Something' Technique you were talking about...?" Reina asked.

"Stomach Flute Technique. Please think of it as a type of Breath attack," Mile replied, thinking.

This is bad... This wyvern can use ranged attack magic...and it has a much farther range than Reina and Pauline...

Until now, Mile had been careful about her magic so that everyone else would not come to rely on her. If they relied on her magic for everything, they would never grow, and they would not be functioning as a party in the first place. Plus, she would hate to have that sort of relationship with others.

As a result, she had resigned herself to a supporting role in this battle, thinking that Reina, Mavis, and Pauline could take center stage in defeating the wyvern.

Yet these new circumstances were making that stance more difficult.

The enemy's attacks could reach them, but no one's attacks but hers could reach the enemy. The wyvern had no intention of entering the range of the others' attacks. Plus, with her carefully devised "Thunderbird Plan" having ended twice in misfires, Reina and Mavis would have absolutely no interest in flying again.

At this rate, the wyvern was going to remain at a distance where its attacks could reach the Crimson Vow, but theirs could not, meaning that they would continue to face a one-sided assault. That said, letting themselves be defeated here would be a stain on the Crimson Vow's record.

What to do?

"I-I'll go next!"

"Huh?"

As Mile pondered, Pauline suddenly announced herself, looking a bit queasy.

"Are you sure about this?" Mile asked.

"I mean, do we have any other choice? Plus, I'm a member of the Crimson Vow, too!" said Pauline.

Mile nodded emphatically.

"All right then. Fly now, Pauline!"

And so, Mile outlined some key items.

"I'm going to aim you straight for its jaw. It's going to get away quick, so you can't use any continuous spells. Strike it with an ice javelin, and if we're lucky, that will give it a concussion and knock it from the sky. At the very least, please try to injure its throat or palate, so that it can't use that special breath again!"

"U-understood!"

This time, there was a chance that Pauline might take a ranged attack while approaching. Plus, unlike Mavis, Pauline did not have the durability to take a blow from the wyvern's tail, talons, or pointy teeth straight on. To ensure her safety, Mile whispered to herself, "Lattice Power Barrier!!!"

Then, Mile grabbed Pauline under the arms and began her mysterious spell once more.

"Thunderbird No. 3, prepare for liftoff!"

Whoom!

Whoom whoom whoom!

"Swingby!"

Ka-whoosh!

She blasted off, at a far higher speed than even the previous two.

"Chin Bombing Thunderbird, Argo!"

Another ooooone!!!

The wyvern, which had just started on its attack path yet again, was momentarily distressed at the appearance of another "flying human," but it quickly regained its cool. This was the third time this had happened now, so the wyvern was starting to grow accustomed to it. Even if it was still a bit frightening...

Seeing that this opponent was one of the individuals that had launched a magical attack, the wyvern opened its mouth and drew in a breath in order to launch a preemptive strike.

Shiiiiiiiing...

Boom!

It should have been a direct hit, but, the enemy was still speeding toward the wyvern, its path unchanged. The wyvern panicked. The human had blasted through its special technique, in which the wyvern had absolute confidence, without moving a muscle. Furthermore, unlike the previous two, this human was flying silently, without making a sound.

The truly strong ones never roared. This was the thought that crossed the wyvern's mind.

It was already too late to launch a second attack. All it had left now were its tail and its claws...

At this thought, the wyvern glared at its enemy, and that was when it noticed.

The flying human's eyes were closed, its body completely limp.

Yes, it was unconscious.

Bang!

In spite of the wyvern's tail attack, Pauline, who was surrounded by the sturdy lattice power barrier, retained her kinetic energy and crashed into the wyvern.

And then, they both fell toward the ground.

"Waaaaaaah! Upward Draft! Air Cushion! Gravity Control!!!"

Pauline and the wyvern were falling together, so it was difficult to cushion only Pauline's fall. Plus, if the wyvern were to fall on top of her , Pauline would be crushed. Mile had to ensure that both of them landed softly. She hurriedly set off her spells.

As a result, the descent speeds of both rapidly declined, and somehow, they successfully made a soft landing.

"Boss! A wyvern just fell from the sky!"

"Don't you think I can see that?! Also, who's this 'Boss'?!?!"

Apparently, Mile had returned to her usual self.

Still, naturally, she did not attempt to catch the falling wyvern in her arms.

Because Pauline was so light, and because Mavis, ever the

gentlewoman, caught her in her arms, Pauline took no damage, even though she was still unconscious. However, it was possible there were still some aftereffects from her collision with the wyvern, and Mile applied healing magic silently.

As for the wyvern, even if Mile had used her magic to cushion its fall, it was still quite heavy, and in order for it to be lightweight enough to stay aloft, its body was rather brittle. As a result, it did appear to have taken at least a bit of damage from the fall.

While the wyvern was still twitching on the ground, Mile pulled something like a spool of thread from her loot box and bound the wyvern's mouth, limbs, wings, and tail.

When the wyvern came to shortly thereafter, it tried to break the bonds, but it could not shred the seemingly thin cord that it was wrapped in.

Carbon nanotubes.

Yes, it was the same powerful material that Mile's slingshot was made of. Nothing bound with that carbon nanotube thread would be able to break free with such halfhearted strength.

After a short while, Pauline regained consciousness, staring widely, perplexed, when the others told her that she had felled the wyvern.

"So, I guess we should transport this guy to the lord. Capturing a wyvern alive is a pretty rare occurrence, and this one is pretty smart, so if you clipped its wings, broke it in, and put it on display, there could be a use for it. Well, actually, they might have to do a public execution in order to appease the citizens—but as long as

we get our completion stamp and our pay, the rest of it's none of
our business. If we can collect an extra free for bringing it in alive,
they can do whatever they want with it after."

The wyvern, which had either given up on breaking its bonds,
or simply relaxed, thinking that no immediate danger was likely
to befall it, was lying quietly, but at this, it eyed Reina uneasily, as
though perhaps, it could understand her words.

Nodding at Reina, Mile called to the youth who had been
standing beneath the trees watching them, in order to ask him to
call the villagers, who could help them transport the wyvern. That
was when *he* appeared.

He had white hair and a white beard. An older man wearing
a robe and holding a wand, looking very much like a stereotypi-
cal mage, appeared from between the trees and said to the four,
"I can't bear to see that poor little wyvern being picked on by all
these people. What do you say? I'll give you a gold piece if you
hand the creature over to me."

Hearing this, all four of them had the exact same thought at
once.

Wh-what a shady guyyyy!!!

And then, Mile alone thought, *It's Urashima Taro!!!*

"Do you think we're stupid? If we bring this thing in, we'll get
paid 30 gold as a reward, plus an additional fee for bringing it in
alive. Why should we turn it over to you for just one gold piece?!
You just want to say that you captured it yourself and collect the
reward, don't you? Plus, if our job is treated as failed, then not

only will we have to pay the penalty, our party's reputation will suffer. There's no way you're taking it!"

The man's brows knitted at Reina's words, but Mile tossed him a lifeline.

"But if you'll let us take just part of the wyvern as proof of the extermination, we might be able to hand it over for just ten gold pieces... couldn't we, Reina?"

"Huh? Yes, well, if we did that we wouldn't get the bonus for bringing it in alive, but we'd still get our completion stamp, so, well, I *guess* that would be fine..."

It was ten times what he had intended to pay, but that should not have been an issue. The man appeared relieved, and asked, "Yes, that's splendid! Well then, which part of it would you need to take as your proof?"

The four of them answered in unison.

"The head!"

"Wh..." The man was nearly speechless.

Naturally, Mile had never had any intention of turning the wyvern over to such a shady old man. She had merely hoped that he would let some information slip if they agitated him.

"But if you take that, it'll die!" the man shouted.

Reina gave the natural response. "That's expected, isn't it? We have to prove that we eliminated it, so..."

"But I want to take Lo—ahem, the wyvern back alive!"

"So we'll compromise. All told, the elimination reward, along with the bonus for bringing it in alive, plus damages for us having our job treated as a failure would total somewhere around 100 gold."

So said Reina, but honestly, no matter how much money he paid, she had no intention of turning over the wyvern. Even if the man were to offer them heaps of money, there was no amount of gold that would make up for having the mark of a failed job on their record and the blow to their reputations that would come with it.

Plus, if the wyvern were to attack the village again later, and anyone died because of it, she wouldn't be able to sleep at night.

"Grrrrrrngh..."

Obviously, to pay one hundred gold or more—the equivalent of over one million Japanese yen—would hurt quite a bit. The man thought hard.

Just then, Pauline asked completely naturally and nonchalantly, "By the way, what was the deal with that cow-like thing that the wyvern was carrying?"

"Oh, that was the dragon-drawn carriage I was riding in. It's disguised so that if anyone sees it, it will just look like a... sto... len..."

The man had begun speaking confidently, but his voice grew small, and then petered out.

There was an idiot in their midst.

"Say, Mile, is this man your father?" asked Reina.

"Just what does that meeeeeeeaaaaaaan?!" Mile shouted back.

"So, is that wyvern named Low or something?" Mavis snarked.

"It's Lobreth!" the man snapped back. "And though it isn't comparable to the Breath of an elder dragon, he can still use Dragon's Breath. That is incredibly rare for a wyvern, so I decided to make that part of his name. 'Low Breath,' or more concisely, 'Lobreth.'"

Compared to the frivolous, unusual names that modern parents liked to give their children, this was far more straightforward reasoning. It gave them a sort of affection for the man. Mile was genuinely moved.

"The Mysterious Bird Lobreth..."

"I told you before, a wyvern isn't a bird!"

"Oh, yes..."

"Anyway, that's not the problem! What kind of villain uses a wyvern to attack people?! What's your angle?" Mile was angry.

"None in particular..."

"Huh?"

"Well, I'm saying that I wasn't really trying to do anything."

"Whaaaat?!"

His response to Mile's accusation was not what the Crimson Vow had expected.

"B-but, you attacked the village..."

"But wyverns always attack villages that are inside their territories, don't they?"

"Er..."

Unable to form a response to the man's words, Mile went silent.

"B-but the wyvern..." Mavis started.

"It's Lobreth," the man interrupted.

Apparently, he was very invested in this name he had come up with.

"Anyway, this Lobreth is in your care, isn't he?! In which case, his attacking the village would have to have been at your command..."

"I'm not taking care of him!"

"Huh???"

"I'm telling you I have nothing to do with caring for Lobreth."

"Th-then, just what exactly is Lobreth to you?!" Pauline asked, raising her voice for once in a blue moon.

The man replied, "He's my friend."

"What?"

"He and I are friends. Now and then he carries me around in that carriage, and I heal his wounds whenever he gets hurt. If my friend wants to eat things that are within his territory, what business is it of mine?"

"............"

All four of the girls were stunned, their mouths agape, not able to manage another word.

"Furthermore, I have asked him never to harm anyone who doesn't harm him, particularly not any women or children. If someone were to ask him, please don't harm any creatures except wolves in the forest who attack people, and people who attack you, and even when you are attacked, try your best not to kill or seriously injure anyone, especially women and children, then what's the crime in that? On the contrary, if *that* is a criminal act, then what would you call a virtuous one?"

"Uh..."

This was suspicious.

This was clearly suspicious, and the things he said were nothing more than trickery.

Even though this was what they were all thinking, if they couldn't disprove what the man was saying, then they had no right to apprehend him as a criminal.

On the contrary, apprehending him without proof would make *them* the criminals.

What to do?

Reina, Mavis, and Mile thought hard, but then Pauline chimed in. "Well then, why don't we just hand the wyvern over to the guild!"

"Wha...?! But I just told you that Lobreth is my friend..."

"And?"

By daring to call the creature "the wyvern" and not "Lobreth," Pauline had emphasized that to them, "Lobreth" was nothing more than some monster.

"Our job was to 'Capture and hand over the wild wyvern that attacked the village and stole their livestock, wounded tons of soldiers and hunters, and just so happens to have a human acquaintance,' yes? What would you have to do with any of that? Would you walk up to a guard who's about to arrest a murderer and say, 'That person is my friend, so you can't apprehend and punish him?' He doesn't *belong* to you or anything, does he?"

"Gnh..."

Pauline was still Pauline, after all. If the man wanted to say that he took no responsibility for the wyvern, then he should be treated accordingly. Yet he had taken the trouble to show himself, so this probably bothered him.

And then Pauline landed the *coup de grâce*.

"It would be awfully hard to transport this thing alive. It might break free along the way and hurt someone... How about this? We give up on turning it in alive and just kill it now? Even if there would be a bonus for bringing it in alive, I'd rather lose the ten gold than run the risk of it escaping during transport. Why not just take the surefire thirty gold and the job completion mark, along with the rank-promotion points?"

This man was middle-aged, and so had probably been a mage for many years, with the knowledge and ability to match. However, considering the way he was speaking and behaving, his interpersonal skills were lacking. Overwhelmingly so. Indeed, it was quite fair to ask whether he was Mile's father.

Perhaps, in his years of research and practice, he had lived a life of almost no human contact.

Realizing Pauline's plan was to rile the man up, Mavis and Reina joined in with that assumption in mind.

"You know, you're right. Losing everything just for the sake of trying to get a bonus is probably pretty stupid of us."

"That's true. Let's do it, then!"

"Wha...?!"

"Huh? But we don't need to do that..."

Naturally, Mile was on the man's side.

"Hm... I can tell that you aren't like those others. You possess a kind heart. Plus, you have that silver hair, and those looks—so adorable, but a bit forlorn, as though you've lost something along the way, and that humble, moderately-sized bosom..."

"Sh-shut up!"

The man's demeanor suddenly changed, and though he seemed to be praising her, his comments were incredibly rude. Mile was, understandably, indignant.

"All right, I'll take you. I'll gladly use that body of yours as a vessel for the mind of my beloved Elsie!"

"What the heck are you talking abouuut?! And, why would I be happy about thaaaaaaaaaaaaaaaaaaat?!?!" Mile screamed.

Reina, Mavis, and Pauline all stood agape at the speed with which this conversation had escalated.

And Lobreth, sensing that the discussion had somehow turned away from him, appeared relieved.

"It was three years ago..."

The man began to tell some sort of tale.

The Crimson Vow were surprised at first, but as they considered it, they supposed that getting an explanation from the man was a welcome turn of events. They had plenty of time, so they decided to sit and listen closely. Even if it took a little while, nothing about the situation was going to change.

"Three years ago, my dearest Elsie passed away... In order to try and resurrect her, I removed the part of her body that holds her mind, and I froze it. Unfortunately, my storage magic only holds ten kilograms, so I couldn't store her entire body..."

Apparently, this man had been putting into practice the

excuse that Mile gave as to how she could keep the rock lizard for such a long time with storage magic: namely, by "insulating the exterior and applying ice magic at regular intervals."

Even if he could only hold a small amount, the fact that this man could use storage magic at all put him in a league above your average mage—and the fact that he had come up with such an idea on his own meant that he was exceptionally talented.

"After that, I just needed to get my hands on a young and healthy body, but transporting one back to my abode deep in the mountains would be troublesome, so..."

Suddenly, this tale was growing unsettling.

"Anyway, to ensure that I had a means of travel and transportation, I thought that I might employ a wyvern."

Ah, so that's why we're talking about this...

Finally the dots had been connected.

"I painstakingly sought out a wyvern's dwelling, waited until brooding season, and then infiltrated a nest, settling in the shell of an egg that had already hatched and covering myself. When the mother returned, I pretended I was a chick, hatching from the egg. Wyverns, not known for their intelligence, are impressionable enough to think that anything that hatched from their own egg must be their young."

Whoa whoa whoa whoa whoa whoa whoa whoa whoa!!!

The four girls interjected internally.

"And then, as I ran for dear life..."

"You just left out the most interesting paaaaaaart!" they all screamed at once.

The man hung his head and muttered, "I don't want to remember that part..."

"O-of course."

They understood.

"As I cowered there, covered in blood, a demon appeared..."

"D-demon?"

Mavis sounded shocked.

Demons dwelled mainly in the northernmost reaches of their continent, cut off from human-inhabited realms by the wide mountain range that ran between the two regions.

It was not that these mountains were entirely impassable, but it was extremely difficult to try and cross them in a wagon. No one ever attempted it unless they had an extremely compelling reason to do so.

Plus, demons and humanoids—in other words, humans, elves, and dwarves—rarely got along.

In fact, even though they were called "demons," they had no interest in worshipping the devil or trying to overthrow mankind. They were merely a slightly different species. As a race, they also possessed far greater magic than humans. That was the real difference.

Over time, their name had actually been shortened from its original form, "decidedly magical persons," to "demagicians," to merely "demons."

There was not a huge distinction between them and humans, so fundamentally, it would not be a stretch for all four races—humans, elves, dwarves, and demons as well—to be considered humanoid. So there could only be one reason why demons should be put in a separate category:

Jealousy.

That was all there was to it.

They had greater magic than humans, better constitutions than elves, and were more skilled than dwarves.

The differences were subtle. It was an incredibly nuanced talent that they possessed.

As far as humans were concerned, elves were beautiful and had strong magic, but they were frail and delicate. This was permissible.

Dwarves were sturdy, and skilled craftsmen, but their magic was weak, and they were short and stumpy. This was permissible as well.

However, demons were not markedly inferior to humans in any way, and in fact exceeded them ever so subtly by most measures. This was unforgivable.

Elves and dwarves felt the same way.

They hadn't done anything to deserve it, but something about the demons drove the other races mad... This happened often.

Even so, it seemed that at some point in the past, they all lived together. But now, no one could say when the division occurred that resulted in the demons moving away. No one in the present day knew what had happened, or the reason for it, but it was clear that the negative feelings were mutual.

However, while it did seem that they had clashed in the past, there was no specific conflict to speak of in the present. Now and then, you might even see a demon merchant or researcher stop by a humanoid settlement.

Furthermore, as there were few differences between demons and humans, if they hid themselves behind a hat or hood and made sure that no one noticed their narrow, elongated pupils, it was not so difficult for demons to simply blend in.

Incidentally, though beastpeople were rather weak at magic, for some reason, they were closer to demons than to humanoids. Therefore, beastpeople rarely showed up in human settlements, either. Not that they didn't *ever* appear.

While Mavis, as a noble, and Mile, as a noble-slash-book-worm, had some knowledge of these circumstances, Reina and Pauline, both commoners, knew nothing about them at all. At best, they thought that demons were evil people who could use strong magic, and that beastpeople were the demons' violent pawns.

Clearly, this was the reason that Mavis was surprised that a demon might have appeared in this area.

Why would they show themselves in a place like this...?

"He patched my wounds and shared his food and water with me. He asked me how I got so injured, and when I answered, he let out a big laugh, and said, 'All right, let me handle this.' Several days later, he brought me this."

The man pointed at Lobreth.

"Huh??"

This story was incredibly bizarre.

No matter how much they questioned this plot-hole-filled tale, though, the facts of the man's explanation did not change.

They knew that *something* had happened. They just could not fathom what the demon's aim could be.

However, they decided to leave that alone for now and focus on the matter at hand: the old man and Lobreth.

"Lobreth was much smaller at that time. However, he was naturally intelligent, and quite accustomed to people, or at least, to the demon. Once the demon turned him over to me, he embraced me as well. I fed him, and taught him many things, and once he grew old enough, he left the nest. And of course, by 'nest,' I mean the nest that I built near my house. The demon had used Lobreth like a horse to ride, or livestock, but I couldn't bring myself to do that. So Lobreth is simply my friend. That is how I think of him."

"What a nice story... *not!!!* Weren't you just intending to scoop out my skull and replace my brains?!" Mile raged.

"Your brains? What are you talking about?"

The man looked perplexed. "I thought I explained this! I need to exchange your mind with Elsie's!"

"Oh, right. A heart transplant, then. I guess that wouldn't really have anything to do with something like the brain, an organ that doesn't do anything but produce snot, would it?"

"Huh?" Mile said.

Beside her, Reina, Mavis, and Pauline all nodded, as though this were a completely natural conclusion.

"Whaaaaaaaat?!"

Apparently, people in this world thought along the same lines as the inhabitants of ancient Egypt. Even though none of the books that Mile had read up until that point had said anything along those lines...

Though, thought Mile, *back in the Kingdom of Brandel, where I was born, I got the impression that the theory was that your mind is in your head...*

At one point, Marcela even said to me, "Miss Adele, just what goes on in that head of yours?!"

But, now that I think about it, even in Japanese we have a separate word for the heart as an organ, which means that in ancient times, even Japanese people probably thought that your heart—as in your mind—was in your actual heart...

And I guess it's true that when you think inappropriate thoughts, it's your heart that's fluttering, not your brain...

In any case, it seemed that Mile's brains were safe. That was, as long as her transplanted heart could pump enough blood to it.

"So what do you think? Will you do this for me? It's not such a horrible idea, is it?"

"It's absolutely horrible!!! Worse than horrible—it's unthinkable! Who would possibly agree to that?!?!"

They had no idea what the old man was even saying anymore.

Mile had thought herself completely reasonable, but apparently, in the old man's view, this was not the case.

The man would not let up.

"I'm begging you! I want to live with my precious Elsie once more! I want to hear that adorable little bark of hers again..."

"She's a dooooooooooooooog?!?!" Mile's scream rang out.

"Why would you put a dog's heart into me—a *human*?! If she's a dog, shouldn't you put her heart in a dog's body?!"

"Huh? Well, I mean, that was certainly my intention up until just a little while ago, but somehow, you're just the spitting image of her... Plus, a young girl's body is clearly much more interesting, for a number of reasons..."

"Whether or not it's interesting is not the issue here! Plus, how do you expect a dog's mind to function in a human body?! What happens when it wants to go to the bathroom?!"

The man stopped and stared at her, apparently pondering something.

"*Are you imagining iiiiiiiiiiiiiit?!?!*"

Her breath ragged from screaming with so much rage, Mile got the feeling that she finally understood exactly how Reina always felt.

"Anyway, I absolutely refuse! If the heart was frozen normally, then its cells would have broken down on freezing. No matter how much healing magic you used on an orc steak, it wouldn't bring it back to life, would it? Even if you could successfully transplant something with healing magic, that magic doesn't have any effect on the dead. That's because the basis of healing magic... is..."

Even if she were to simply tell him that this heart transfer was impossible, Mile realized, he wouldn't believe her. Therefore, she abandoned her explanation mid-thought.

"Sh-shut up! Don't act like you know everything! You couldn't possibly understand the way I feel! To me, Elsie is—Elsie is..."

"To *me*, she's just some complete stranger's pet dog!"

"Guh... Y-you... Fine, Lobreth, do it!"

With a screech, Lobreth stood up and spread his wings. The cord binding his legs, wings, and mouth had been completely undone.

"H-how...?" Mile asked, surprised.

The man explained with a sneer.

"Did you really think I was just talking your ear off for no reason? Bwahaha! While I was talking, I was using part of my mind for silent casting, blasting those ropes with miniscule but powerful fire magic in places you all couldn't see! That's how I burned through Lobreth's bonds! You stupid little girls know nothing about battle—you have a thing or two to learn!"

Carbon nanotubes were still carbon, after all. They were not particularly flammable, but that meant nothing more than saying it was difficult to ignite coal with a single match. If the thin cords were exposed to high-powered flames, they would burn like anything else. Just as even diamond might burn.

Because he was at such a close range, Lobreth did not use his Breath, but instead launched a direct attack.

However, perhaps because his opponents were women, and he had been told to take it easy on them, he attacked not by biting or clawing at them, but by flapping his wings. He was a sporting fellow.

But then, Lobreth saw Reina and Pauline brandishing their staves and beginning to chant spells, and Mavis wielding her sword. Remembering the magical attack he had desperately dodged earlier, and the pain in his tail, he began beating his wings frantically, whipping up a powerful whirlwind.

And then, whipped by the winds, Reina, Pauline, and Mile's skirts began to rise.

"Eeeeeeeek!!"

Reina and Pauline stopped their incantations and hurriedly pushed their skirts back down.

Unconcerned by her own fluttering skirt, Mile muttered,

"There it is, his 'Kamikaze Technique'..."

Mile had been pondering this since she had first seen Lobreth use his "Stomach Flute Technique." If he could use the "Stomach Flute Technique," then surely he could use the "Kamikaze Technique" as well.

"Don't just stand there talking nonsense and nodding to yourself! Hurry up and attack hiiim!!!"

Brought back to the present by Reina's scream of rage, Mile quickly drew her sword.

However, Lobreth had been trying his best to never kill anyone so far, and he never attacked anyone except those who hurt him first.

That extended even into this moment. He was still holding back.

Mile was hesitant to launch a fatal attack on an opponent like that.

Yet just as she had that thought, a biting attack came her way. It did not seem like Lobreth intended to kill, but merely to clamp down and toss her away.

As she tried to field the rapidly descending bite attack with her sword, suddenly, Lobreth's tail came whipping around from the side.

A side attack was bad. The only force she had to steady her was the friction of her own weight pressing her feet into the ground, so it would be easy to send her flying.

To cut it off with her sword would be too cruel, and as for magic, water or fire combined with the physical energy of the tail would...

Snap!

"Oh..."

Time was up.

Too deep in thought to react in time, Mile took a direct hit from Lobreth's tail and went flying.

"Mile!!!" the other three screamed.

The distance she flew this time was much shorter than when she had been struck by the rock lizard, and this time there was no cliffside for her to crash into.

However, a wyvern's tail was much thinner than a rock lizard's and supple like a whip. Therefore, the damage done by the rock lizard's tail could not compare to the damage done this time.

Still, now was not the time to go rushing over to Mile. As long as she wasn't dead, Pauline should be able to do something with her healing magic. Knowing this, the other three turned to face Lobreth.

Even if his opponents were female, landing some damage on them was unavoidable if it meant that he and his master could escape safely. Having come to this conclusion, Lobreth decided to finally unleash his claw strike along with his tail and his teeth, and charged at the girls brandishing all three.

Mavis bided her time in an attempt to somehow block this, while Reina and Pauline started their spells. But then...

"Water Impact!"

The silently cast spell that flew out then was not Reina's, Pauline's, nor (obviously) Mile's.

The spell that was cast while the Crimson Vow were preoccupied with Lobreth had come from the suspicious old man.

It's over! the old man thought, grinning at his spell, which had gone perfectly according to plan. Just then...

Ka-shing!

It bounced back at him.

The water spell was meant to strike the girl closest to him, the one with the big chest, and envelop both her and the others, then blow them away, knocking the fight out of them without hurting them too much. Yet just before it struck the first girl, the spell came flying back as though it had been repelled by something.

"Wh..."

"Ah, I forgot to remove that barrier..." said Mile, who, after she had been sent flying and crashed into the ground, hopped to her feet completely unharmed and ready to return to the fray.

Of course, this was Mile's doing. Even if it was unintentional.

"Tch! Water—"

Slash!

There was no more time for that.

Reina fired off a spell to keep Lobreth in check, Mavis thwarted the tail attack with her sword, and Pauline redirected her offensive from Lobreth to the man.

And then, as the man was blown away, crashing into the ground, they saw Lobreth stiffen up with a crackling sound, and collapse.

"Bwuh... Just one hit...?"

Mile, judging that a close-range battle would be dangerous, and figuring that allowing her fellow party members to capture the wyvern on their own once was enough, had stricken Lobreth with a magical electric shock.

"Now then, what to do with them...?"

Once again they bound Lobreth, along with the mysterious man. As Reina glared at him, the man pleaded.

"I-I'm begging you! Please don't kill him!"

Tossing another glare at him, Reina said, "If you try anything funny this time, it's off with your heads. Both yours and his!"

The man nodded, his face pale.

None of the Crimson Vow had ever had any intention of killing the captured wyvern in the first place. Naturally, there was no sense in needless killing, and it meant more money for them if they brought it in alive.

In truth, until this man had cloistered himself away in the mountains to begin a life of magical research, he had been a fairly well-known mage. Even now, his past renown carried some influence, and the people he had aided over the course of his career still held fairly important positions in the royal palace. If he played his

cards right and cooperated in his role as the mage who successfully tamed a wyvern, he could probably avoid punishment for
any of his crimes. In fact, the probability of it was quite high.

But in order for that to happen, Lobreth had to be in good
health. For his own sake—and because the wyvern was his good
friend—Lobreth's survival was paramount.

Transporting Lobreth by manpower alone would have been
impossible, but they figured that if the man told him what to do,
the wyvern would obediently follow instructions. While the man
considered Lobreth to be his friend, as far as Lobreth was concerned, this man was probably more like his owner or master. So
Mile undid only the wires that were wrapped around Lobreth's
legs so that he could walk on his own.

Just in case, Mile bound a thin wire around both Lobreth's
neck and the man's, then brought Lobreth back to consciousness
with awakening magic. The man whispered something or other
into Lobreth's ear, and Lobreth began walking dutifully ahead.
Perhaps they had some sort of magic with which to understand
each other, or perhaps, Lobreth merely had a high enough intelligence to understand human speech...

The strength of the wires was clear to the man. He recognized
that, should Lobreth try to run, or make any other sudden moves,
the wire would squeeze their necks, or even—because it was so
thin—cut straight through them. The man had no intention of
risking his life on stupid gambits with a low chance of success.
The man was no fighter, after all, just a scholar and researcher.

Plus, having learned from her previous mistake, this time Mile had bound them not with the carbon nanotube fiber, but with steel wires. It was a superfine material made of piano wire, more durable than even a standard steel line. Even if fire were put to this wire, it would not be destroyed.

Of course, she still had no intentions of letting them out of her sight.

The young villager who was a little too fond of children watched as the five humans walked alongside Lobreth, who wobbled, unable to balance with his upper half bound. The young man was trembling.

Th-they're scary! City girls are absolutely terrifying!!!

Perhaps, he would have one of the familiar village girls as a lover, after all. Women from the city were scary. However, the rough, crude ladies of his generation were also...

"Yep, I'll just have to make friends with a little girl and raise her how I like!" he concluded.

If Mile had heard him say this, she probably would have said something like, "Are you Hikaru Genjiiiiii?!"

When the group returned to the village, they were surrounded by villagers, who, though initially petrified at the sight of the wyvern, were soon rejoicing, praising the Crimson Vow. The girls called the village elder and requested that a messenger be dispatched to the regional capital in order to bring them a transport team.

Though the royal capital was far away, the regional capital was much less so, and in order to increase his popularity by "doing things for the citizens," the lord, who was also their client, would absolutely comply with the request. It was possible that a transport unit led by the lord himself might even meet up with them before they entered the city, so that he could lead the triumphant return through the gates. They could safely expect a bonus for capturing the wyvern alive, too.

The Crimson Vow, having achieved even more than they had set out to, enjoyed the feast provided by the grateful villagers and swiftly forgot about two things:

The suspicions they held about the existence of the demon.

And the worry in their hearts over what that demon might be trying to do...

It was still morning when the messenger set out from the village, so by the evening of the following day, a transport team arranged by the guild had arrived at the lord's request. They would depart again for the capital early the next morning.

All of the members of the transport team were hunters, so a high-ranking guild employee had accompanied them as their lead. He seemed to be a former B-rank hunter, someone whose orders the other hunters would not go against.

The Crimson Vow were relieved to see that no commander from the regional army or the like had shown up to try and steal their thunder.

On the contrary, the hunters all bowed their heads in

deference to the Crimson Vow, captors of the wicked wyvern who had struck a huge blow to so many of their fellow hunters in the form of medical costs for the injured and job failure penalties. The previously defeated hunters had been forced to replace broken equipment and seen their finances go up in smoke, some of them even having to disclose their newfound bankruptcy to their families.

The hunters had wished to take a stab at eliminating the wyvern themselves, for the sake of their pride as local hunters, and regretted that they could not. However, they couldn't be expected to take on a reckless job that might land their party members or their families in the depths of misfortune.

"Countless promising but stupid young parties ended up way in the red thanks to this thing, between having to replace their gear, get their injuries healed, and other things like that—not to mention the significant delay to their next promotions. Plus, morale was at an all-time low among us hunters and guild employees. The local villages were being attacked, and there was nothing that we could do about it. So sincerely, from the bottom of our hearts, we thank you for capturing this fiend," the commanding guild employee said, bowing his head, and signing the girls' job completion slip.

They had handed the wyvern over to the guild on the condition that it could be killed at any time, and now their job was over.

In truth, as far as the killing went, the Crimson Vow had asked the staff leader, "If we wanted him alive, what would you think about turning him over just like this?" to which he replied, "Gladly!"

Because they'd gone through all the trouble of bringing Lobreth in alive, they decided to relinquish the wyvern there, and leave the rest in the guild's hands.

The benefits of this outweighed the risk of the wyvern escaping, or stirring up a fuss and killing someone, so naturally, everyone agreed.

Thus, the Crimson Vow had completed their job with an A-grade and the promise of a bonus for their successful capture—and without of the burden of transporting their quarry. However...

"Oh, who is that?"

Seeing the man bound beside the wyvern, the commander of the transport squad asked the obvious question.

Indeed, they had yet to tell him the tale of the mysterious man.

"I am Byrnclift. I was once in service of the palace, as a court magician."

"Huh? A-are you *that* Byrnclift? The head of the royal court magicians?" the transport commander asked in surprise.

"Indeed. To think that anyone still remembers my name..."

They were humble words, but the old man's expression betrayed him completely. He was clearly very pleased with himself.

"In truth, I was living deep in the mountains, researching ways of training wyverns not to attack people, and to understand human speech. As a result, I successfully prevented this wyvern from attacking any of the villagers that live within its hunting grounds. Unfortunately, he was still forced to employ a bare minimum of countermeasures against the people who came to attack and kill him... I thought that the results of this research might be able to be put to good use for the sake of this country, but..."

Truthfully, this man had made a request to the Crimson Vow.

"I'm going to tell the transport team the truth, so please don't interrupt me.

"I won't tell any lies. Once I'm finished talking, if you think any part of it is false, feel free to point it out then. Don't make any conjectures of your own—merely present them with the objective facts, as you witnessed them yourself."

In fact, most of the information was the same as what the man had told them himself, so they would not truly be able to dispute it.

At this juncture, there were no clear falsehoods for them to contest.

"Even though the results of my research were fairly effective, those girls there came to capture and kill this wyvern. I tried to pay them to take the wyvern off their hands, but the job they accepted took priority, they said, so we could not negotiate an exchange...

"Then, I tried with all my might to rescue him. And so, I intend to go with this wyvern and plead for his life. Please reconsider this! I thought it would be good for me to care for this wyvern, and put him to use in your lord's service, should he be so inclined..."

Indeed, there were no lies. And now...

"That is all."

"Huh?" The Crimson Vow were stunned at this incredibly simple explanation.

Indeed, it was all as he had said.

He had not lied.

However... somehow, the four of them felt dissatisfied with this tale.

"........."

The guild employee and the hunters looked rather concerned as well.

This was understandable. The man was talking like a would-be villain out for revenge, speaking out against the hunters who had tried to attack and kill a supposedly innocent wyvern in the course of duty during a legitimate job they had taken, risking dire physical and financial damage along the way.

"Is that all true?" the guild employee asked the girls, who could only reply, "Y-yes... There is at least nothing false in what he just told you... Even though I feel like there's something more to it..." Reina replied, reluctantly.

The comments about Mile's body and so forth were stories that Byrnclift had told only them, so for now, they had to uphold his request.

Plus, if he said that he wasn't being serious, only buying time to save Lobreth, there was nothing more they could do. That they had attacked him was clear, so they would have to apologize...

Of course, interfering with a hunter's work was still illegal, so at least they were in the right as far as that went. Normally such disputes would be handled by the parties involved, or the hunters' guild would intervene and decide if any reparation or disciplinary action was needed.

However, in this case, the assailant was not a hunter, so the guild had no authority, and there was no choice but to leave it all in the hands of the officials. He had not done any real damage to them, so there would be minimal repercussions.

The incident, so far, was nothing more than a reason to keep Byrnclift's movements restricted. His crimes in relation to the wyvern would have to be investigated later.

The exchange went on for a bit longer, but in the end, it was judged that Byrnclift, the former court magician, would travel along with the transport team not as a captured criminal, but as a benevolent third party.

Attacking the girls had only been for the sake of saving Lobreth, he claimed, and he had no intention of threatening, killing, or even injuring them; in fact, Lobreth had clearly been holding back, and the spell that Byrnclift had fired off was one that would have only blown them back with water, causing little injury.

Perhaps, he truly wasn't such a bad person after all.

Besides, Reina, Mavis, and Pauline were all familiar with people like him. So, none of the three were in a position to make a strong objection to his release.

"It was only because he didn't want to harm my body," Mile thought to herself, but she did not voice her theory aloud.

In any case, these people were only a transport team. They did not have much authority of their own. No matter how much they said to these hunters, it would be of little use. At best, it changed nothing more than how they might treat the man while escorting him, so they decided to give up on explaining the situation to the team any further.

In the first place, most of what they knew was what Byrnclift had told them, so if he himself objected to any of it, then that was that. The fact that he had done everything in his power to rescue the wyvern was simply the honest truth. They had nothing else that they could convey to the transport team that was "an objective fact they had witnessed themselves."

Plus, any detailed testimony that the Crimson Vow gave would be delivered to their client via the guild. In other words, they would have to write down everything, including what Byrnclift said. If they did that, this information would certainly make it to the ears of the lord, their client, who was responsible for everything that went on in this region.

The Crimson Vow wanted nothing more to do with Byrnclift after this point, and they couldn't bear the thought of having to share their journey with him, or take some share of the responsibility if something happened. So, they decided to separate themselves from the situation as quickly as possible in order to focus on something else. Other than the commander, who was an essential part of the operation, all the members of the transport team were active hunters, and even the commander himself was a former hunter, so there was absolutely no need for the Crimson Vow to accompany them as an additional escort.

Plus, while they had traveled here fairly swiftly, having to return while transporting a cart with a wyvern on it would take considerably more time. None of them were raring to stick along and keep Lobreth company.

The next morning, the Crimson Vow left the village a little before the transport team, headed for the regional capital.

They would feel awkward about leaving at the same time as the transport team, and then leaving them in the dust, and leaving later and then passing them would be just as bad. Therefore, they had no choice but to leave ahead of the other group.

It was then, along the road to the capital, that the four of them finally remembered that concerning piece of information from earlier.

"That demon... I wonder what he was trying to do. Really, what was he even doing in a place like that in the first place...?"

"Good point... I wonder if he was plotting something...?"

"I have a weird feeling about this..."

This time, not only Mavis, who knew a bit about demons, but also Reina and Pauline, began to feel a creeping sense of doubt.

"Well, we don't even know if that man was telling us the truth, and anyway, it has nothing to do with our jobs. There's no point in investigating it—or even thinking about it anymore."

The other three were shocked that Mile could be so nonchalant, but as they thought about it, they realized that she was correct.

"I guess it's true." Reina agreed with Mile's assessment. "We completed our job with an A-grade, and we're getting a bonus. I'd call this a huge success—let's just enjoy it!"

There was still something unsettling about that man, Byrnclift, but there was nothing to be done about that. No matter what had happened, in the end, the matter was out of the Crimson Vow's hands. They would report everything they knew, including the matter of the demon, to the guild, and the rest would be for the lord to handle. There really was no more point in them worrying over it.

The man would be dealt with according to the laws of this territory. That was all there was to it.

They were laws that could far too easily be bent by someone in a position of power, but that was none of their affair.

Later that day, just before noon, the Crimson Vow arrived at the capital. They proceeded to the guildhall to process their job completion forms and report the details of their job to the guild master. They then received their payment, along with the bonus that the guild master had negotiated with the lord on their behalf. Apparently, even the lord, who always pinched pennies, was in good spirits and had been more than happy to open his purse.

After that, they excused themselves from the guild, receiving the blessings of the staff and all the hunters present, and ate their fill of luncheon at an inn, before the four of them, exhausted, went straight to bed.

The next day, they headed out toward the capital to begin the journey home.

"All right, it's been a while! It's time for another 'Japanese Folktale'!" Mile announced, thinking that everyone could use a change of pace.

This time, however, she was strapped for material.

Hmm, hmm... What would be a good allusion to make here...?

Lobreth, Urashima Taro, bottom... stripes... huh? No no...

Lobreth, Urashima Taro, Uramima Taro... No no no no no! That's too far away from Lobreth!

Sales Princess... Is this Comiket?!

Unbuying Lady... Is this the Handmade Bride?!

The Hard Old Man... Is there such as thing as a "Soft Old Man"? And there's the Sleepy Old Man...

"Are you ready yet?"

"Hurry up and start, please!"

As the requests flooded in, Mile became more and more aggravated.

She was in a slump. Mile was ailing.

Dr. Slump? Ailing-chan? No no no no no no no no no!

It was five more days until they reached the capital.

Was little Lenny safely making use of the baths?

Had she turned them into some kind of black-market orphan sweatshop?

Hoping that a least a momentary peace awaited them in the capital, the four marched on, leaving the great, wide mountains to unfurl at their backs ...

"Are you ready *yet?*"

"P-please just give me a moment!!!"

Didn't I Say
to Make My Abilities
Average in the
——— Next Life?!

Adele's MAGNIFICENT ACADEMY LIFE

STORY 4 |
Adele's First Date

"Next rest day will be a day off."

"Hm? Oh, yes, of course. Rest days are a day of rest!"

"No! I'm saying that this shop is taking a day off!" said Aaron, the owner of the bakery, weary and disappointed with Adele, who, despite her usual impression of clarity, could be a bit dense now and then.

"Every once in a while, we need to take a full day to do maintenance on the ovens. It's much less of a pain for our regulars if we do this on a rest day, rather than a weekday, when everyone is working, yeah? You need to take it easy sometimes too, Adele. Why don't you go on a date with a boy or something? I'm sure you'd have your pick of the litter when it comes to boys, right, Adele?" he suggested at the end of Adele's shift, as she collected her wage of two silver.

"A d-d-d-date, you say...?"

Adele suddenly froze up.

Including her previous life, Adele had a track record of 19 boyfriend-less years. If you included her time spent in this world before her reawakening, that was 29 years.

In her time as a singleton, AKA her entire life, she had never even held hands with a boy, let alone gone on a date.

"Miss Adele, you're behaving rather strangely today. Did something happen?"

"Ah, yes, it seems that on our next rest day, I'm supposed to go on a date..." Mile answered glumly.

"Whaaaaaaaaaat?!?!"

A shout filled the classroom.

"Wha-wh-wh-wh-wh-wh-wh..."

The most shaken among all of them was Marcela.

"Uh, ahh, Miss Adele, wh-what did you just...?"

"I'm asking, what should I do about my date next rest day?"

"W-with who?! Who are you going on a date with?!"

"I'm telling you, that's the part I need to figure out first..."

"Whaaaaaaaaat?!"

In order to survive in Class A, you needed to have a voice of steel.

After Marcela's interrogation of Mile, the class finally came to understand the situation.

"In other words, the bakery is closing for the day, and the owner ordered you to go on a date or something?"

"Yes, that's exactly it! But, I've never been out with a boy even once before now, so what in the world do I even do...?"

Why do you have to do anything at all?!

Her classmates interjected silently. Naturally, Marcela was thinking the same thing.

"So what you're saying is, you're going on a date, but you've yet to actually decide who you're going with?"

"Y-yes. That's the sum of it." Adele replied.

Marcela rubbed her temples with her middle fingers.

"Understood. Don't you worry about a thing, Miss Adele. Please just be your normal self. We will handle the rest of this."

It happened after class had ended and Adele had exited the classroom.

At the instructions of the girl with the chairwoman-like air, the students swiftly closed and locked the door. The windows, of course, were shut as well.

Adele alone had left the room to return to the dormitory. Everyone else remained there.

"Now then, let the Class A emergency meeting begin!"

With the chairwoman presiding, an emergency conference was taking place.

"The crisis we are currently facing should go without

explanation: the incredibly dire prospect of what to do about Adele's first date. First, we have to begin with the fundamental issue of whether we will allow this date or quash it..."

"Chairwoman, a question!" one girl interrupted, raising her hand.

"Yes, what is it?"

"Will girls be included in the pool of date candidates?"

"Whooooooooooooooooooooooaaaaa!!!"

The more than half of the class that was female raised their voices in admiration, perhaps not having even conceived of such a spectacular possibility themselves. Even the chairwoman was moved by this idea, her eyes sparkling.

However, as the chairwoman, she could not allow the conference to be swayed by her own opinion. This matter had to be decided on everyone's...

"Girls are forbidden to participate!"

The chairwoman pointed at the boy who had interjected. His hand was raised, and she nodded, allowing him to state his opinion.

Even if it was in opposition to her own, she had to allow all assenting and dissenting voices to be heard equally. The chairwoman had to uphold the rules of her position.

"It's not that I don't understand how the girls feel. But, as we all know, Adele hasn't yet awakened to the world of romance. Do you really think it's all right for her first date to be with a girl? What happens if she starts thinking that dates with girls are especially enjoyable, and that she hates boys because they're crude and tactless? If she starts down that path, are you all willing to take on the responsibility of explaining it to Adele's family?"

"Er..."

"I'll take it!! If I can be with Adele forever, then..."

Everyone pretended they hadn't heard the chairwoman's shout.

"Now, let us summarize today's meeting. Point one: It is necessary for Adele to go on a date for the sake of her own personal growth, so we shall permit it. Point two: Only boys will be eligible partners for this date..."

The chairwoman ground her teeth, her eyes bloodshot.

"Point three: All eligible partners shall be examined and the final candidate appointed by a council of all the girls in Class A. Point four: If the date in question should attempt to do anything untoward to Adele then... then... I'll kill them!"

All the girls glared directly at their male classmates.

After that, all the male students were sent back to their lodgings, and the conference continued with only the girls of Class A.

"I think we should exclude any nobles. Adele is more than likely the daughter of a noble family with some extenuating circumstances, so it would be best for her to avoid any special relations with other nobles. Plus, as cute and intelligent as she is, there are probably some idiots who would try to bring her into their own family... Adele is living her life entirely as a commoner for now, so I think it would be better not to put her in a position where she would be in danger of being spotted by the agent of some noble family, or compelled into anything strange."

The third daughter of a baron stated this extremely sensible opinion.

Everyone thought about this earnestly.

The chairwoman was quite pleased about it.

"Which means, it has to be a commoner," said the daughter of a merchant. "However, putting her with someone who's *too* poor is also... I'm sure that Adele herself wouldn't mind, but even so, if she got close to someone who is too poorly off in terms of money, he might use her, and that's just as bad. Between her cute face, the social position that she probably has, and that intelligence of hers... Even though she's strapped for money now, it's likely that she never lived like that before she came here, so she probably knows nothing of living among the common folk. It would be so upsetting for her first date to be with some penniless beggar..."

This was a reasonable opinion as well.

"In that case, it must be a merchant's son. Preferably the eldest. He must not yet have someone he's betrothed to or courting, and he must be kind and chivalrous. And he must be able to protect her from enemies, even if it means putting his life on the line. That is the sort of man he must be. As for his abilities, if he is in Class A, then we can at least be certain of a minimum there."

"Agreed!"

"Agreed!"

"Agreed!"

"If there's a man like that, then *I* want him!" one girl cried out desperately, only to be shushed.

And so, the difficult selection process began.

"Huh? You want me?"

It was the day after the Class A emergency meeting.

Ignace, the eldest son of a mid-sized mercantile family, suddenly found himself surrounded by his female classmates, who informed him that he had been selected to go on the date with Adele.

"Be aware that the only reason we are allowing you to go on this date with Adele is so that she can develop some experience with courtship! It does not mean that Adele is interested in you or that she will continue to date you in the future. Don't misconstrue this!"

"Well, I was at yesterday's meeting too, so I am already aware of that..."

Ignace was at the school to receive an education as the heir of a merchant. He gave a rather mature reply, but was unable to conceal his surprise at being selected.

"Anyway, yes, we did select you. Handle this well!"

As he watched the girls walk away, their declaration made, Ignace muttered to himself, "Why is this happening?"

Of course, it was not that Ignace was totally unhappy about this occurrence.

On the contrary, he was thrilled.

Adele was incredibly cute. She wasn't a dazzling, elegant maiden like the daughters of high-ranking nobles were, but she had the sort of cuteness that endeared one to her, and made one wish to protect her. Plus, just looking at her gave one a sense of peace and calm.

Also, she was extremely talented.

She was top of the class in intelligence, and could use combat magic, and was so strong in sports that even Kelvin had never once beaten her.

However, even with all of that, it was clear that she was holding back.

For some reason, no matter how much time passed, Adele's tea never seemed to grow cold.

She always used incantations for her magic, but when she was spacing out or flustered, she tended to use powerful, silently cast spells.

Most unmistakably, she lost on purpose to everyone but Kelvin during sparring bouts.

And then there was the bread and other items that suddenly appeared in her hands when she hadn't been holding anything moments prior.

Even if she could fool their teachers, who only saw her during class time, her classmates were always with her and saw everything. However, they were also kind, so they never revealed this to anyone.

Should I do it?

Indeed, Ignace was rather lazy, but this did not mean he lacked an interest in girls.

He was going to inherit his family's shop.

In order to do this, he could not allow any stupid girl or gold-digger to sink their claws into him. To avoid such a fate, the optimal course of action was to be a feminist, being kind to all girls and playing the role of a laid-back fellow who would never lay a hand on a woman.

By birth, Ignace was a commoner, so there was quite a low bar, should he wish to offer his hand to any girls in need. Therefore, he affected a progressive demeanor. If he were slavering over girls all the time, they were certain to doubt him when he did offer his assistance, and that would make things much more difficult.

Such was Ignace's way. But when it came to Adele...

She was cute. Being with her put him at ease. She was good-natured and clear-headed. Her magical skills and physical ability were far beyond the average. She had storage magic, which, for a merchant, was the dream of a lifetime. With that, you could smuggle as much as you wanted... *Ahem!*

If they worked together, they could safely transport high-priced goods and wouldn't need a guard. Plus, there was a chance that any children or grandchildren might inherit those exceptional abilities of hers.

Though they were still four or five years away from even considering marriage, the day was going to come sooner than they knew it.

He wouldn't be at all surprised if a prize catch like Adele had been betrothed since her infancy. That she might have been up for grabs this entire time would be the more surprising thing.

Even if this were the case, it had nothing to do with him. It wasn't as though he were looking to gain any connections to Adele's family, after all. What he wanted was Adele, and Adele alone.

Well, even if they had to disclose the circumstances of her birth when it came time to marry, it wouldn't be a *problem* if he ended up being part of a noble family's line. Absolutely, thoroughly, not a problem. Such an un-problem that his parents and grandparents would be dancing with joy.

All right, I'll do it! And I'll give it my all!!

The girls who had so carefully selected him had completely missed the mark.

At least Ignace wasn't *entirely* a bad guy...?

"I-I hope we have a nice time today!"

It was the next rest day, just around the second morning bell at 9 AM Ignace bowed his head to Adele, who was jittery with nerves.

"Same here! So, anyway, I was thinking that first we would do some shopping, and then some sightseeing at Riverside Park, where we could have our lunch. What do you think?"

"Y-yes! That sounds good!"

Even counting her previous life, this was Adele's first date ever.

Her first time holding hands with a boy or even going out alone with one, to say nothing of having a boyfriend.

Though at least here she was already doing better than in her previous life, in which she'd hardly ever had anything more than a two-line exchange with any man besides her father...

The reason that Adele's teeth were chattering was not that she was embarrassed or excited, but merely because she was "not used to boys"—and because this was her first date!

Really, she was twenty-nine years old, if you included her previous life. Even if you excluded the ten years before her reawakening, she was still nineteen. She was absolutely uninterested in some ten or eleven-year-old child. No matter how much one might say that "The body influences the mind," or "It's all a matter of circumstances!" these things had their limits.

Still, in Ignace's eyes, this was how things appeared:

She's a novice, nervous about her first date. So cute!

Ignace and Adele toured the capital's shopping district, wandering around in the various shops.

Adele always worked on rest days, and without money, she had zero interest in buying anything, so she was hesitant to enter these establishments, and had never really seen the inside of them. So, her very first time window-shopping was quite a bit of fun. At least as far as it allowed her to confirm the production levels and variations in goods that were present in this world.

Seeing Adele earnestly checking the selection and quality of the merchandise, and investigating the prices of goods that she

never even intended to buy, Ignace was stunned. *No, he thought,
I don't think you're supposed to do this sort of thing on a date. She
should be all, "Ooh," and "Teeheehee"...Or not.*

Rather, he observed the way Adele was acting, and thought:
This girl already has the makings of a merchant!

Then came lunchtime.

Riverside Park was at the riverside. It wasn't a particularly
clever name—just one that was straightforward and easy to
understand.

The river had a wide floodplain, on the banks of which plum
trees stood in full bloom.

In this country, when one went out to admire flowers, it was
the plum blossoms that were most beloved.

Adele, a girl beneath the plum trees, was fluent in the languages of both Japan and this continent.

One might say she took to new languages with *a-plum*.

"Now then, why don't we have lunch somewhere around
here?" Adele suggested to Ignace as they stood in an open spot
among a relatively crowded cluster of trees.

"Ah, good idea. I'll go and buy us some food and drinks from
the kiosk. You just go ahead and pick a..."

"Oh, that won't be necessary," said Adele, stopping Ignace in
his tracks. "I, um, asked the lady at the cafeteria, and she let me
use the kitchen to make us some boxed lunches. I'm not sure if
you'll like them though..."

Indeed, Adele had no disposable funds with which to be eating out.

When Adele, who was working her hardest to make ends meet, asked to use the leftover foodstuffs—food that she probably would have eaten anyway if she had stayed in her room that day—to make a boxed lunch, the lady from the cafeteria happily consented. She liked to accommodate the girl now and then, and when she heard that the lunches were for Adele's first date, she was even more thrilled, heaping piles of luxury ingredients on her.

Incidentally, when Adele offered the older lady some of the extras she made to sample, her eyes opened wide, and she asked Adele to teach her how to make the dishes later.

"Huh? But, Adele, you don't have anything... Oh, right!"

Indeed, this was another thing that all of her classmates had realized. For while Adele did not go out of her way to advertise it, she didn't exactly hide it, either.

"Now then..."

Pop!

"Wh...?"

He had assumed that Adele would pull a lunch box from her storage space. Based on everything that he had learned about Adele so far, Ignace could expect at least that much.

However, what she actually produced was a table and two chairs, a number of apparently freshly cooked dishes with steam rising off of them, and some teacups. These items, which appeared in an instant, were at least 45 times more substantial than his initial prediction.

"Are you a wizard?!"

"Well, yes, I am a mage..."

Naturally, that was not what Ignace had been implying. He did not mean that she was a regular mage, but rather, the type of wizard who uses impossible magic and only appears in fairy tales.

"Eheheh, the truth is, I can use storage magic. I've been keeping it a secret from everyone, but it's troublesome to carry things around, so I ended up using it today!" she added, smiling.

Ignace wondered, deep down in his heart, *Does she really think that no one's noticed?*

Besides, that's not how "storage magic" works! At least regarding the food not getting cold, and her being able to move it in and out still arranged on top of the table. That is absolutely not how it works!!!

"That was delicious."

Adele's homemade meal received full marks.

Though it was not a large operation, Ignace's family's business was still fairly successful. They maintained a decent larder in their home, and in order to teach Ignace, the heir, how to recognize good and bad material, they had cooked with reasonably pricey ingredients as well.

It would have been one thing if Ignace was attending the superior Ardleigh Academy, but he hadn't thought he could be so stunned at the quality of the food produced by an amateur using the ingredients available in the kitchens of Eckland Academy.

She made this *food with* those *ingredients?! If a new cooking trend like this were to spread, then a new market would... No, actually, there would be some way to process and sell this food...*

"Now then, I'll clean things up!" Adele announced, as she and Ignace stood from their seats.

With that, she stored away the table and chairs, along with the now-empty plates and serving dishes.

And then, the two stood there, on the empty grassy knoll.

I'm sure Adele, who has no experience with men, is expecting me to kiss her here! I have to make my move, so that things don't end between us today—so that she and I have a future!

Ignace made his move. As Adele stared out at the water, he quickly brought his lips closer to kiss her, when...

Lady Adele, duck!

Huh? Oh, okay!

At the voice in her ear, Adele ducked instinctively, while Ignace stumbled forward, his puckered lips thrust out and his arms grabbing at the air.

"Uh—huh? What are you doing?"

"Oh, uh, nothing... Wah!"

As Ignace tried to disguise his own actions, hurriedly apologizing, he was suddenly seized by the shoulders from behind.

Timidly, he turned around, to see...

"Eek!"

It was the class chairwoman, rage clear upon her face, along with a task force of six that included three girls and three boys

selected from Class A, who were all seething with anger.

"Will you come with us a moment?"

And so the force dragged Ignace away, off to who knew where.

Indeed, there was no way that Class A, whose members were so overprotective of Adele, would possibly let her be alone with a boy without a chaperone.

"Huh? Um, what just..."

As Adele dithered in confusion, the chairwoman, the last person remaining, walked over to her with a smile and said, "That concludes your practice at dating boys. Now, it's time for you to practice dating a girl—with me!"

"A-all right? That's fine, I suppose..."

Going on an outing with a girl had been another one of Adele's lifelong dreams, even in her previous life, so there would be no complaints from her on that count.

"Well then, let's go!"

The chairwoman grabbed Adele by the hand and quickly rushed away. She had to hurry before the task force caught on.

"Ah, wait! Please don't pull so hard!"

Adele panicked at the sudden force with which she was being dragged.

But the chairwoman, blood pounding in her ears, did not hear her.

The following day, there were two injured parties in the Class A classroom.

The identities of these two "perverted fiends," who had been roughed up by the task force, were Ignace and the chairwoman, who was now being held accountable for her scheme.

Ignace was listless, but for some reason the chairwoman was beaming, a cunning smile spread across her face.

Later, Adele thought it mysterious that both of the people who had so kindly gone on dates with her the previous day now both had bruises all over their faces...

By the way, Nanomachines, what was that all about, yesterday? When you told me to duck...

A VENOMOUS INSECT WAS ABOUT TO LATCH ONTO YOUR CHEEK, LADY ADELE.

Oh, so that was it! Thank you. I'll have to continue listening for your warnings from now on!

YES, PLEASE LEAVE IT TO US, the nanomachines replied confidently.

Adele, of course, had no idea what in the world it was that she had just instructed the nanomachines to do.

For some reason, no more boys ever came to court her.

Adele would not discover the reason for this until much, much later...

Children

"**M**EOW."
     As always, Cricket Eater's voice came loudly from out-side the door.

He could, of course, come in through any open window as he pleased, but when the windows were shut, he would have to plead, "Let me in," from the other side.

"Just a moment..."

Marcela paused in her studies and stood to open the door.

Cricket Eater was the cat that Adele had been taking care of.

No, more accurately, he was the cat that Adele had "also" been taking care of. The cat who wandered from room to room in the girls' dormitory.

However, the cat had taken a particular interest in Adele, and was most often in Adele's room whenever she was present. When he wasn't wandering from room to room to beg for food, of course.

And so, the female students all referred to the creature as "the cat Adele looks after," which is why, after she left, Marcela had been the one to take over that duty... In fact, it had nothing to do with what the humans wanted. It was merely that the cat decided that Marcela's room would be his next abode.

As she opened the door, Cricket Eater slipped into the room, his tail held aloft.

And then, as Marcela tried to shut the door...

One more shape slipped in afterward. A tiny black cat, with its tail held aloft also.

"Huh...?"

Slip, slip, slip, slip.

One after another, four more of them slipped in.

There were five little black cats in total, all the spitting image of Cricket Eater.

"Whaaaaaaaat?!"

Marcela, flustered, grabbed Cricket Eater with both hands, and lifted him up high.

When she looked hard at the cat, she saw...

"So you *are* a boy, after all... Then what happened to their mother?!"

Realizing that the cat couldn't be expected to understand what she was saying, Marcela questioned him with a sort of gestured pantomime. She grabbed up one of the kittens and made a motion like birthing the kitten and nursing it, and then conveyed her question to the cat with her body language: Where did that other cat go?

If anyone else were to have seen this, Marcela would have been quite embarrassed, but thankfully, she was not thinking of this at the moment.

Perhaps Marcela's painstaking actions were exceedingly clear to Cricket Eater, for it seemed that the cat had understood the question. Cricket Eater's response to the question was this:

He averted his gaze from Marcela, and simply hung his head.

"Huh...?"

Marcela started at Cricket Eater, perplexed.

"You were abandoned...? And the kids were thrown out with you?"

Cricket Eater looked as though he was about to cry.

"This is a problem... There are six of you. I can't possibly keep taking care of you in secret like this. Thankfully, it looks like they're no longer nursing, but unlike you, an adult, they still have to eat special food. Also, sir, will you be able to look after these children the whole time while I'm away at class? If you take your eyes off of them for even a moment... This is hopeless, isn't it? You're always wandering around to hither and yon..."

Marcela, hopeless, called for help.

Soon, Monika and Aureana arrived.

"Let's try and get them adopted." Aureana, the first to speak, offered a solution.

"Hm?"

"Normally it's cruel to separate them from their parents, but their mother abandoned them, and their father... he is the way he is. For these children, this is a much better option..."

Glancing over at Cricket Eater, Marcela and Monika silently nodded.

"O-of course! If it is the child of the cat that Miss Adele was caring for, then I shall gladly take on its care!"

It was far too easy.

The kittens were almost devilishly cute. Plus, if they were "the children of the cat Miss Adele took care of," she could explain it to her father by playing the "when we find Miss Adele" card. There was a chance he might even let her keep them all herself. The third princess was more than capable of caring for a pet on her own, and this was a chance she was absolutely unwilling to pass up.

With that in mind, the third princess, Morena, happily accepted the five kittens into her home.

The three girls were pleased.

"It's according to plan..."

Just as Morena had schemed, she was allowed to take care of the kittens herself. As the king saw it, when Adele returned, it might win her favor, if only a little, and give them something to discuss.

Morena was fond of the kittens and spoiled them with all her heart.

Then, because the court ladies misheard Morena calling them

"the messenger's cats," and assumed she was saying "the messenger cats," as in, "a cat who is a messenger," other people began to treat them with especially high regard.

And so, this was the result.

After some time, Morena emerged from her kitten-filled reverie and appeared once more at Marcela's door.

"Please save me..."

Her hair was disheveled, her arms covered in scratches, and five kittens were hanging from her back, swinging from their dug-in claws.

"I've failed to discipline them..."

"Ah..."

And so, the Wonder Trio and Cricket Eater, along with the other female students who had cared for cats at home, ran an Etiquette School for Kittens for ten days, after which they returned the cats to the princess's hands.

Didn't I Say
to Make My Abilities
Average in the
—— Next Life?!

Seafood Cuisine

T HE CRIMSON VOW had just returned from their swimming and fishing expedition to Amroth.

Between what they bought, and what they caught themselves, they had obtained quite a lot of fish while there.

Now was the time to go wild with fish dishes!

For this purpose, Mile chartered the use of the kitchen and dining room, once dinner was through.

Tentatively, they thought of having a cooking competition, but, when they thought hard about it, there was no way that any of them, having been raised inland, so far from the sea, would be much good at cooking fish. Even if Mavis and Reina were able to at least envision the word "fish," their hopes of culinary accomplishment were dim.

Because of this, it was decided that Mile would handle all the cooking. The ones who would get to eat it would be Mavis,

Reina, and Pauline, along with the matron of the inn, the owner, and little Lenny. And, for some reason, all of the overnight guests at the inn, who had stayed in the dining hall instead of returning to their rooms.

"Why is this happening...?"

This was no time to complain, though. She had to start cooking. Thankfully, her ingredients were plentiful.

Mile's high-speed cooking began. She even relaxed the limitations she had placed on the speed of her own reflex actions.

Her knife moved faster than the eye could see. Everyone was waiting in the dining room for the food to be complete, save for the owner, who was in the kitchen watching Mile work, his mouth agape.

"Sorry to keep you all waiting."

After some time, Mile began carrying the completed dishes out of the kitchen.

Lenny and her mother assisted as well.

The owner still had not fully recovered from his shock, and there was no way that any amateurs would be allowed into the kitchen. From both the perspective of restaurant safety and health standards, this was the right course of action.

Gradually, a number of fish dishes were lined up across the tables. They were on large platters, separated by cooking method.

Broiled, glazed, steamed, poached, meunière, fried, tatsuta-age, nizakana, nanbanzuke, pickled... and of course, sashimi.

The sashimi was served with Mile's recently developed "something like soy sauce," and, because she could not find anything like true wasabi, western-style horseradish.

To safeguard against parasites, she had flash frozen and thawed all the fish before cooking, and used a foreign-body-removal magic and a cleaning magic on the food.

Because it was flash frozen, there was no expansion of the water crystals or breakdown of cells, so the fish lost none of its delicious flavor.

The first to eat, of course, were the members of the Crimson Vow. After them came the matron and Lenny. The owner eventually made a full recovery as well. After them, the other guests sampled the rest of the food that remained on the plates.

"This is delicious!"

"It's so good!"

"Wh-what is this?! I've never eaten such a delicious fish dish! Well, in fact, this is the first time I've even eaten anything other than dried fish..."

All of the various dishes, as well as the dipping sauce made from a mixture of the pseudo-soy-sauce substance, sugar, and Mile's recently developed mirin and sake-like liquids—plus the berry sauce she had made from mixing a number of things—all received favorable reviews. By and by, the food piled up on the plates slowly began to vanish.

However.

No one appeared to be interested in the pickled fish or the sashimi.

This was probably to be expected. This place was far from the sea, and it was not a place where you could normally eat raw fish—or at least, not a place where you *should*. Not if you valued your health and your life.

Even in this world, people did have some knowledge of the parasites that lived in mammals and fish. This was something that impacted their lives, so it was only natural.

In other words, there was no one in this world who would eat raw fish so far away from the sea. That was the sum of it.

"But it's so delicious..."

So saying, Mile put some of the sashimi onto her own plate somewhat glumly. Then, she put some of the wasabi on top of the fish, pierced it with her fork, and gingerly dipped the bottom of it in a small dish filled with pseudo-soy sauce. The "wasabi" was a bit watery, so putting it directly into the soy sauce would have ruined some of the spice.

Then, when she tried to put it in her mouth...

Yoink! Chomp!

"Huh??"

Someone had grabbed her hand that was holding the fork and eaten the piece that had been pierced on it. It was Mavis.

"Mm, that's tasty! You really can't ever go wrong with your cooking, huh?"

In truth, sometimes her cooking did go wrong.

"Knowing you, you removed the parasites with magic somehow, didn't you? There's no way someone like you, who's always talking about hygiene, would ever overlook something like that, I'm sure."

With these words, Reina, and then Pauline, followed Mile's lead, putting the wasabi and pseudo-soy sauce on pieces of sashimi, which they then placed in their mouths.

"What is this?! It's good!"

"A flavor I've never tasted before is spreading across my tongue!"

"But each of these things tastes so different individually!"

Seeing the girls chowing down, the others in the room timidly followed their example.

The first was the owner, who was moved by his curiosity as a chef, and Lenny, a challenger who knew no fear.

"I-It's really good..."

"That's Miss Mile for you!"

Their forks flew out for another, and another, and another.

"W-we can use this! Here Father, try this... We need to study this and add it to our specialty menu! This would make us so much money!"

"Y-yeah!"

Lenny and her father were getting fired up, but Mile had to be the bearer of bad news.

"Uhm, I don't mind at all if you want to refer to my methods, but where are you going to get your hands on fresh fish that hasn't gone rancid, as well as the dipping sauce, my experimental soy sauce, and the wasabi?"

"Huh?"

The two, who had intended merely to get Mile to tell them her means of acquiring all these goods, were deflated.

"The fish is one matter, but the soy sauce was an experiment, so it's all been used up, and you need soy sauce for the dipping sauce as well. You'd have to find another place where the wasabi grows and order it from them..."

"I-If you could make that 'so-ee' sauce again..."

"Well, it's fermented, so making it takes time. Plus, I'm still experimenting with it, so I can't guarantee the flavor. I'm not even sure that you would be able to use the same preparation methods yourself, so..."

Mile's reply crushed all of Lenny's hopes into the dirt.

"N-no way..."

Without regard for the devastated Lenny and her father, the seafood-tasting party continued, with words of praise and cheerful laughter abounding...

Afterword

FUNA here. It's been a while, hasn't it?

Welcome to Volume 3 of this series, *Didn't I Say to Make My Abilities Average in the Next Life?!*

Just when they thought they were settling into earning an honest living, trouble came knocking on the Crimson Vow's door again.

But they'll do anything they can for their friends!

Take this! The flurry of my secret technique!

"Did you really think I needed to undertake special training for such a paltry secret technique as that?"

And so the hellish wheels of fate have begun to turn...

Huh? "'Hell' according to whom," you say?

That's a secret!

Even though they said, "That's a registered trademark," and

"They're gonna file claims against you!" and warned me, "Do you really think they can publish it like this?" these words were safely preserved for publication (even though there was one part that did have to be removed for the serial version). What does the future hold for this work, which continues to test the limits?

"FUNA-san, just what, exactly, are you battling against?!"

Sh-shut up!

It's been one year since I first registered on the novel posting website, *Shousetsuka ni Narou*, and half a year since I made my debut as a novelist.

It's been more of a whirlwind of a year than I ever expected. Will the next year be even more sensational for me? Or will I return to myself as it all comes crashing down, and end up huddled in the corner crying and saying, "I knew this would happen, I knew this would happen"?

Please, buy enough volumes to keep this show on the road! Really, I mean it!

Our battle has only just begun!

I've only just started to climb that distant, endless hill of light novel writing...

It can't end now! I won't let it end this way!

In other words, I would really like to continue.

I spend most of my day writing my novels or brainstorming ideas or reading articles online.

I'm on my computer while I'm working, I'm on my computer

on my breaks, and I'm on my computer even for my mindless entertainment.

I spend far too long looking at my screen, and my eyes are so tired... Clearly, I have problems with eyestrain.

Even when I'm on the train, I close my eyes and brainstorm new ideas.

Ha, could this be... a false punch line?!

Volume 1 was the "Uneven Parallel Bars" arc, Volume 2 was the "Japanese Folktales" arc, and Volume 3 was the "Puns and Wordplay" arc.

So I guess that would make the next volume (assuming it comes out), the "Serious Arc," when we finally get to meet "those guys"!

Riddles and mysteries.

And, for the Crimson Vow, a new battle and a new path...

The real story has finally begun for these normal, unassuming girls.

Even for the most mundane people, adventure eventually comes calling!

Mysteries abound!

Thank you for continuing to enjoy this work, along with the mangafied version by Neko Mint (which can be read for free on Earth Star Comics [heep://comic-earthstar.jp]), currently in serialization.

Finally, to the chief editor; to Itsuki Akata, the illustrator; to Yoichi Yamakami, the cover designer; to everyone involved in the proofreading, editing, printing, binding, distribution, and selling of this book; to all the reviewers on *Shousetsuka ni Narou* who gave me their impressions, guidance, suggestions, and advice; and most of all, to everyone who's read my stories, both in print and online, I thank you from the bottom of my heart.

Thank you very much.

Please continue to look forward to these novels, and the manga, from here on out.

— FUNA

Didn't I Say to Make My Abilities Average in the Next Life?!

AFTERWORD?

UNOFFICIAL DESIGN
EWAN
*THIRD
BROTHER*

THE MIDDLE
BROTHER WIL
COME LATER IF
GET A CHANC

*ITSUKI
AKATA*

LET'S TRY MAKING SOME MORE CHARACTER
DESIGNS THAT I DISCUSSED WITH NO ONE!

THIS IS THE "WILL
THIS BE PUBLISHED
OR IGNORED?"
CORNER, SO...

UNOFFICIAL DESIGN
THERESA
KNIFE-WIELDER
AGE ?

Didn't I Say
to Make My Abilities
Average in the
——— Next Life?!

Experience these great light novel titles from Seven Seas Entertainment

See all Seven Seas has to offer at
SEVENSEASENTERTAINMENT.COM
TWITTER.COM/GOMANGA